LIVING COMES NATURALLY.

LIVING WELL IS AN ART.

And with this new edition of the trusted, proven wisdom that has helped millions, you can begin the fascinating and rewarding task of getting the most out of life...

THE ART OF LIVING

•   •   •   •   •   •

READER'S DIGEST PAPERBACKS
Informative..... Entertaining..... Essential.....

Berkley, one of America's leading paperback publishers, is proud to present this special series of the best-loved articles, stories and features from America's most trusted magazine. Each is a one-volume library on a popular and important subject. And each is selected, edited and endorsed by the Editors of Reader's Digest themselves!

Berkley/Reader's Digest books

THE GREAT ENTERTAINERS
"I AM JOE'S BODY"
LAUGHTER, THE BEST MEDICINE®
MORE TESTS AND TEASERS
ORGANIZE YOURSELF
SUPER WORD POWER
TESTS AND TEASERS
THEY BEAT THE ODDS
WORD POWER

THE EDITORS OF READER'S DIGEST

THE ART
OF LIVING

A BERKLEY/READER'S DIGEST BOOK
published by
BERKLEY BOOKS, NEW YORK

Cover design by Sam Salant.

THE ART OF LIVING

A Berkley / Reader's Digest Book
published by arrangement with
Reader's Digest Press

PRINTING HISTORY
Berkley / Reader's Digest edition / April 1980
Second printing / March 1981
Third printing / March 1982
Fourth printing / July 1982
Fifth printing / September 1982
Sixth printing / August 1983
Seventh printing / February 1984

ISBN: 0-425-05891-3

A BERKLEY BOOK ® TM 757,375
The name "BERKLEY" and the stylized "B" with design
are trademarks belonging to Berkley Publishing Corporation.
PRINTED IN THE UNITED STATES OF AMERICA

Grateful acknowledgment is made to the following organizations and individuals for permission to reprint material from the indicated sources:

New York Magazine (January 17 '72) for "How To Get Control Of Your Time— And Your Life," by Jane O'Reilly, copyright © 1972 by the New York Magazine Co.; David McKay Co. Inc. for "The ABC'S Of It," by Alan Lakein, condensed from HOW TO GET CONTROL OF YOUR TIME AND YOUR LIFE, copyright © 1973 by Alan Lakein and reprinted by permission of the David McKay Co. Inc.; Pete Hamill for "Going Home," by Pete Hamill, appearing in *The New York Post* (October 14 '71), copyright © 1971 by the New York Post Corp.; W.W. Norton for "Too Much Sex, Too Little Joy?" by Rollo May, condensed from LOVE AND WILL by Rollo May, copyright © 1969 by W.W. Norton; Judith Viorst for "What Is This Thing Called Love?" by Judith Viorst, appearing in *Redbook* (February '75), copyright © 1975 by the Redbook Publishing Co.; *Kiwanis* Magazine (October '78) for "You're Smarter Than You Think," by Dudley Lynch, copyright © 1978 by Kiwanis International; *Family Weekly* (January 12 '64) for "The Remarkable Self-Healing Powers of the Mind," by Morton Hunt, copyright © 1964 by *Family Weekly*; *Guideposts* (July '77) for "My Journey To Faith," by Jim Bishop, copyright © 1977 by Guideposts Assn. Inc.; Viking Penguin Inc. for "Have You An Educated Heart?" by Gelett Burgess from THE BROMIDE AND OTHER THEORIES by Gelett Burgess, copyright © 1933 by Gelett Burgess. Copyright renewed 1961 by Ruth Morisey. Reprinted by permission of Viking Penguin Inc.; Mrs. John Green for "How To Sell An Idea," by Elmer Wheeler, appearing in *Your Life* (September '48); *Women's Day* for "The Loving Message In A Touch," by Norman M. Lobsenz, copyright © 1970 by Fawcett Publishing Inc.; *New York Times* Magazine (December 5 '68) for "The Heart Of Soul," by Adrian Dove, copyright © 1968 *New York Times*; Conde Nast Publishing Inc. for "'How To Read Body Language," by Flora Davis, courtesy of *Glamour* Magazine (September '69), copyright © 1969 by the Conde Nast Pub. Inc.; Harper & Row for "The Fine Art Of Complaining," by George Weinberg, condensed from THE ACTION APPROACH by George Weinberg. Reprinted by permission of Harper & Row Publishers Inc.; Simon & Schuster for "Touched By Something Divine," by Richard Selzer, M.D., copyright © 1974, 1975, 1976 by Richard Selzer. Reprinted by permission of Simon & Schuster, a division of Gulf & Western Corp.; *Medical Dimensions* (March '76) for "I'm A Compulsive List Maker," by Naomi R. Bluestone, M.D., copyright © 1976 by MBA Communications Inc.; *New York Times* (October 6 '73) for "Pied Piper of Seventh Avenue," by James Comer, copyright © 1973 by the New York Times Co.; Roger J. Williams for "You Are Extraordinary," by Roger J. Williams, copyright © 1967 by Roger J. Williams; Prentice-Hall for "How To *Live* 365 Days A Year," by John A. Schindler, M.D., copyright © 1954 by Prentice-Hall Inc.; *Christian Science Monitor* (January 1 '74) for "Listen!" by Alison Wyley Birch, copyright © 1974 by the Christian Science Publishing Soc.; Prentice-Hall Inc. for "How To Relax," by Joseph A. Kennedy, condensed from RELAX AND LIVE by Joseph A. Kennedy, copyright © 1953 by Prentice-Hall Inc.; Stephen S. Price for "Put Your Best Voice Forward," by Stephen S. Price, copyright © 1955 by Stephen S. Price; Doubleday & Co. for "The One Sure Way To Happiness," by June Callwood, from LOVE, HATE, FEAR, ANGER AND OTHER LIVELY EMOTIONS by June Callwood. Copyright © 1964 by June Callwood, reprinted by permission of Doubleday & Co.; *Guideposts* (October '55) for "The Wisdom of Tears," by

CONTENTS

STRATEGY, TACTICS

HOW TO GET
CONTROL OF YOUR TIME

by Jane O'Reilly

MANY PEOPLE go through life without finding any satisfaction in the simple fact of being alive. Yet this lifetime is the only time we will have—we had better make the most of it. Few of us do, of course. We act as if this time were just a practice run for the next. As George Bernard Shaw said, we seem not to live long enough to take our lives seriously.

Fortunately, however, we live in an age when people have developed methods to help us— if we choose—to use our time wisely. One such person has been Alan Lakein, a time-management consultant who as of the early 1970s had given his seminar in this useful art to some 11,000 people. The purpose: to try and help men and women improve their motivation, reset direction (if it seems desirable or necessary), or find ways around or through situations that block them.

"Most people don't think in terms of minutes," says Lakein. "They waste all the minutes. Nor do they think in terms of their whole life. They operate in the mid-range of hours or days. So they start over again every week, and spend another substantial chunk of time in ways unrelated to their lifetime goals. They are doing a random walk through life, moving without getting anywhere."

The real question is: What do we really want to *do?* If we do not know, sooner or later we will realize that, whatever it was, there just isn't enough time left to do it. Our lifetime is not entirely our own, and yet it is all we have, and it is absurd to spend that time in constant reaction and accommodation to someone else's plan—whether that plan is imagined as God's, the boss's or a spouse's. Distinctions must be made. If it is the boss's time, then we must do his thing. Done properly, this should leave us time of our own to do *our* thing.

It takes organization and concentration to carve out your own time, but most important of all it takes self-knowledge to *know what you want to do with it*. Without goals and motivation the time will evaporate.

"A typical best use of time is to plan," says Lakein. Some people don't even make lists, much less imagine that today is connected with next week and five years from now. "But you can't effectively plan the next few days without deciding on the next ten years," says Lakein.

And so he begins by asking you to sort out your own personal priorities:

What are your lifetime goals? Write down everything you can think of, including money, career, physical, family, social, community, spiritual and personal goals. Try to fill up an entire sheet of paper. Now, place an "A" in front of three goals that are most important to you. On another sheet of paper, be specific about each of the three: identify subgoals, logical next steps, immediate plans. Then, from each A goal, select one "next step" to take next week. Now you have an action program! This list should be redone once a month, to keep up a continuous and evolving spiral of improvement.

"Great power comes from having a clearly identified list of lifetime goals," says Lakein. It is not unknown for a client at this point to decide that his minutes are not adding up to a lifetime he wants.

A busy woman lawyer, for example, told Lakein that her problem was not having enough time. After she'd made a list of her lifetime goals, which began, "To be left alone," he pointed out that there were inconsistencies between her overcrowded life and her stated goal. It emerged that her problem was an inability to say no to anyone. She and Lakein worked together on a list of tactful ways to get her off the hook. Not only was time saved, but she improved her self-esteem by developing the courage to say no.

How would you like to spend the next five years? Not how *will* you, or how *should* you, but how would you *like* to? If you have just written down as a lifetime goal a desire to be rich, and now find yourself answering, "I would *like* to be building birdhouses in British Columbia," you have not been honest in Question 1.

The point is to discover your own goals, not the ones you have been taught. We do too many things because of some atavistic sense that we have to. But do we? Even if the action was originally sensible, is it sensible now?

Herbert A. Shepard, a behavioral consultant to government and industry, asks clients to explore their wildest dreams—the fantasies or impossibilities they have filed permanently away because "People don't do that" or "I don't have time."

Milton Glaser asks his students at New York's School of Visual Arts to *design a perfect day for yourself five years from now.* There are all kinds of similar games—such as writing your own obituary—which, if taken seriously, can release people who are trapped not so much by circumstances as by lack of imagination.

One August, a reporter made a survey of young matrons sitting around a Long Island club pool. Their days were filled with sunshine and bathing suits and tennis lessons. The reporter asked them about their favorite fantasies. "They had none," she reported, "only fears." Fears of losing their money or their looks. Without imagination there can be no alternatives, and no motivation.

How would you like to live if you knew you would be dead six months from today? With this question, Lakein forces the client to face what is basically important to him.

Similarly, Shepard asks people, "When are you really glad you're alive?" and "What do you regret not doing lately?" Many people have never consciously thought out the answers, and once they recognize their own feelings, they can begin to set firm policies to see that their lives are arranged to make them happier more often while reducing guilt and frustration. And that is the point of the process: to meet the stranger that is often ourself, and to establish priorities that take that person into account.

"There is always enough time to do what is important," says Lakein. (Many people take the most productive hours of the day, between 8 and 11 a.m., to read newspapers, drink coffee, chat.) Once we have realized that there *is* time for the important things, the next problem is to do them. *Now!* After all, as Lakein says, "Time is life."

THE ABC'S OF IT

by Alan Lakein

WHEN I first started delving into the matter of getting more done every day, I asked successful people what the secret of their success was. I recall an early discussion with a vice president of a large oil company. "Oh, I just keep a To Do List," he said. I passed over that quickly, little suspecting the importance of what he said.

I was in another city the next day and I had lunch with a businessman who practically owned the town. He was chairman of the gas and light company, president of five manufacturing companies, and had his hand in a dozen other enterprises. I asked him how he managed to get everything done. "Oh, that's easy," he said. "I keep a To Do List."

The first thing in the morning, he told me, he would come in and list what he wanted to accomplish that day. He would arrange the items in priority. During the day he would cross off items as they were completed and add others as they occurred to him. In the evening he would check to see how many of the items he had written down still remained undone and then give himself a score. His goal was to cross off every single item.

Again and again in the years since, when I have talked to successful people, the To Do List has come up. I have found that one difference between people at the top of the ladder and people at the bottom is that those at the top use a To Do List every day to make better use of their time; those at the bottom don't.

Because the To Do List is such a fundamental time-planning tool, let's take a closer look at it.

Some people try to keep To Do Lists in their head, but this is rarely effective. Why clutter your mind? It's much better to leave it free for creative pursuits.

What do you write down? I recommend that you not list routine items but do list everything that has high priority today and might not get done without special attention. Don't forget to put down the activities related to your long-term goals. Although it may appear strange to see "begin learning French" or "find new friends" in the same list with "bring home a quart of milk," you want to do them in the same day. Since you'll use your To Do List as a guide when deciding what to work on next, you need the long-term projects represented, too.

You must *set priorities*. Some people do as many items as possible on their lists. They get a very high percentage of tasks done, but their effectiveness is low because the tasks they've done are mostly of C priority (lowest). Others like to start at the top of the list and go right down it, again with little regard to what's important. The best way is to label each item according to ABC priority and then polish off the list accordingly.

For people who have trouble living with priorities, I have found that it's helpful to use one piece of paper for the A's and B's and another page for the more numerous C's. The A and B paper is kept on top of the C list, and every time you raise it to do a C, you're aware that you're not making the best use of your time. Remember, it's not so much completing the list that counts, but making the best use of your time.

One reason many people poke through routine matters is that they like the feeling of doing something efficiently, even if it is inconsequential. Desk-neatening, for example, is hardly an A activity, but results show immediately. The homemaker who collects another delicious-sounding recipe when she has 500 untried clippings may kid herself into thinking that she is becoming a better cook, but the truth is that she is clipping rather than cooking.

Many activities of top value, on the other hand, cannot,

by their very nature, be performed well. The problems associated with them are new, untried and uncertain. Doing them means taking risks, which, whether calculated or not, will sometimes bring an unsuccessful outcome. Is there any wonder that you look around for something you can do well? One of the things you can do well is clear up all the easy C's. And you justify it by saying you are clearing them away so that you will then be free to do the A items later.

There's a rule to help people like that—the 80/20 rule. It says, "If all items are arranged in order of value, 80 percent of the value would come from only 20 percent of the items, while the remaining 20 percent of the value would come from 80 percent of the items." The 80/20 rule suggests that in a list of ten items, doing two of them will yield most (80 percent) of the value. Find these two, label them A, get them done.

Many C items can be turned into what I call "CZ's." CZ's are C's that can be deferred indefinitely without harm. Definite CZ's include watering the lawn when it looks like rain, inventorying the freezer (when you just did it last month and nothing has changed significantly in the interim), mopping the kitchen floor just before the children come home on a rainy day. You can probably think of many other items that are too trivial to do, or will settle themselves by the passage of time.

If you can let the dusting, washing, filing or checking go one more day, then let it. You will have spent less of your life dusting, filing and washing. If you continually resist the temptation to do the C's, you can significantly increase the number that become CZ's. Always keep in mind the question, "How terrible would it be if I didn't do this C?" If your answer is, "Not too terrible," then don't do it.

Do your A's instead. Make the most of your time.

A SIMPLE

SHORTCUT TO

SET YOU FREE

by Elise Miller Davis

SOME YEARS ago, Dr. Henry Cohen, the well-known rabbi, asked my opinion of a short manuscript. "A boy sent it from Europe, hoping I could sell it for him," he said. "I haven't had time to read it."

After I had read only a few paragraphs, it was apparent that the article had been copied from a travel folder. But I didn't say so. I hedged. "I don't know about this," I said. "I'll send it to my agent for you."

Rabbi Cohen scanned the pages as I handed them back. After a minute he looked at me in surprise. "Do you mean to tell me you'd take the time and trouble to send this to New York, and impose on a man there to read it and write you a letter, only to have to return in a week or so to tell me what you can tell me now?" he asked incredulously. My embarrassment must have been apparent, because he smiled gently. "Always remember this," he said. "Honesty is the world's greatest labor-saving device."

I thought about his advice for some time afterward. For how long, I kept asking myself, had I been engaging in deceptions that were squandering precious time and irreplaceable energies—both mine and those of others? And all under the virtuous cloak of diplomacy. Gradually, I came to realize that honesty is more than just a labor-saving device: it is the ultimate of economy in *all* human relations. For example:

• *Honesty Saves Time.* I'm often interrupted by telephone calls from strangers offering everything from "free" dancing lessons to "free" cemetery lots. There was a time when I remained mute during such calls, listening to a memorized speech that took valued minutes and left me frustrated and resentful. Now, however, I interrupt my caller immediately. "It wouldn't be fair to take your time," I say, "when I already know I'm not interested." And I hang up.

A couple I know made a New Year's resolution to be completely honest in their social life. "It all began with a friend calling every Monday morning to make plans with us for the following weekend," the wife explained. "I'd say okay—whether we wanted to see them or not—because I could never come up with a quick excuse. Then my husband and I would spend all week trying to figure out a way to cancel. We finally realized that it is all right to refuse any invitation."

• *Honesty Is Good Manners.* Some months ago, at a club meeting, I heard an exchange student speak glowingly about his year in our country. "But there's one thing I still don't understand," he added. "Americans often promise more than they deliver. 'Come to see me,' they're always saying, or 'we must get together.' Yet, few follow up. Everybody seems to want to be a good guy, but I find their dishonesty unkind. Maybe it's meant to be good manners, but it turns out to be bad manners."

An honest question deserves an honest answer—that's only common courtesy. A neighbor of ours recently acquired a new puppy. She called a veterinarian's office three times, but her calls were not returned. Finally, on the fourth call, she asked the receptionist outright, "Do you think the doctor already has too many patients?" A silence hung in the air. Then the receptionist said. "You've been frank, so I'll be frank. Yes, I think the doctor has more patients now than he can properly handle. If I were you, I'd call one of the younger doctors at a less-established animal clinic."

• *Honesty Saves Needless Contriving.* A friend of mine recently underwent the chores of moving. As the movers were gathering their barrels and boxes, she realized that she hadn't seen a valuable vase. Carefully, the four men went through every barrel of excelsior, every box of papers, while my friend and her young daughter searched closets and cupboard shelves. After an hour, on the verge of giving up, the woman's eyes caught the gleam of a bit of crystal on the kitchen floor. The girl looked at her mother and burst into tears. "I dropped it early this morning," she confessed. My friend was distressed over the loss of a treasure, naturally. But she was more distressed over the unnecessary trouble her child had caused. "You have wasted an hour for six people," she pointed out. "That's six hours—almost a day's work." The girl wiped her eyes. "But I think I learned a lesson, Mother," she said. "If the truth hurts, putting it off only hurts worse."

- *Honesty Generates Trust.* A little boy who greatly feared the sight of blood was taken to a dentist to have a tooth pulled. Both his father and the dentist assured him there would be no blood. There was, of course, and the child was outraged. Now an 80-year-old man, he said to me, "I remember it to this day. Parents shouldn't lie to children even if they think it's for their own good. Lies deteriorate relationships, can ruin them permanently."

- *Honesty Brings Inner Peace.* When she first went to Hollywood, an actress I know posed as a foreigner in an effort to appear more glamorous. "I knew nothing but hectic days and sleepless nights," she told me. "It was a horrible existence— trying to be what you're not." One day a columnist told her he knew the truth and was going to release the story. "The fact that people really believe you're British *proves* that you're a good actress," he said. "But you can't continue running scared. Because if you do, you won't have energy left for your real profession." The actress said that she would be grateful to the columnist for the rest of her life. "He forced me to admit the truth, and the truth set me free."

A final word of warning about honesty: solicited or unsolicited, it should never be confused with rude, intrusive comment. "Aggressively outspoken people get satisfaction from saying that they don't like your new dress or your new chair," a minister told me. "Worse, there are those who say they wouldn't be your friend if they didn't tell you something ugly that was said about you. In my work, I sometimes have to tell a hard truth. But I don't do it unless I'm absolutely certain it's meant in a loving way. The rule I use—and think anyone could use—is to refuse to employ painful honesty unless the unpleasant task breaks my own heart. Hence, I'll never wound to gain feelings of self-righteousness or superiority. Or to punish someone I really don't like."

From time to time, each of us should step back and take a look at our daily lives. Are we wasting time and energy carrying out deceptions, both polite and impolite? Having stepped back myself, I have learned that being honest is not a talent, not an art, not even a skill. It is a habit. And like the forming of most habits, this one requires concentration and practice. But once formed, it is as rewarding as a good-luck coin—for truth lies on one side, well-being on the other.

IT PAYS

TO INCREASE YOUR

WORRY POWER

by Joyce Lubold

FOR YEARS I was just an ordinary, run-of-the-mill circular worrier, like everyone else. No plan, no organization, pick up a worry here, drop another there, never *getting* anywhere, worry-wise. I'd head for the grocery store, let's say, my mind clear as a bell, all ready to plunge into those tricky decisions between the Giant Economy Size at 97 cents and the Super Savings Size at two for 83. But the car would wheeze windily as it started, which would make me think of the cost of new cars (high) and the state of my bank account (low). Thinking about cars would bring on dark concern about the pollution problem, which would lead to fretting about the kind of world we'll be turning over to the young. By the time I got to the store I could hardly remember why I came, much less divide 11½ ounces of tomatoes into 43 cents.

We're living, let's face it, in the Golden Age of Worry. Worry is everywhere these days, piling up—more solid, non-biodegradable worry than most people can dispose of. It's a kind of mental pollution, and we're all showing the strain.

But then one day I began to discover that, like pollution experts finding ways to turn trash into treasure, I could turn my worry into work. After all, Ben Franklin found electric power at the end of a kite string. James Watt saw steam power in his mother's teakettle. So there's really nothing unusual in finding Worry Power in the odds and ends of worries hanging around the house. Here is what I've learned:

Concentrate your worrying. Worry power, like steam power, works only when you put a lid on it. I discovered this by accident the day my eldest son got his driving permit. I'd had a pretty busy summer, worry-wise. Between the state of the world, the dry spell, the funny noise the washing machine kept making, my young daughter's teeth and my husband's waistline, I just hadn't got around to worrying about my son's starting to drive. So it wasn't until they pulled away from the curb, my six-foot baby boy at the wheel, his father at his side, that the worry hit me. All at once. Talk about Watt's teapot blowing its top!

I went back in to start my chores, concentrating heavily on faulty brakes, tire blowouts and other things that could happen. Before I'd run through them all, I'd waxed and polished all the floors. Then, tensely, I began to review automobile accidents I'd heard or read about, as I cleaned three closets and my husband's bureau drawers. Then I turned to special hazards like drunken drivers, jackknifing trailer trucks, and icy patches on the road. (It was summertime, but worry knows no season.) When they came back, I had an immaculate house—and no memory at all of having done the work.

"He's going to be really good," my husband reported matter-of-factly. "He's got the touch." Then he looked around. "Wow! It's the Waldorf! What got into *you?*"

Worry power! It's the housewife's greatest help since somebody decided to pipe water right into the house.

Worry creatively. Worry doesn't have to furrow your brow and wear you out. Used imaginatively it can refresh and restore your strength. My husband took a plane trip recently. An ordinary, foolish fretter would have sat rigidly throughout the trip, listening to the shrieking argument in his brain: "This plane is going to crash.... Don't be silly, of course it won't.... It will *so*...." But my husband, a master at creative worrying, did it differently.

Even before he was airborne, he spotted a large rivet which he could easily believe held the whole wing together. It wasn't hard to imagine the bolt's working loose and being sucked into the jet engine, thus forcing a crash landing at sea.

(The flight was entirely over land, which just shows you how creative a man he is.) Such an emergency would demand that some brave, quick-witted passenger (guess who?) would open the emergency door, thereby saving all the passengers' lives *and* earning the affectionate gratitude of the friendly stewardess, with whom he would then float cozily in a life raft just big enough for two until—well, until his plane landed in Toledo. By the time he deplaned, he was ready to lick his weight in corporate vice presidents.

If we can just break away from the "No it won't . . . Yes it will" pattern, imaginative worrying can make heroes of us all.

Don't call it worry if it's only procrastination. Once, in the middle of the night, I woke up coughing. I realized that I'd been coughing for weeks. "I wonder if I'm smoking too much," I worried to myself. "I'll bet I'm a mess in there."

Through the days that followed, I tried in vain to turn this into worry power, to use it, for example, to help me through two weeks' back ironing. But I simply stood weakly at the board, moving the iron slowly, slowly, as cigarette ashes fell on the clothes. I finally confided to a sympathetic friend, my fingers shaking just a little as I struck another match, "I'm so worried that I'm smoking too much."

"Then quit," she said.

She was right, of course. Whenever you find yourself agonizing over something you can actually do something about, you're not worrying—you're just kidding yourself.

Make a list. Most of us walk around with a large, foggy cloud of worries hanging over our heads, some of them old friends, some of them near strangers. If you sit down, make a list and really examine them, you may be surprised. For a month last summer I worried steadily about my second son, who was camping in the Canadian woods. Finally, when I wrote all the faceless worries down, I discovered that "appendicitis attack" was in the crowd. Since he'd had his appendix out years ago, I discarded that one—along with "typhoon," because you don't really get many typhoons in the Canadian woods. As I read down the list, I kept lightening my pack and feeling better.

Another day, weighed down with concerns, I made a two-column list: Worries, and What to Do About Them. My list of worries was a long one, ranging from "war" and "pollution" to "Jeannie's teeth." Then opposite each I entered something that was in my power to do immediately: "Write Congressman *today*"; "Call Boy Scouts about old newspapers"; and even that terrifying phrase, "Call orthodontist's office." The major worries I carried still, even after the small gallant actions had actually been taken. But at least some part of the worry had been turned into worry power.

If we can get our worries working for us, instead of the other way around, we may eventually find ourselves having less worry to work with. But let's not worry about *that* until the time comes.

SIMPLIFY! SIMPLIFY!

CONDENSED FROM "WALDEN"
by Henry David Thoreau

WHEN I wrote the following pages, or rather the bulk of them, I lived alone, in the woods, a mile from any neighbor, in a house which I had built myself, on the shore of Walden Pond, in Concord, Massachusetts, and earned my living by the labor of my hands only. I lived there two years and two months [July 4, 1845, to September 6, 1847].

I went to the woods because I wished to live deliberately, to front only the essential facts of life, and see if I could not learn what it had to teach, and not, when I came to die, discover that I had not lived. I did not wish to live what was not life, living is so dear; nor did I wish to practice resignation, unless it was quite necessary. I wanted to live deep and suck out all the marrow of life, to live so sturdily and Spartan-like as to put to rout all that was not life, to drive life into a corner, and reduce it to its lowest terms, and, if it proved to be mean, why then to get the whole genuine meanness of it, and publish its meanness to the world; or if it were sublime, to know it by experience, and be able to give a true account of it.

The mass of men lead lives of quiet desperation. What is called resignation is confirmed desperation. But it is a characteristic of wisdom not to do desperate things.

We live meanly, like ants. Our life is frittered away by

detail. An honest man has hardly need to count more than his ten fingers, or in extreme cases he may add his ten toes, and lump the rest. Simplicity, simplicity, simplicity! I say, let your affairs be as two or three, and not a hundred or a thousand; instead of a million, count half a dozen, and keep your account on your thumbnail.

Simplify, simplify. Instead of three meals a day, if it be necessary eat but one; instead of a hundred dishes, five; and reduce other things in proportion. The nation itself, with all its so-called internal improvements, which, by the way, are all external and superficial, is just such an unwieldy and overgrown establishment, tripped up by its own traps, ruined by luxury and heedless expense, by want of calculation and a worthy aim, as the million households in the land; and the only cure for it, as for them, is in a rigid economy, a stern and more than Spartan simplicity of life and elevation of purpose.

Why should we live with such hurry and waste of life? We have the Saint Vitus' dance, and cannot possibly keep our head still.

Let us spend one day as deliberately as Nature, and not be thrown off the track by every nutshell and mosquito's wing that falls on the rails. Let us rise early, and fast or break fast gently and without perturbation; let company come and company go, let the bells ring and the children cry. Why should we knock under and go with the stream? If the bell rings, why run? Let us settle ourselves, and work and wedge our feet downward through the mud and slush of opinion, and prejudice, and tradition, and delusion, and appearance, till we come to a hard bottom and rocks in place, which we can call *reality*, and say, This is, and no mistake. If we are really dying, let us hear the rattle in our throats; if we are alive, let us go about our business.

The gross necessaries of life for man in this climate may, accurately enough, be distributed under the several heads of Food, Shelter, Clothing and Fuel; for not till we have secured these are we prepared to entertain the true problems of life with freedom and a prospect of success. But most of the luxuries, and many of the so-called comforts of life, are not only not indispensable, but positive hindrances to the elevation of mankind. The ancient philosophers were a class than which none has been poorer in outward riches, none so rich in inward.

None can be an impartial or wise observer of human life but from the vantage ground of what *we* should call voluntary poverty.

No man ever stood the lower in my estimation for having a patch in his clothes; yet I am sure that there is greater anxiety, commonly, to have fashionable clothes than to have a sound conscience. If my jacket and trousers, my hat and shoes, are fit to worship God in, they will do, will they not? I say, beware of all enterprises that require new clothes, and not rather a new wearer of clothes.

As for shelter, I will not deny that this is now a necessary of life. But when I consider my neighbors, the farmers of Concord, I find that for the most part they have been toiling 20, 30 or 40 years, that they may become the real owners of their farms—and we may regard one third of that toil as the cost of their houses.

With consummate skill, the farmer has set his trap with a hair spring to catch comfort and independence, and then, as he turned away, got his own leg into it. And when the farmer has got his house, he may not be the richer but the poorer for it, and it be the house that has got him.

Most men appear never to have considered what a house is, and are actually though needlessly poor all their lives because they think that they must have such a one as their neighbors have. It is possible to invent a house still more convenient and luxurious than we have, which yet all would admit that man could not afford to pay for. Shall we always study to obtain more of these things, and not sometimes to be content with less? Our houses are cluttered and defiled with furniture. I would rather sit in the open air, for no dust gathers on the grass.

But to make haste to my own experiment in the woods by Walden Pond. I have built a tight shingled and plastered house, ten feet wide by fifteen feet long, and eight-feet posts, with a garret and a closet, a large window on each side, two trapdoors, one door at the end, and a brick fireplace opposite. The exact cost of my house, paying the usual price for such materials as I used, but not counting the work, all of which was done by myself, was $28.12.

Before I finished my house, wishing to earn ten or twelve dollars to meet my usual expenses, I planted about two acres and a half of light and sandy soil chiefly with beans, but also part with potatoes, corn, peas and turnips. My income was $8.71.

I learned that if one would live simply and eat only the crop which he raised, and raise no more than he ate, he could do all his farm work as it were with his left hand, and thus he would not be tied to an ox, or horse, or cow. I was more independent than any farmer in Concord, for I was not anchored to a house or farm, but could follow the bent of my genius, which is a very crooked one, every moment.

I have maintained myself solely by the labor of my hands, and I found that, by working about six weeks a year, I could meet all the expenses of living. The whole of my winters, as well as most of my summers, I had free and clear for study.

In short, I am convinced both by faith and experience, that to maintain one's self on this earth is not a hardship but a pastime, if we will live simply and wisely. It is not necessary that a man should earn his living by the sweat of his brow, unless he sweats easier than I do.

I would say to my fellows, once for all: As long as possible live free and uncommitted. It makes but little difference whether you are committed to a farm or the county jail.

I would not have any one adopt *my* mode of living on any account. For, beside that before he has fairly learned it I may have found another for myself, I desire that there may be as many different persons in the world as possible. I would have each one be very careful to find out and pursue *his own* way. Let every one mind his own business, and endeavor to be what he was made.

Why should we be in such desperate haste to succeed and in such desperate enterprises? If a man does not keep pace with his companions, perhaps it is because he hears a different drummer. Let him step to the music he hears, however measured or far away.

MAKE AN

APPOINTMENT WITH

YOURSELF

by Louis Finkelstein

A STUDENT in a class conducted by Dr. Harry Emerson Fosdick, minister emeritus of New York's Riverside Church, once made a shrewd comment on the celebrated incident of Isaac Newton and the apple. Too much emphasis, the student said, had been placed on the apple; the important fact was that Newton was alone in the garden, in a position to be receptive, when the apple fell.

As one writer has put it, contemplation is to knowledge what digestion is to food—the way to get life out of it. Reading gives us information and suggests ideas, but it is in meditation that we form our judgments.

All of us acknowledge that we ought regularly to withdraw from the round of routine and renew ourselves. Yet we do not set aside the time for this renewal, this examination of the self that we can meet only in contemplation. It is for this reason that a firm and specific date with one's inner self seems to me the best, if not the only, way to establish the practice of daily meditation.

One must choose the time and the place, and keep the date with the same fidelity as one would a date with a friend—remembering that the self is one's best friend and ought to be treated as such. I stress the importance of routine because I know my own nature, and I suspect that I should not have maintained daily periods of private thought and study if I had not been brought up in a tradition which made it obligatory, and finally easy. Yet the benefits have been enormous, and the pleasures so great that I would not exchange these sessions for any number of idle hours.

At the Jewish Theological Seminary of America, where I was chancellor, we have a rule that anyone who is in meditative study must not be disturbed. The telephone operator or the secretary explains. The explanation makes a curious impression, I am told, on some of our friends in the business world, but I have often wondered if such an inviolable time might not be adopted with profit in some businesses. It is odd how likely we are to respect the privacy of people talking, but not of one who is thinking.

Dr. Fosdick had an absolute rule that he was not to be disturbed during his contemplative hours, save by his wife in an emergency. There were only two interruptions in 18 years. The remarkable clarity and force of Dr. Fosdick's preaching and writing were unquestionably due in no small measure to the fact that he regarded thinking as vital, and the time set aside for it as sacred.

How to find the place and set aside the time for a daily appointment with oneself is the crucial question. Especially is this true if one is not in a profession where what we call thinking is indulged, if not honored. In our culture, some are paid to think and some are paid to do. But we *all* need to think, to get the benefits and satisfactions that come from meditation.

How feasible is it for a housewife or businessman or college student to have a regular appointment with his soul? It requires a lot of thought, but the very difficulties involved make all the more important a plan of inaction. It is well to have a private stage for the act of meditation. If living arrangements are such that you can't shut yourself off, fix your schedule so that you will have solitary moments by being up while others are down.

Once the place and hour are fixed, there is still the danger of letting the mind wander aimlessly. Most of us in the Western world are by nature and training activists, accustomed to coming to grips with tangibles. We find unassisted straight meditation hard. As one woman put it, "I can't keep my mind on my mind that long." Not a few may be tempted to give up.

For this reason we should consider taking a profound but companionable book as an aid to meditation. A great book gives us even more of a sense of an appointment because we can look forward to the presence of another mind without the distraction of another personality. My whole working day is quickened by the awareness that next morning will be devoted to the discovery and exploration of ideas offered in a book of substance and brilliance.

If you meditate with a book, choose your book thoughtfully and stay with it until it has become a part of you, and you have become a part of it. You may elect Scripture, Plato, Montaigne, Whitehead, or a modern such as Tillich or Buber. The criterion should be depth—the depth of interest to be plumbed by you and the stirring that takes place as you read and think about what you read. The aim is to understand how the great men approached life, and to discover what advice they may have to offer us in the perplexities and confusions of today.

The book I use is the Talmud. This is, in effect, a vast commentary on the Bible, explaining verse after verse and preserving the discussions carried on over thousands of years about passages of Scripture. The works that make up the Talmud were at first handed down orally from teacher to pupil, being memorized before they were reduced to writing. Part of their wisdom is formulated in maxims—distillates of reflection. Some of these one memorizes as a child, but the full light of their meaning reaches one only gradually. In this way, one's whole life becomes a commentary on the Bible and the Talmud, as they are commentaries on life itself.

Through thinking on the Talmud, I have a real and profitable acquaintance—to take but one instance—with Simon the Righteous, who lived more than 2000 years ago. He was one of a group of Jewish sages who believed that what the world needs is less action and more contemplation. "Do something" may be good advice under certain circumstances, one learns, but quite frequently better advice is, "When in doubt, do nothing; try to discover what is best to do."

Such a maxim lends sanction to meditation. It does not counsel us to lie supine. It allows latitude for the labor of further thought and study, brings to mind a line of poet Marianne

Moore: "But patience, that is action." What's more, the counsel and the questions that arise out of such exploration and discovery show how one idea touches off another. A thought that may be insubstantial at the outset will linger to enrich our later days.

In sum, thought prompted by great literature brings rewards that we cannot anticipate but can always appreciate. They may be tangible, and help a person, if only through increased clarity of mind. But even if fruitful inspirations do not come about from the daily appointment, there is still much for which we can give thanks, including repose. It was one of the wisest men of the Bible, Isaiah, who heard the Holy One of Israel say, "In returning and rest shall ye be saved; in quietness and in confidence shall be your strength."

MAN AND WOMAN

GOING HOME

by Pete Hamill

I first heard this story a few years ago from a girl I had met in New York's Greenwich Village. The girl told me that she had been one of the participants. Since then, others to whom I have related the tale have said that they had read a version of it in some forgotten book, or been told it by an acquaintance who said that it actually happened to a friend. Probably the story is one of those mysterious bits of folklore that emerge from the national subconscious every few years, to be told anew in one form or another. The cast of characters shifts, the message endures. I like to think that it did happen, somewhere, sometime.

THEY WERE going to Fort Lauderdale—three boys and three girls—and when they boarded the bus, they were carrying sandwiches and wine in paper bags, dreaming of golden beaches and sea tides as the gray cold of New York vanished behind them.

As the bus passed through New Jersey, they began to notice Vingo. He sat in front of them, dressed in a plain, ill-fitting suit, never moving, his dusty face masking his age. He chewed the inside of his lip a lot, frozen into some personal cocoon of silence.

Deep into the night, outside Washington, the bus pulled

into a Howard Johnson's, and everybody got off except Vingo. He sat rooted in his seat, and the young people began to wonder about him, trying to imagine his life: perhaps he was a sea captain, a runaway from his wife, an old soldier going home. When they went back to the bus, one of the girls sat beside him and introduced herself.

"We're going to Florida," she said brightly. "I hear it's beautiful."

"It is," he said quietly, as if remembering something he had tried to forget.

"Want some wine?" she said. He smiled and took a swig. He thanked her and retreated again into his silence. After a while, she went back to the others, and Vingo nodded in sleep.

In the morning, they awoke outside another Howard Johnson's, and this time Vingo went in. The girl insisted that he join them. He seemed very shy, and ordered black coffee and smoked nervously as the young people chattered about sleeping on beaches. When they returned to the bus, the girl sat with Vingo again, and after a while, slowly and painfully, he told his story. He had been in jail in New York for the past four years, and now he was going home.

"Are you married?"

"I don't know."

"You don't know?" she said.

"Well, when I was in the can I wrote to my wife," he said. "I told her that I was going to be away a long time, and that if she couldn't stand it, if the kids kept askin' questions, if it hurt too much, well, she could just forget me. I'd understand. Get a new guy, I said—she's a wonderful woman, really something—and forget about me. I told her she didn't have to write me or nothing. And she didn't. Not for three and a half years."

"And you're going home now, not *knowing?*"

"Yeah," he said shyly. "Well, last week, when I was sure the parole was coming through, I wrote her again. We used to live in Brunswick, just before Jacksonville, and there's a big oak tree just as you come into town. I told her that if she'd take me back, she should put a yellow handkerchief on the tree, and I'd get off and come home. If she didn't want me, forget it—no handkerchief, and I'd go on through."

"Wow," the girl said. "Wow."

She told the others, and soon all of them were in it, caught up in the approach of Brunswick, looking at the pictures Vingo showed them of his wife and three children—the woman handsome in a plain way, the children still unformed in the cracked, much-handled snapshots.

Now they were 20 miles from Brunswick, and the young people took over window seats on the right side, waiting for the approach of the great oak tree. The bus acquired a dark, hushed mood, full of the silence of absence and lost years. Vingo stopped looking, tightening his face into the ex-con's mask, as if fortifying himself against still another disappointment.

Then Brunswick was ten miles, and then five. Then, suddenly, all of the young people were up out of their seats, screaming and shouting and crying, doing small dances of exultation. All except Vingo.

Vingo sat there stunned, looking at the oak tree. It was covered with yellow handkerchiefs—20 of them, 30 of them, maybe hundreds, a tree that stood like a banner of welcome billowing in the wind. As the young people shouted, the old con rose from his seat and made his way to the front of the bus to go home.

This article when it appeared in Reader's Digest in the early 1970s inspired a popular song, one that is still sometimes heard.

TOO MUCH

SEX, TOO LITTLE

JOY?

by Rollo May

IN VICTORIAN times, when one never mentioned sex in polite company, males and females dealt with each other as though neither possessed sexual organs. Even William James, who was far ahead of his time in everything else, treated sex with polite aversion. In two volumes of his epoch-making *Principles of Psychology,* he devotes only a page or so to sex, at the end of which he murmurs, "These details are a little unpleasant."

Such repression, of course, was scarcely healthy. Thus Sigmund Freud, one Victorian who *did* look at sex, was right in his delineation of the neurotic symptoms which result from cutting off so vital a part of the human body and the self.

Then, in the 1920s, a radical change took place. In an amazingly short period following World War I, we shifted from acting as though sex did not exist to being obsessed with it. Sexual expression rather than repression became dogma in liberal circles, until today we place more emphasis on sex than any society since ancient Rome. Far from not talking about sex, we might well seem, to a visitor from Mars dropping into Times Square, to have no other topic of conversation.

Partly as a result of this radical shift, therapists today rarely see patients who exhibit repression of sex in the manner of Freud's pre-World War I patients. If anything, they find the opposite: a great deal of talk about sex, a great deal of sexual activity, and practically no one complaining of cultural prohibitions. What patients do complain of is lack of feeling and passion. "The curious thing about this ferment," says one authority, "is how little anyone seems to be *enjoying* emancipation." So much sex and so little meaning or even fun in it!

Thus, one paradox of sexual freedom: enlightenment has *not* solved our sexual problems. To be sure, there are important positive results, chiefly in increased freedom for the individual. Books on sexual technique can be bought in any bookstore; contraception is available; couples can, without guilt or squeamishness, discuss their sexual relationship and undertake to make it more meaningful. Let these gains not be underestimated. *External* anxiety and guilt have lessened.

But *internal* anxiety and guilt have increased. And in some ways these impose a heavier burden upon the individual. The challenge a woman used to face from men was simple and direct: Will she or won't she?—a direct issue of how she stood vis-à-vis cultural mores. But the question men now ask is, Can she or can't she?—which shifts the challenge to the woman's personal adequacy. In past decades, women could blame society's restrictions for their hesitancy and thus preserve their self-esteem. But when the question is simply how one *performs,* one's own sense of adequacy is inevitably called into question.

Sexual enlightenment has proved frustrating in other areas. For example, the battle for freedom of expression in the arts has been won, but has it not merely become a new straitjacket? The realistic chronicles on stage and in novels are self-defeating, for realism is neither sexual nor erotic. Indeed, there is nothing *less* sexy than sheer nakedness.

A second paradox of sexual freedom is that the new emphasis on *technique* can backfire, that tenderness and joy in fact bear an inverse relationship to the number of how-to-do-it books rolling off the presses.

Certainly nothing is wrong with technique as such, whether one is playing golf or making love. But emphasis on technique beyond a certain point makes for a mechanistic attitude, and the age-old art tends to be superseded by bookkeeping and timetables. Did he (or she) pay the right amount of attention to me during the evening? Have we made love often enough in recent months? Are we behind schedule? One wonders how the spontaneity of this most spontaneous act can survive.

Even the sexologists, whose attitude is generally the more sex the merrier, are raising their eyebrows these days about the anxious over-emphasis on achieving orgasm, on "satisfying" the partner. Such technical preoccupation robs the act of its essence—spontaneous abandon—and can lead to alienation, depersonalization and feelings of loneliness. For when we cut through all the rigmarole about performance, what still remains is how amazingly important the fact of intimacy is—the meeting, the growing closeness, the excitement of not knowing where it will lead, the assertion of the self and the giving of the self.

A third paradox is that our highly vaunted sexual freedom has turned out to be nothing more than a new form of puritanism—not to be confused with the original Puritanism which came to us via our Victorian grandparents. In those days, sin meant giving in to one's sexual desires. Today's puritan believes it is sinful not to have *full* sexual expression. The tendency in psychoanalysis to speak of sex as a "need"—in the sense of tension to be reduced—plays into this puritanism.

This use of the body as a machine means, of course, that people must not only perform sexually but must make sure that they do so without letting themselves go in passion or unseemly commitment (which might be interpreted as the exertion of an "unhealthy" demand). Thus the final irony: Where the Victorian sought to have love without falling into sex, today's puritan seeks to have sex without falling into love!

Where have we gone wrong? Why has sexual freedom proved so disappointing? Perhaps because, in our headlong rush to "enlightenment," we have left behind the concept of *eros*.

Early Greek mythology tells us that when the world was barren and lifeless, it was Eros who breathed the "spirit of life" into the nostrils of the clay forms of man and woman. Ever since, "eros" has signified the giving of life, in contrast to sex, which is the releasing of tension. The end toward which sex points is gratification; eros, on the other hand, is a desiring, a longing, a forever reaching out.

And here's the problem: In anesthetizing feeling in order to perform better, in using sensuality to hide sensitivity, we have separated sex from eros. We have, in fact, used sex to avoid the anxiety-creating involvements of eros.

Understandably, the experience of falling in love—of surrendering to eros—is frightening to some. When we fall in love, the world is vastly widened; it confronts us with regions we never dreamed existed. Are we capable of giving ourselves to our beloved without losing ourselves in this dizzying new continent?

The answer, of course, is yes. For a basic truth of human experience is that eros drives us to transcend ourselves, to leap barriers, to unite with another person in relation to whom we discover our own real self-fulfillment. Eros—not sex—enables us to realize the deepest meaning of love.

STRAIGHT TALK ABOUT

THE LIVING-TOGETHER

ARRANGEMENT

by Louise Montague

As THE author of two books on divorce, I try to accept as many speaking engagements in high school and college classes as I can. For it is my feeling that one answer to the soaring divorce rate is "preventive thinking"—the time to face many of the problems of divorce is *before* marriage. Lately, however, I find that at every session someone will stand up and state that marriage is outmoded and that the answer to the divorce problem is to live with a partner without the legal commitment of marriage.

Unhappily, "living together" is a modern phenomenon, a national trend today. Between 1960 and 1970, according to the U.S. Department of the Census, there was an eightfold increase in the Living-Together Arrangement (LTA). Why are so many people opting for this arrangement? And how do they get into it?

Certainly it's a very attractive idea sexually. But many young people also say it's a good way to "test" marriage. Others claim it's a terrific financial boon. And some don't even know how they ended up together. He started staying over or she began to leave clothes in his closet. These young people feel that by not making their relationship permanent they can maintain the spontaneous atmosphere of new love. By eliminating the legal commitment, they feel they have eliminated the "bad" part of marriage.

But the phenomenon is not limited to young people. Many divorced persons burned in marriage are trying it. Some have religious convictions forbidding a second marriage. Divorced men who are financially strapped feel they can't take on the responsibility of a new wife. Or the divorced woman may be reluctant to give up the alimony which would stop with her remarriage.

With all these "pluses" why do so many people engaged in an LTA write to me about the problems they have encountered? Why *is* the Living-Together Arrangement a detriment to those involved? Let's first consider the college students who decide on or slide into an LTA. You'd be surprised, once the subject comes up for discussion in a classroom, how many youngsters tell unhappy stories about themselves or their best friends.

Take the case of the young couple at Stanford. After they moved in together, the boy lost his scholarship and was not able to meet the high tuition costs from his part-time job. The girl quit school in order to work and let him finish his education. When he graduated, he applied for—and received—a scholarship to do graduate work in England. The girl was extremely hurt and angry; she felt he owed it to her to stay and help her finish *her* education. They argued bitterly for a day, and then the young man packed and left!

This situation is typical of dozens I have heard. The LTA simply can't work when it breeds the mutual dependency of marriage without the mutual responsibility.

Another example is a young couple at Georgetown University who moved into an apartment together. The girl's parents, shocked and hurt, cut off all their daughter's funds. The boy suggested they split up and go back to their dorms, but the girl, having had a terrible row with her family, insisted that it was now his responsibility to take care of her! Both got jobs, and the young man, not a strong student, fell behind and was unable to graduate.

Certainly it's difficult to think in realistic terms when a couple imagine themselves in love. But it is unfair to expect parental values to be dropped at a whim. The censure of family and friends is one of the greatest burdens the LTA carries. Young people who need the support of family are very foolish to chuck their long-term goals for short-term pleasures.

To be sure, intimate relationships are widely accepted today, but any resourceful couple can find ways of being together without moving in together. Moreover, living alone at times and developing individuality should be a prime concern of young people. For few can handle the LTA until they have learned to live with themselves.

Some of the most heartbreaking stories I hear about LTAs concern children. Whatever life-style a single male or female chooses is that individual's responsibility. But to bring a child into this atmosphere is to involve an innocent third party in an experiment that can leave all parties damaged. Although the law generally requires a father to support his children, it is often difficult to enforce these laws. Women are frequently left with the burden of support while the air of illegitimacy hangs heavy on the child.

A divorced or widowed woman who involves her children in an LTA may also be subjecting them to undue stress. Children experience great pressures to conform. What the mother and her companion view as a marvelous, free life-style, a child could see as a freaky embarrassment. The man in question, not being either father or stepfather, has no social definition as to the role he should play in the child's life. In some states, a divorced mother in an LTA stands a good chance of losing not only support payments but custody of her children.

Even a highly motivated working couple should be aware of the consequences of their actions. How you present yourself to the world is how you will be judged. A young petroleum engineer, living with a dental hygienist, applied for a much-wanted overseas job with an oil company. When the company conducted its routine investigation, and found that the young woman with whom he was living was not his wife, he was turned down; the firm felt that his LTA smacked of indecisiveness, instability, and failure on his part to accept responsibility. Who is to say if the oil company made the right decision? But, judging from a great many instances, it happens to be the way things are. What a couple may view as a sophisticated way to live, the business community may see as a career impediment.

Heartbreak and setbacks are also in the cards for a

woman who moves in with a man in the hope of getting married. My advice is to avoid this strategy. When you demand nothing of a relationship, that's often exactly what you get. The very impermanence of the LTA suggests that that is what each partner has settled for. If marriage is what you want, marriage is what you should have. So why commit yourself to a shaky arrangement that keeps you out of the mainstream of life where you quite possibly will meet someone who shares your views?

Many divorced women with a great need for a little security, and with little faith in themselves, seek an LTA as a temporary answer to help them get on their feet. All this does is prolong their adjustment and reinforce their self-doubts. I'm reminded of one such woman who told me she had been living with a man for four years and wanted out but was afraid to leave. "Why?" I asked. Because, she said, she feared to give up the free rent and all that "security" she had with him. "Wrong," I said. "You have no security of any kind. You stand a good chance of being replaced by a younger version of yourself. And as for free rent, that's no security either. Security is owning the building."

Probably the greatest single hazard of the LTA is that it can actually spoil a good relationship between two people who should eventually marry. Because it is entered into out of weakness rather than strength, doubt rather than conviction, drift rather than decision, it offers unnecessary obstacles. Knowing this, you shouldn't casually toss aside those inherited institutions that have had a history of success.

If I were asked to give one reason only why I am opposed to the LTA, I would state quite simply that I am morally against it. As Barbara Tuchman wrote in *McCall's:* "Standards of taste, as well as morality, need continued reaffirmation to stay alive, as liberty needs eternal vigilance." There are valid standards of judgment which come from confidence in yourself and your values. To accept a living pattern that goes against your better judgment is to chip away at your personal freedom.

And what of love? You cannot hope to find love by experimenting biologically. You don't build love by creating a living situation designed to test it. You don't create love by setting up a forced proximity. Love *is*. And when you love you commit to it—for better or for worse. When we finally realize that all our experiments in alternate life-styles, communal marriage and open-ended covenants are simply a means of running *from* responsibility and love, not *to* them, we will have reached the beginning of maturity.

WHAT IS THIS THING

CALLED LOVE?

by Judith Viorst

LOVE IS much nicer to be in than an automobile accident, a tight girdle, a higher tax bracket or a holding pattern over Philadelphia. But not if he doesn't love you back.

Question: What is the difference between infatuation and love?

Answer: Infatuation is when you think that he's as sexy as Robert Redford, as smart as Henry Kissinger, as noble as Ralph Nader, as funny as Woody Allen and as athletic as Jimmy Connors. Love is when you realize that he's as sexy as Woody Allen, as smart as Jimmy Connors, as funny as Ralph Nader, as athletic as Henry Kissinger and nothing like Robert Redford—but you'll take him anyway.

One advantage of marriage, it seems to me, is that when you fall out of love with him, or he falls out of love with you, it keeps you together until you maybe fall in again.

According to my friend Jonathan the Jock, it's easier to love a woman more than life itself than to love her enough to turn off the Super Bowl.

41

Love is when it's 10 p.m., and you get this gnawing need for peach ice cream, and even though you're not sick or pregnant, he drives to a drugstore and buys you some. *Note:* If he then goes around telling people about it, deduct 20 points.

Brevity may be the soul of wit, but not when someone's saying, "I love you." When someone's saying, "I love you," he always ought to give a lot of details: Why does he love you? How much does he love you? When and where did he first begin to love you? Favorable comparisons with all the other women he ever loved also are welcome, and even though he insists it would take forever to count the ways in which he loves you, you wouldn't want to discourage him from counting.

Love is agreeing with him completely when he needs you to agree with him completely, and telling him the plain, unvarnished truth when he needs you to tell him the plain, unvarnished truth, and knowing when he needs which.

Love means never having to say you're sorry. Except when it's your fault. Or when it's his fault but he's too immature to admit it. Or when it's the children's fault but he's holding you responsible. Or when it's nobody's fault but he's looking for a scapegoat. Or when....

According to my friend Ada The Anthropologist, love is a great improvement over other forms of warfare.

Love is what makes a person who is philosophically opposed to monogamous sexual relationships on the grounds that jealousy and possessiveness between women and men are not intrinsic to human nature but simply the outmoded by-products of a decadent capitalistic system take it all back.

Question: How do you distinguish love from like?

Answer: Love is the same as like except you feel sexier. And more romantic. And also more annoyed when he talks with his mouth full. And you also resent it more when he interrupts you. And you also respect him less when he shows any weakness.

And furthermore, when you ask him to pick you up at the airport and he tells you that he can't do it because he's busy, it's only when you love him that you hate him.

Roses are red/ Violets are blue/ Sugar is sweet/ And so/ Because you once said that you would rather go through life drinking diet cola with me than Dom Perignon with Jacqueline Onassis/ Are you.

MIND AND FAITH

YOU'RE SMARTER

THAN YOU THINK

by Dudley Lynch

- POLICE IN a midwestern city were stumped. A fast-moving burglary team kept breaking into clothing stores, stripping the garment racks like hungry piranhas and slipping away before police could respond to the alarm systems. Was there any way to stop them—or at least slow them down?

Suddenly, one detective had an idea. "Alternate your hanger hooks," he told the city's merchants. "Turn one toward the wall, and the next toward the aisle—all the way down the rack." When the next alarm went off, police caught the hapless thieves still removing garments one at a time.

- An old frame church in New England stood in desperate need of exterior paint, so the minister recruited a half-dozen volunteers from his congregation. But he couldn't get them to show up for the job—until he had a devilish inspiration. He divided the building into six segments, then, in bold letters three feet high, painted a volunteer's name on each segment. Shortly thereafter, each recruit dutifully arrived to paint his segment, fulfill his pledge—and avoid all that public notoriety.

- Not long ago, when I was pushing my wife's stalled car with my own, our bumpers locked. With a strong friend, I tried to bounce the bumpers loose. No go. Next I tried a jack. That didn't work either. Then my wife suggested backing my car up on the curb and leaving her smaller car at street level. Eureka! The cars immediately sprang apart.

We've all met people like this, with an uncanny knack for solving problems, and we wonder how they do it. They don't appear to be geniuses; yet, somehow, they *think* differently from the rest of us.

Over the last 15 or 20 years, social scientists have been taking their first serious look at this power of creative thinking, and have written more than 1500 doctoral theses and 2000 books on it. On available evidence, scholars now believe creativity is far more common than previously thought. In fact, most researchers claim there is a spark of genius in each of us, waiting to be freed.

Here, from experts in several fields, are five tips for freeing your own creativity potential:

Rekindle childhood curiosity. A man I know spent an hour trying to rescue his young son's pet frog from the bottom of a narrow shaft on their property. He used a long stick, then a rope with a loop at the end, then an open-ended can on a string. Nothing worked, and he finally gave up. Minutes later, his five-year-old son appeared at the front door—with the frog! The boy had hit on the idea of flooding the shaft with a garden hose and floating the frog to the surface.

In the wild kingdom of their imagination, children are forever coming up with creative solutions. Unlike adults, children have an open pipeline to the seat of creativity: the right hemisphere of the brain. But when they start school, the "left brain"—the seat of logic—begins falling victim to the fears, rules, obligations and concerns of the adult world and, before long, imagination is in retreat.

What sets the creative person off from the rest of us is that he or she has somehow managed to hold onto a childlike curiosity and an unbounded sense of creative possibility. To help rekindle your own curiosity, start by widening your horizons—especially your reading horizons. Ray Bradbury, a prolific writer of science fiction, stuffs his mind with everything he can lay his hands on—essays, poetry, plays, lithographs, music. "You have to feed yourself information every day," he says. "When I was a kid, I sneaked over to the grown-up section in the library. Now, to make sure I'm fully informed, I often go into the children's section."

Ask the right question. For months, a group of YMCA Indian Guides had planned a "father-and-son" weekend in the wilds, where they hoped to make plaster casts of animal tracks. When the weekend finally arrived, it poured rain, and no one could go out. Then one imaginative leader had an idea. Why not use the plaster to make casts of each father's hand, along with that of his son. "It was one of the best things we ever did," a YMCA official recalls. "It saved the weekend."

The idea would never have developed if the leader who thought of it had stayed with the obvious question: "How can we make plaster casts in the rain?" They couldn't, of course. The "right" question was: "How can we have fun with the plaster we've bought?"

Dr. Frederic Flach, New York psychiatrist and leading authority on creativity, says that restating the question can often be the first step toward discovering the solution. "Instead of asking, 'Should I get a divorce?'" suggests Dr. Flach, "you might ask, 'Does it make more sense to be on my own?' Similarly, instead of wondering, 'Should I quit my job?' you might ask, 'To what degree does the work I am doing reflect my basic interests?'"

Angelo M. Biondi, executive director of the Creative Education Foundation, likes questions that begin, "In what ways might I...?" He recently offered advice to a friend in business. Head of a small company, the friend was debating whether or not to fire an unproductive assistant. A better question, Biondi suggested, might be: "In what ways might I improve this employe's performance?" That led to questions about *why* the employe was having trouble; the employer soon discovered that his assistant had marital problems that were diverting him from his work. A family counselor saved the marriage—and the man's job.

Put ideas together. More often than not, creativity is the spark that's struck from pairing two or more existing ideas. SES ASSOCIATES, a Cambridge, Mass., "think tank," was asked by a major food manufacturer to find a better way to package potato chips. So SES associated two ideas: potato chips and wet leaves.

Why leaves? Because the first question the SES creative types asked was: "What is the best packaging solution you ever saw?" Someone said the bagging of wet leaves. "Try to shove a load of dry leaves into a bag, and you have a tough time," he explained. "You are packing air, just the way the potato-chip manufacturers do. But if the leaves are wet, you can pack a lot of them in."

Good idea, the researchers thought, and they tried packing wet potato chips. But it didn't work; when the chips dried in the package, they crumbled. That led to the development of a tougher chip that, when wet, could be pressed into a uniform shape. Today, this product is recognized by millions of Americans as the potato chips that come in a can instead of a bag.

William Gordon, president of SES, stresses that such creativity cannot happen without "the emotional willingness to risk failure." In other words, even the craziest of ideas should be considered, since every truly original idea may look a little crazy at first. Thomas Edison, a man with 1093 American patents in his name, once confessed: "I'll try anything—even Limburger cheese!"

Sleep on it. When faced with an intractable problem, try putting it completely out of your conscious mind; let it incubate. At the moment you least expect it, a creative solution may pop up.

In 1865, German chemist Friedrich Kekule fell asleep puzzling over the structure of the benzene molecule. Kekule dreamed of thousands of atoms dancing before his eyes, some forming patterns and twisting like snakes. Suddenly one snake grabbed its own tail. In a flash, Kekule awakened with the idea of a closed-chain structure of benzene—a brilliant scientific discovery.

Others have also hit on their best ideas while their mental engines were idling. It was said of Mozart, for example, that his music wrote itself while he traveled, strolled or dozed. Nobel Prize-winning physicist Dennis Gabor says that, like Einstein before him, he gets his best ideas while shaving. Then there was seven-year-old Susie, whose problem was simply that the braided string belt had been pulled out of her pajama bottoms. *How on earth,* she wondered, *can I ever thread it back through again?* She put the problem out of her conscious mind. A short time later, as she was getting an ice cube out of the freezer, an idea suddenly hit her. She could wet the belt, freeze it in a circle, then guide it through the pajama opening. It worked!

Practice. Like jogging or speaking a new language, using creative techniques may feel awkward until old habits have been unlearned. To help, try some of the following creative calisthenics. For example: Write three-word phrases beginning with each letter of the alphabet ("Buy better bargains" or "Tell tall tales"). Devise a new, witty definition for these words: a bore, a politician, an expert, a grapefruit, a revolution, hope, patience, lust. Make a list of 5 blue foods, or 15 ways to use a feather, or 6 new names for the United States of America. Or try this: think how it might feel to be, say, a stapler, or a Volkswagen, or a fish. Then write down what you think.

Most of all, develop and practice a "passion for living." Pablo Picasso marveled at everything. "I look at flies, at flowers, at leaves and trees around me," he said. "I let my mind drift at ease, just like a boat in the current. Sooner or later, it is caught by something."

By being alert to what is around you, your mind and imagination can't help but begin to stir in new, mysterious ways. "The larger the island of knowledge," said the late clergyman-scholar, Ralph Sockman, "the longer the shoreline of mystery surrounding it." And, somewhere behind that shoreline, pushing it out toward the horizon, is our power of creativity.

THE REMARKABLE

SELF-HEALING POWERS

OF THE MIND

by Morton M. Hunt

DURING WORLD War II, I was an Eighth Air Force pilot, flying lonely reconnaissance missions deep into Germany week after week. Under this stress I became strange and alien to myself: my handwriting became crabbed and illegible, I drank and gambled night after night, I could read nothing more substantial than the scandal sheets, and music, one of my chief joys, became boring and meaningless. One night, on my way to the briefing room, I even seriously considered trying to break my ankle—to avoid being sent out on another flight.

I was on the verge of a breakdown when the fighting ended. Then for weeks I slept, daydreamed and drifted through my duties. Meanwhile, deep inside, where the wellsprings of joy and health reside, a healing and a regrowth must have been taking place. For gradually I began to read books again, my handwriting ceased to look like that of a crippled old man, and one day, hearing a familiar Mozart aria on a nearby radio, I suddenly felt a flood of good feeling wash through me. I had the eerie sensation that all at once I was in the presence of a long-lost friend—myself. "It's me!" I thought in joyful amazement. "I'm back!"

Spontaneous recoveries from emotional ailments are

vastly more common than most of us realize. What does it? The mind itself.

A decade or so ago, most psychiatrists thought that an ill mind had little chance to cure itself; their thinking was still focused on the mind's frailties. Today that's changing. Many psychiatrists now stress that the human mind, like the body, has a whole battery of weapons to heal its own ills. Without denying the value of psychiatry for the severely disturbed, the new viewpoint suggests that millions of people with emotional problems have the resources to heal themselves.

The Balance Restorers.

The mind's self-healing mechanisms are surprisingly parallel to those of the rest of the body. Take one of the body's basic principles, "homeostasis," or maintenance of equilibrium between its organ systems: when we get too hot, for example, we sweat, in order to keep our temperature constant. In a comparable way, the mind tries to restore emotional balance when it is upset. People plagued by feelings of unworthiness, guilt or inadequacy often unconsciously turn to an occupation which upsets these feelings—a mental device known as "compensation." An excellent illustration of this is Glenn Cunningham, who, having been burned as a child and told he would never walk again, not only walked but became one of the world's greatest milers.

A parallel also exists between the body's ability to wall off an invading foreign object within a cyst and the mental-balance restorer called "rationalization." When we talk ourselves into thinking an agreeable thought about a disagreeable fact, we are encysting the thing that hurts us. A friend of mine, for example, lost money in a foolish investment, and now cheerfully says of the experience, "It was an expensive lesson—but it was worth it."

In the past, many psychiatrists thought of rationalization, compensation and the other mental defenses as unhealthy. Today, some boldly state that although exaggerated defense reactions *can* be harmful—like fevers that run too high—more often mental defenses are curative balance restorers. In the *American Handbook of Psychiatry,* Dr. Melitta Schmideberg

expresses the current view: The mental defenses are as essential
as any vital organ of the body.

No End to Emotional Growth.

The new viewpoint is changing another pessimistic notion: the
theory held by some psychoanalysts that we stop growing
emotionally after adolescence, that the flaws built into a
person's character in the early years can be removed only by
intensive therapy. The latest data indicate that the personality is
often quite capable of straightening itself out during maturity.

Many a college student who drops out is diagnosed as
having a "character disorder"—as being impulsive, willful,
irresponsible, lacking in conscience. Folk wisdom has been
optimistic about the wild one, however. "He'll settle down," it
says. Pollyanna-ish? No; researchers at Yale recently surveyed a
number of men who had dropped out because of emotional
problems, found that many of them had gone back to college
and finished well, and that most of the group had done well in
later life.

Why? Because emotional growth never stops. It often
takes only the sunshine and rain of love, work, parenthood to
make the bent plant straighten up.

The Healing of Love.

Freud said that each love we experience, whether for parent,
beloved or friend, leaves a deposit in the self, enlarging and
maturing it. When we fall in love, we gain a sudden new
perspective on ourselves: we know how we want the loved one to
see us, and we try to transform ourselves to match that image.
Moreover, love is a completion, a satisfying of deep needs; most
of us fall in love with someone whose personality is the
complement of our own (the strong, driving person with the
frail, timid one, for instance) and through whom we can try to
fulfill ourselves.

A few years ago, the Dallas Child Guidance Clinic studied
34 adults who had been uncommonly shy and withdrawn
children. Most of them, it was revealed, had turned out quite
well—and, significantly, three quarters of these had married
extroverts, who completed their personalities and healed their
old hurts.

The Challenge of Work.

Thomas Carlyle once wrote, "Work is the grand cure for all the maladies and miseries that ever beset mankind." Neuroses are, in a sense, childish things, and some persons are fortunate enough to find challenges so serious and adult that they are able to put away childish things. Many years ago, a young midwestern lawyer suffered such depressions that his friends thought it wise to keep knives and razors out of his reach. He wrote: "I am now the most miserable man living. Whether I shall ever be better, I cannot tell; I awfully forebode I shall not."

He was wrong. The challenges that life offered him brought him a health and a strength that saved him and his country from dissolution. His name was Abraham Lincoln.

Forgetting and Reconditioning.

One of the most important self-curing agencies is our human propensity to forget unpleasant things. Psychological researchers have given subjects tasks and puzzles to do, arranging them in such a way that not all could be completed. Afterward, when the subjects were asked to recall which tasks they had finished and which they had not, those with shaky self-esteem tended to remember only the tasks they had managed to complete. As someone has said, "Remembrances embellish life; forgetfulness alone makes it endurable."

More demanding than forgetting is a laborious process we might call "reconditioning"—a kind of rewiring of the brain in which our reactions are changed, one by one. We do it, for example, when we grieve for a dead person. The very process of going over the fond thoughts again and again gradually conditions us to our new status. The healthy mind slowly arrives at the point where it can look back with a loving smile instead of tears.

Psychological Antibodies.

Just as a cured infection leaves antibodies behind, a hurt, once healed, may leave us with a net gain—greater self-awareness, increased maturity.

An event that shocks can set off a process of reorganization and growth in the whole personality. Many a playboy has grown up only after his parents died. Going off to military service has transformed more than one disturbed young man. "The loss of supportive persons," writes Dr. Ian Stevenson in the *American Journal of Psychiatry,* "seems often to contribute to recovery from the psychoneuroses."

Even a severe mental illness can sometimes leave a person who recovers from it healthier than he was, thanks to deeper self-understanding, according to famed psychiatrist Dr. Karl Menninger. Thus, many famous writers—including John Stuart Mill and William James—did their best work after severe depressions or nervous breakdowns.

Self-Acceptance.

The most valuable and pervasive of all the mind's defenses is belief in self and in life. Psychologists refer to it as "self-acceptance," the power that enables us to see ourselves realistically and to concentrate on our assets so that we come to like what we see. William James spoke of this power as the "religion of healthy-mindedness." Dr. Menninger calls it an "inner strength," which he feels all people have in varying degrees.

None of this means that we can always sit back and complacently assume that all will go well. Though it is true that the mind has remarkable self-restorative powers, it is sometimes necessary to give those powers help. A person with a serious emotional problem *should* seek professional counsel.

Yet, having looked closely at the self-healing powers of the human mind, I am encouraged to think that our natural and unconscious inclination is to mend ourselves rather than to destroy ourselves. Though a thousand wise and gloomy philosophers have called man a frail, wretched and miserable creature, I prefer to side with the Psalmist, who sang, "I am fearfully and wonderfully made."

THE STRANGE POWERS

OF INTUITION

by John Kord Lagemann

"WOMEN KNOW everything," my grandfather once told me, "and heaven help us if they ever find it out."

He was referring, of course, to feminine intuition—that mysterious faculty which enables women to answer questions before they're asked; predict the arrival of unexpected guests; identify social climbers, alcoholics and rivals as if they were plainly labeled; know without being told when their husbands have quarreled with the boss or daydreamed—just daydreamed, mind you—about another woman.

Ever since Eve took the first bite out of the apple, man has been asking woman how she knows all these things without any apparent reason for knowing. Nothing infuriates him more than to be told: "I just know, that's all."

Does intuition really exist? And if so, is it feminine? I decided to put the question to science.

Intuition, I learned, is a normal and highly useful function of human intelligence. This fact has been confirmed by each of the half dozen authorities I consulted. Though associated with high IQs in both sexes, it is more characteristic of women than of men.

Why? As Dr. Helene Deutsch, author of *The Psychology of Women,* points out, in adolescence a boy is interested primarily in asserting himself in action, while a girl's interests center around feelings, her own and others. Dr. Deutsch compares the adolescent girl to "someone listening in the dark and perceiving every noise with special acuteness." From the understanding she gains of her own emotions she is able by analogy to relive the emotions of others.

Women don't pay nearly as much attention as men to what people say, but they are apt to know a great deal more about the way people feel. One winter when I was living in New Hampshire my friend Mr. White coveted a corner pasture which his neighbor Mr. Perry stubbornly refused to sell. The men were no longer on speaking terms, but their wives went right on visiting over the phone. One night after a long and rambling party-line visit—in which the land issue was never mentioned— Mrs. White said to her husband, "I think Mr. Perry will sell that corner lot if you still want it." When I saw the Whites a few months later the deal had been completed.

Reduced to simplest terms intuition is a way of thinking without words—a short cut to the truth, and in matters of emotion, the only way of getting there at all. Dr. Carl Jung defines it as "a basic psychological function which transmits perceptions in an unconscious way." This perception is based on the evidence of our physical senses. But because it taps knowledge and experience of which we aren't aware it is often confused with telepathy, clairvoyance or extrasensory perception. We all know the "psychic" card player who seems to read another's hand; actually he notes a telltale flutter of your eyelid or lip, a hesitation in speech, the tightening of a wrist muscle when your hand touches a card. He may not be aware himself of the clues he follows.

Civilization has substituted words and various other abstractions for the direct experience of seeing, hearing, smelling, tasting, touching and feeling. But our neglected senses still go right on operating, far better than we realize. Take the sense of smell, perhaps the least developed of the senses. We used to laugh at backwoods doctors who diagnosed certain diseases by sniffing the air near the patient. Then we discovered that these diseases really did produce chemical changes resulting in characteristic odors. Experiments have shown that the odor of a person's breath actually varies with changes in his emotional attitude. The distance over which we can unconsciously pick up the scent of another human being is unknown, but it is almost certainly greater than the length of a room. How can an odor of which you are not even aware mean anything to you? If you've ever been awakened slowly and deliciously by the aroma of coffee and bacon, you know the answer.

Last summer I saw an example of how the senses cooperate to produce intuition. On the boat from Woods Hole to Martha's Vineyard my wife nodded toward a young woman sitting nearby and remarked, "I'm sure I know her. Yet I can't remember having seen her before."

Impulsively we introduced ourselves and mentioned my wife's feeling. After the young woman had spoken, my wife said, "Now I know. You take phone calls for Dr. Miller."

"Why, yes, I do," the girl answered.

Why did my wife feel there was something familiar about the girl? "But don't you see?" she explained to me later. "She *looked* just the way she sounded over the phone." Simple as that. Come to think of it, though, can't almost any teen-ager spot a blind date from the way he or she sounded on the phone?

Most women are quite good at guessing age, particularly if the subject is another woman. If you don't believe it, try it sometime at a party. The difference between a girl of 23 and a girl of 25 is far too subtle to put into words. Men try to reason it out and usually their guesses are not better than chance or gallantry will allow. Yet with the aid of almost imperceptible clues women can often spot the difference.

One of the few attempts to observe intuition systematically was made by Eric Berne, a former staff psychiatrist with the Army Medical Corps and later the originator of Transactional Analysis. While interviewing men at an Army Separation Center, Dr. Berne and his colleagues tried to guess, before the patient had spoken, what his occupation had been in civilian life. All the patients were dressed in standard maroon bathrobes and cloth slippers. The doctors' guesses averaged well above chance. "On one occasion," Dr. Berne reports, "the occupations of 26 successive men were guessed correctly." Clues unconsciously detected in the men's eyes, gestures, facial expressions, speech, hands, and so on, probably explain this success.

As psychiatry and common sense have actually proved,

you know a lot more than you are aware that you know. The mind tunes into consciousness only a few of the impressions which flow in from your sense organs. But your brain does not waste these impulses. It stores them up in your unconscious mind where they are ready to be used. Some physicians, for instance, have only to glance at a patient to diagnose correctly a disease which others cannot identify without painstaking examination. These intuitive doctors note many faint clues and match them with relevant information accumulated over a lifetime.

Likewise, every intuitive person knows how to draw on his reserve of unconscious knowledge and experience in coping with the problems of everyday life. The American Chemical Society questioned 232 leading U. S. scientists, found that 83 percent of them depended on intuition in their research after intense conscious effort had failed to produce results. A similar study by Dr. Eliot Dole Hutchinson revealed that intuition played an important part in the creative work of 80 percent of a sample of 253 artists, musicians and writers.

The unconscious part of your brain never stops working. So when you're faced with a perplexing job, work on it as hard as you can. Then if you can't lick it, try sleeping on it or taking a walk or relaxing with friends. If you have primed yourself with all available facts, the answer is likely to "dawn" on you while your mind is seemingly at rest.

In the case of a purely personal decision, the important facts are your own deep feelings, and in this case you know intuitively what to do without the need for long preliminary deliberation. Dr. Sigmund Freud once told a friend, "When making a decision of minor importance I have always found it advantageous to consider all the pros and cons. In vital matters, however, such as the choice of a mate or a profession, the decision should come from the unconscious, from somewhere within ourselves. In the important decisions of our personal lives we should be governed by the deep inner needs of our nature."

Life is much more interesting for the intuitive person than for the nonintuitive. People mean more when you understand them from the inside out—and because of this, you mean more to them. That is what intuition is, really—finding new and deeper meanings in people and events, making more sense out of life. How can you develop your intuitive powers? Like any other form of thinking, intuition requires an alertness, sensitivity and discipline of mind which have to be cultivated.

Take off the blinders of habit and open your mind to what's going on around you. See people as they really are, not as you think they ought to be. Don't let prejudices distort your vision. Half the trick is to let people tell you about themselves unconsciously. The way a person stands, sits, shakes hands, smokes or sips a drink will be, to the intuitive man or woman, important clues in sizing up character.

Intuition isn't the enemy, but the ally, of reason. Effective realistic thinking requires a combination of both.

MY JOURNEY

TO FAITH

by Jim Bishop

AT THE age of four, I knew that God was everywhere. I spoke to Him, and sometimes He listened with sympathy. It was an unforgettable occasion in boyhood when He did indeed send a bicycle with a coaster brake.

As I grew toward manhood, the more I learned, the less I believed in God. I told myself that He had been invented by ancients who feared the eternal darkness of death. Even worse, they had fashioned Him unto their likenesses.

When I was 21, my superior intellect told me that God was a fake. Heaven could not be up and Hell down, because in space there is no up or down. And I knew that everything in creation dies, including the smallest insect and the biggest star.

In following years, there were times of industry and some small success, but they were not happy years. There was a bedtime carrousel of the mind in which the horses of doubt swung in slow circles to tinny music. They carried empty saddles and they pranced with a fury of faithlessness in God, in myself, in my work, in my wife, in mankind, even in my mother and father.

Then one day I felt a new experience. I saw the miracle of birth, and it turned my wandering mind around. I had seen babies before, of course, in bassinets, had cooed at them, chucked them under the chin, observed their gummy grins and hoped they would not cry.

But this miracle was Virginia Lee, a child of my own. She was just another infant (an exceptionally beautiful one, to be sure), but so close to me that this time I questioned birth and life.

She was the result of the fusion of two bodies in love, but how did an ovum learn to roll to the womb? What caused spermatozoa to fertilize an egg? And what far-off deity told that ovum to split and split to form a fetus, to devise its own chemical factory and absorb nourishment from its mother?

How, I wondered, could an infant, unconscious of life and the struggle for existence, fashion the correct number of limbs and toes and fingers and eyes and ears? Did all of that do itself?

If it was a matter of genes, did they fashion themselves? Maybe they evolved over millions of years. From what? I began to doubt my doubts.

Gradually I lost faith in my intellect. It was far from supplying the needed answers. I could not see air, but without it I would die. Thus it is, I decided, with the spirit of man. I needed Something to breathe life into a soul that had been crushed by the dominance of the human mind.

Then in a span of nine weeks I saw my mind proved a helpless instrument. My mother and my wife were both taken. They went off quietly, rich in faith, strong in the knowledge of where they were going. But for me the weeks dragged. The months appeared to be in a freeze frame.

Sometimes, lost in a labyrinth of complexities, I was forced to return to the beginning. Over and over I argued: (1) There is no God. (2) There is. Day by day, I began to see that nothing is accidental. All the good and bad events are part of a divine scheme in balance.

I was a slow learner. But somehow, somewhere, as I groped my painful way, I found my soul. Overnight, I knew it was there—wounded, bleeding perhaps, but alive.

If there is a soul, there must be a God. Science cannot measure a soul. Call it conscience; call it reasoning between right and wrong; call it a spiritual being—it is there because He willed it.

I began to pray. I found that I could murmur a quick prayer at any time—while driving, while shaving, while thinking of Him and His Almighty Presence. I began to ask for things. Not small things. I asked for world peace. I asked for faith for the faithless. I prayed for the poor, the sick, the injured, the old, the lonely. As faith returned to me, I feared that it might dissolve again. So I prayed for continuing faith, too.

Faith does not come as quickly as these words. It starts. It stops. It floods and recedes. For a time I felt that I was wooing faith. Cultivating it as one might a friend whom no one ever met. Grasping. Clawing. Reaching. Then calmness came. When I gave up, I could feel His presence. There were no apparitions; no wraiths on the wall. He was there and I knew it.

I understood that I was here as part of an enormous test. He had given me custody of my soul; someday He would ask me to account for my stewardship. I had spent half of my life kicking and punching that soul to a state of unconsciousness. So I murmured: "Forgive me. Make me more pleasing to Thee." I murmured it over and over. And I also said, "Dear God, I was a little boy once who prayed, not knowing what faith was, and You gave me a bicycle I didn't deserve. Please remember me."

And finally, like the bicycle, light came. I had wanted proof. He wanted me to believe without revealing Himself.

If He revealed Himself to us, none of us would require faith. None of us would want to toil. There would be no point in struggling to keep alive if we were so easily assured that eternal life in paradise is waiting on the far side of this life.

No, it is a far better test of our devotion if He remains mystical and obscure, just beyond the range of our senses.

I had wanted proof, something for my eyes or ears or hands. He wanted me to believe without it. Faith was what He required of me. And He never rested till I found it.

THE BIBLE'S TIMELESS

—AND TIMELY—

INSIGHTS

by Smiley Blanton, M.D.

THE OTHER day a new patient noticed a Bible lying on my desk. "Do you—a psychiatrist—read the Bible?" he asked.

"I not only read it," I told him, "I study it. It's the greatest textbook on human behavior ever put together. If people would just absorb its message, a lot of us psychiatrists could close our offices and go fishing."

"You're talking about the Ten Commandments and the Golden Rule?"

"Certainly—but more, too," I said. "There are dozens of other insights that have profound psychiatric value. Take your own case. For the past hour you've been telling me how you've done this, tried that, all to no avail. It's pretty obvious that you're worrying yourself into a state of acute anxiety, isn't it?"

"That," he said dryly, "is why I'm here."

I picked up the Bible. "Here's some advice that St. Paul gives to the Ephesians. Just four words: *Having done all, stand.* Now, what does that mean? Exactly what it says. You've done your best, what more can you do? Keep running in circles? Plow up the same ground? What you really need—far more than a solution to this particular problem—is peace of mind. And there's the formula: relax, stand quietly, stop trying to lick this thing with your conscious mind. Let the creative power in your unconscious mind take over. It may solve the whole thing for you, if you'll just get out of your own way!"

My patient looked thoughtful. "Maybe I should do a little Bible reading on my own," he said.

It does seem foolish not to make use of the distilled wisdom of 3000 years. Centuries before psychiatry, the Bible knew that "the kingdom of God is within you." We psychiatrists call it the unconscious mind—but only the words are new, not the concept. From beginning to end the Bible teaches that the human soul is a battleground where good struggles with evil. We talk about the forces of hostility and aggression contending with the love-impulses in human nature. It's the same thing.

What psychiatry has done is to bring scientific terminology to the truths that the Bible presents in poetry, allegory and parable. What, in essence, did Freud and the other pioneers discover? That the human mind functions on the conscious *and* the unconscious level. That the thing we call conscience does, too, and that many emotional pressures and dislocations are caused by its hidden action.

It is tremendously exciting to read the Bible with even this much knowledge of psychiatry. Here are a few of my favorite passages, words so full of insight that I think they might well be memorized and repeated periodically by anyone who values his mental health.

- *Underneath are the everlasting arms.* For hundreds of years, troubled people have found comfort in these words from the Book of Deuteronomy. This is not surprising. One of the few fears we are born with is the fear of falling, so the idea of a pair of loving arms, sustaining and eternal, is an answer to the yearning in all of us to feel safe, to find security. Furthermore, one of the deepest forms of communication is *touch*. And so this Biblical image brings a great sense of peace. If you suffer from tension and insomnia, try repeating these words to yourself at bedtime. You may find them more effective than any sleeping pill.

- *Love thy neighbor as thyself.* Many people think this noble concept comes from the New Testament. Actually you can also find it in Leviticus. The remarkable thing, to a psychiatrist, is its recognition that in an emotionally healthy person there must be self-love as well as love of others.

Lack of self-esteem is probably the most common

emotional ailment I am called upon to treat. Often pressure from the unconscious mind is causing this sense of unworthiness. Suppose a woman comes to me, weighted down with guilt. I can't undo the things she has done. But perhaps I can help her understand why she did them, and how the mechanism of her conscience, functioning below the conscious level, is paralyzing her. And I can urge her to read and reread the story of the Prodigal Son. How can anyone feel permanently condemned or rejected in a world where this magnificent promise comes ringing down the centuries, the promise that love is stronger than any mistake, any error?

• *Take no thought for the morrow.* A modern rephrasing might well be, "Stop worrying about the future." Worry causes tension. Tension blocks the flow of creative energy from the unconscious mind. And when creative energy wanes, problems multiply.

Most of us know perfectly well that worry is a futile process. Yet many people constantly borrow trouble. "Sufficient unto the day," says the Bible, "is the evil thereof." There are plenty of problems in the here-and-now to tackle and solve. The only moment when you're really alive is the present one, so make the most of it. Have faith that the Power that brought you here will help you through any future crisis, whatever it may be. "They that wait upon the Lord," says Isaiah, "shall renew their strength; they shall mount up with wings as eagles." Why? Because their faith makes them non-worriers.

• *As he thinketh in his heart, so is he.* This penetrating phrase from Proverbs implies that what you *think* you think is less important than what you really think. Every day in my office I see illustrations of this. I recall talking to a woman who had married during the Korean war. Her husband, a reserve officer, had volunteered for war duty and gone overseas, leaving her pregnant. He had been killed; she was left to bring up their son alone. Eventually she remarried, but now she was having difficulty with the 15-year-old boy.

It was apparent that she treated her son with unusual harshness and severity. "Why are you so strict with him?" I asked.

"Because I don't want him to grow up spoiled," she said instantly.

"Did it ever occur to you," I asked, "that when this boy's father went away voluntarily, leaving you, and got himself killed, something in you was enraged, something in you hated him? And isn't it just possible that some of this unadmitted hate has been displaced onto the child he left you with, although your conscious mind doesn't want to admit that either? Look into your heart and search for the truth there, below the rationalizations of your mind. Until you do, we're not going to get anywhere with this problem."

* *Where your treasure is, there will your heart be also.* Of course! *What* we shall love is the key problem of human existence, because we tend to become the reflection of what we love. Do you love money? Then your values will be materialistic. Do you love power? Then the aggressive instincts in you will slowly become dominant. Do you love God and your neighbor? Then you are not likely to need a psychiatrist!

We psychiatrists warn against sustained anger and hostility; we know that unresolved conflicts in the unconscious mind can make you physically ill. How does the Bible put it? *Let not the sun go down upon your wrath.* And: *A merry heart doeth good like a medicine.* Exactly so. These flashing sparks of truth from the pages of the Bible are endless!

If I were asked to choose one Bible passage above all others it would be this: *And ye shall know the truth, and the truth shall make you free.* In one tremendous sentence these words encompass the whole theory and method of psychotherapy. Nine times out of ten, when people come to me tormented by guilt, racked by anxiety, exhausted by unresolved hate, it is because they don't know the truth about themselves. It is the role of the psychiatrist to remove the camouflage, the self-deception, the rationalizations. It is his job to bring the unconscious conflicts into the conscious mind where reason can deal with them. As Freud said, "Reason is a small voice, but it is persistent." Once insight is gained, the cure can begin—because the truth *does* make you free.

We shall never have all the truth. Great questions of life and death, good and evil, remain unanswered—and must so remain, as the book of Job eloquently tells us. But this much seems plain to me: locked in the unconscious of each of us are the same elemental forces of love and hate that have haunted and inspired the human race from the beginning. With this hidden area of the human spirit psychiatry concerns itself—sometimes helpfully, sometimes not. But there is also an ancient book that deals with it, that understands it profoundly and intuitively, a book that for 3000 years has been a help in time of trouble to any person wise enough to use it.

PERSON TO PERSON

HAVE YOU

AN EDUCATED HEART?

by Gelett Burgess

LAST OCTOBER I sent Crystabel a book. She acknowledged it, and promptly. But two months afterward she actually wrote me another letter, telling me what she thought of that book; and she proved, moreover, that she had read it. Now, I ask you, isn't that a strange and beautiful experience in this careless world? Crystabel had the educated heart. To such as possess the educated heart thanks are something like mortgages, to be paid in installments. Why, after five years Crystabel often refers to a gift that has pleased her. It is the motive for a gift she cares for, not its value; and hence her gratefulness.

Everything can be done beautifully by the educated heart, from the lacing of a shoe so that it won't come loose to passing the salt before it is asked for. If you say only "Good morning," it can be done pleasingly. Observe how the polished actor says it, with that cheerful rising inflection. But the ordinary American growls it out with surly downward emphasis. Merely to speak distinctly is a great kindness, I consider. You never have to ask, "What did you say?" of the educated heart. On the other hand, very few people ever really listen with kindly attention. They are usually merely waiting for a chance to pounce upon you with their own narrative. Or if they do listen, is your story heard with real sympathy? Does the face really glow?

Consider the usual birthday gift or Christmas present. By universal practice it is carefully wrapped in a pretty paper and tied with ribbon. That package is symbolical of what all friendly acts should be—kindness performed with style. Then what is style in giving? Ah, the educated heart makes it a business to know what his friend really wants. One friend I have to whom I can't express a taste that isn't treasured up against need. I said once that I loved watercress, and lightly wished that I might have it for every meal. Never a meal had I at his table since, without finding watercress bought specially for me.

Do you think it's easy, this business of giving? Verily, giving is as much an art as portrait painting or the making of glass flowers. And imagination can surely be brought to bear. Are you sailing for Brazil? It isn't the basket of fine fruits that brings the tears to your eyes, nor the flowers with trailing yards of red ribbon—all that's ordinary everyday kindness. It's that little purse full of Brazilian currency, bills and small change all ready for you when you go ashore at Rio.

There was old Wentrose—he understood the Fourth Dimension of kindness, all right. Never a friend of his wife's did he puffingly put aboard a streetcar, but he'd tuck apologetically into her hand the nickel fare to save her rummaging in her bag. Real elegance, the gesture of inherent nobility, I call that.

Is it sufficient simply to offer your seat in a streetcar to a woman? The merely kind person does that. But he does it rather sheepishly. Isn't your graciousness more cultured if you give it up with a bow, with a smile of willingness? Besides the quarter you give the beggar, can't you give a few cents' worth of yourself too? The behavior of the educated heart becomes automatic: you set it in the direction of true kindness and courtesy and after a while it will function without deliberate thought. Such thoughtfulness, such consideration is *not* merely decorative. It is the very essence and evidence of sincerity. Without it all so-called kindness is merely titular and perfunctory.

Suppose I submit your name for membership in a club. Have I done you (or my club) any real service unless I also do my best to see that you are elected? And so if I go to every member of the committee, if I urge all my friends to endorse you, that is merely the completion of my regard for you. It is like salt—"It's what makes potatoes taste bad, if you don't put it on."

Must you dance with all the wallflowers, then? I don't go so far as that, although it would prove that you had imagination enough to put yourself in another's place. All I ask is that when you try to do a favor you do it to the full length of the rope. Don't send your telegram in just ten carefully selected words. Economize elsewhere, but add those few extra phrases that make the reader perceive that you cared more for him than you did for the expense.

No one with the educated heart ever approached a clergyman, or a celebrity, or a long-absent visitor with the shocking greeting: "You don't remember me, do you?" No, he gives his name first. No one with the educated heart ever said, "Now do come and see me, sometime!" The educated heart's way of putting it is apt to be, "How about coming next Wednesday?" And strongly I doubt if the educated heart is ever tardy at an appointment. It knows that if only two minutes late a person has brought just that much less of himself.

Truly nothing is so rare as the educated heart. And if you wonder why, just show a group picture—a banquet or a class photograph. What does every one of us first look at, talk about? Ourself. And that's the reason why most hearts are so unlearned in kindness.

If you want to enlarge that mystic organ whence flows true human kindness, you must cultivate your imagination. You must learn to put yourself in another's place, think his thoughts. The educated heart, remember, does kindness *with style*.

HOW TO SELL

AN IDEA

by Elmer Wheeler

HAVE YOU ever approached your boss with a red-hot idea for increasing efficiency—only to have him become resentful instead of enthusiastic? Have you ever offered your wife or the neighbors "good advice"? If you have, you know what I mean when I say that people resent having other people's ideas forced on them.

When someone approaches us with a new idea, our instinctive reaction is to put up a defense against it. We feel that we must protect our individuality; and most of us are egotistical enough to think that our ideas are better than anyone else's.

There are three tested rules for putting your ideas across to other people so as to arouse their enthusiasm. Here they are:

Rule One: Use a fly rod—not a feeding tube. Others won't accept *your* idea until they can accept it as *their* idea.

It was said during World War I that Colonel House was the most powerful man in the world because he controlled the most powerful man in the world—Woodrow Wilson. "I learned that the best way to convert him to an idea," explained House, "was to plant it in his mind casually, to get him thinking about it on his own account."

When you want to sell someone an idea, take a lesson from the fisherman who casts his fly temptingly near the trout.

He could never ram the hook into the trout's mouth. But he can entice the trout to come to the hook.

Don't appear too anxious to have your ideas accepted. Just bring them out where they can be seen.

"Have you considered this?" is better than "This is the way." "Do you think this would work?" is better than "Here's what we should do."

Let the other fellow sell himself on your idea. Then he'll stay sold.

Rule Two: Let the other fellow argue your case. He instinctively feels called upon to raise some objection to save his face. Give him a chance to disagree with you—by presenting your own objections!

"The way to convince another," said wise old Ben Franklin, "is to state your case moderately and accurately. Then say that of course you may be mistaken about it; which causes your listener to receive what you have to say and, like as not, turn about and convince you of it, since you are in doubt. But if you go at him in a tone of positiveness and arrogance you only make an opponent of him."

Franklin used this technique, against great opposition, in his sale of the idea of adopting the Constitution of the United States.

"I confess," he began, "that I do not entirely approve of this Constitution; but, Sir, I am not sure I shall never approve it; for having lived long, I have experienced many instances of being obliged by better information or fuller consideration to change opinions, even on important subjects, which I first thought right. I cannot help expressing a wish that every member of the convention who may still have objections to it would with me on this occasion doubt a little of his own infallibility, and, to make manifest our unanimity, put his name to this instrument."

Abraham Lincoln used the same technique in selling his ideas to a jury. He argued both sides of the case—but there was always the subtle suggestion that his side was the logical one. An opposing lawyer said of him: "He made a better statement of my case to the jury than I could have made myself."

Another technique is to sell the other fellow the idea as

his, not yours. "You gave me an idea the other day that started me thinking," you begin.

Tom Reed, for many years Speaker of the House, was an adroit persuader. At a committee hearing he would remain silent until everyone had had his say, making notes of all objections. Then, when everyone else was argued out, Reed would say, "Gentlemen, it seems to me that what has been said here can be summarized as follows...." Reed would then present *his* ideas—and sell them.

Once Dudley Nichols, the movie director, wasn't satisfied with a scene in one of his pictures. To remedy the situation, he said to Rosalind Russell, the star, "Wonderful, wonderful, but I could see, Miss Russell, when you hesitated that brief instant, that you were thinking about the possibility of playing the scene down just a trifle more. Shall we try it once the way you were thinking?"

Rule Three: Ask—don't tell. Patrick Henry, another famous idea salesman, was a political unknown when first elected to Virginia's House of Burgesses—but every resolution he introduced was passed. Listen to him in his famous "Liberty or Death" speech and see how he uses questions to get his ideas across:

"Our brethren are already in the field—why stand we here idle?"

"Shall we lie supinely on our backs?"

"What is it that gentlemen wish? What would they have? Is life so dear or peace so sweet as to be purchased at the price of chains and slavery?"

Try saying the same thing in positive statements and see how much antagonism it would invoke.

When you put your ideas across with questions, you give the other fellow a share in the idea. You don't tell him—you ask him for the answer. You're giving him a chance to sell himself.

Try these rules the next time you want to put an idea across to your boss, your family or the neighbors.

THE LOVING MESSAGE

IN A TOUCH

by Norman M. Lobsenz

NOT LONG ago, a couple went to a marriage counselor with a problem. The wife objected violently to being touched. Although she freely enjoyed her sexual relationship with her husband, she could not, to his bewilderment and hurt, bear the affectionate caresses he liked to give her hand or arm or hair.

Another family, concerned about a teen-age son's rebelliousness, consulted a psychiatrist who spent weeks trying to restore communication between the emotionally estranged boy and his father. One day, the father suddenly got up and embraced his son. The boy hugged back, and both began to cry. "It's the first time you've held me since I was a child," the boy said.

These incidents are not as unusual as they may seem. Whether we can admit it or not, many of us are painfully inhibited about touching and being touched even by those we love.

Reasons are not hard to find. The average American tends to think of bodily contact in terms of sex or combat—both of which are prickly with cultural and psychological taboos. Our Puritan heritage leads many of us to disapprove of any touching as "sensual."

Those who have created this invisible barrier have lost

something important: the part touch plays in giving encouragement, expressing tenderness, showing emotional support. Touch is a crucial aspect of all human relationships. Yet, except in moments of extreme crisis, we often forget how to ask for—or to offer—this boon. We forget, for instance, how it can heal the wounds of a quarrel. I was told about a mother who tried reasoning with two daughters, 11 and 12, who were fighting bitterly over clothes for a party. When reasoning failed, their annoyed father *ordered* them to be quiet. But it wasn't until the mother impulsively flung her arms about both girls and held them close that the bickering stopped.

We also tend to forget how comforting physical contact can be when we are under stress. When my wife was seriously ill I spent hours in the hospital simply holding her hands—a gesture that was wonderfully sustaining for both of us. Yet, in the ordinary run of life, it seems that even the most loving couples seldom link hands—either in times of sorrow and anxiety, or in moments of peace and pleasure.

An instinctive awareness of the power of touch to convey deep feeling is reflected in such expressions as having a "touching" experience, being "touched" and keeping "in touch." When "words fail," we reach out physically. Helen Keller—blind and deaf from birth—wrote in her diary: "My dog was rolling in the grass. I wanted to catch a picture of him in my fingers, and I touched him lightly. Lo, his fat body revolved, stiffened and solidified into an upright position. He pressed close to me as if to crowd himself into my hand. He loved it with his tail, his paw, his tongue. If he could speak, I believe he would say with me that paradise is attained by touch."

Studies of infants and children have shown repeatedly that nothing is more important to early physical and mental growth than touching. In various experiments with normal and subnormal youngsters, those who had the most physical contact with parents or nurses or attendants learned to walk and talk the earliest and had the higher I.Q.s.

Research with animals yields similar results. In a famous experiment, psychologist Harry F. Harlow built two "surrogate" mothers for monkey babies. One, a motherfigure built of wire, gave milk. The other, built of sponge rubber and terry cloth, gave no milk. Given a choice, the baby monkeys went to the terry-cloth mother for the comfort of her soft "touch." These results contradicted the accepted theory that a baby loves its mother primarily because she provides food.

Despite what science, instinct and common sense tell us, many Americans seem to cut down—almost deliberately—on the amount and quality of physical contact. After infancy, words replace touches; distance replaces closeness. With toddlers, touch is used to guard and control children, but less often to play with or show affection to them.

The warning is drummed into them: "Don't touch!" Touching is "not nice." Moreover, care is often taken to make sure that youngsters don't see even their own parents touching each other affectionately. And many parents, who confuse the sexual touch with the tender, caring, restorative or sympathetic touch, are either afraid or ashamed to make physical contact with growing sons and daughters. Little wonder, then, that so many of us learn to do without touching or being touched.

Where does one begin? How does an undemonstrative person learn to touch? Here are suggestions—and cautions—gathered from psychologists who have taken an interest in the matter:

• Discuss the idea with your family first. "Don't just suddenly and singly become a 'toucher,'" says psychiatrist Dr. Alexander Lowen. "Nothing is more upsetting than an unexpected and unexplained change in another person's behavior."

• Begin by performing simple acts of physical contact that are customary in some, but far from all, families: kissing good night or good morning; hugging when greeting or saying farewell.

• Learn to discern when others are in a mood to be touched; otherwise physical contact can be irritating. Children often go through stages of rejecting a parent's touch.

• Be emotionally honest when you do touch. Dr. Nicholas Dellis, a New York psychologist, told me that once, when he was extremely busy, his daughter came to him seeking attention. "I put my arm around her, but my mind was on my own problems. She sensed at once that I was not emotionally with her. She said, 'You're holding me *away* from you.' I looked, and the arm I had around her shoulder actually was forcing her apart from me rather than bringing us together."

• Try to make the act of touch a source of comfort and reassurance, rather than a veiled demand. Touch should never be a vehicle for clinging to or possessing another person.

• Realize that touching does not always have a sexual connotation. Many of us have failed to learn that different kinds of touching, meaning different things, are possible.

Dr. Herbert A. Otto, a pioneer in the search for ways to foster personal growth and expand human potential, believes that much more takes place through touch than most of us realize. It can, he says, almost magically dissolve barriers between people. It can break down the emotional walls we build within ourselves. "Touch," says Dr. Otto, "is always an exchange, if not a sharing. Through touch we grow, and we enable others to grow."

THE

HEART OF

"SOUL"

by Adrian Dove

IT WAS a stormy Monday morning in Watts in 1968 when Willie Lee Jackson, high-school graduate and a black, applied for a routine assembly-line job. After meeting all the other requirements, he enthusiastically took the written exam—a widely used personnel or intelligence test devised in 1942. But because Jackson didn't know the meaning of "R.S.V.P." and had trouble with proverbs like "Many a good cow hath a bad calf," he was labeled "hard-core unemployed."

I was then on a special committee on testing which had been trying to locate a "culture-free" intelligence test. Some of us felt that the measurable aspects of intelligence are so interwoven with culture that the only fair way was to devise separate tests for separate cultures. I had just finished writing such a test, with a bias in favor of the ghetto dweller, when I heard about Jackson's getting done in. Jackson took my test and passed it strong. The white middle-class employers on our committee did not pass it.

Next day, a group of us, all black, showed Jackson's would-be employer exactly how biased his test was. But he didn't understand. "I won't segregate my testing just because you say blacks have a separate culture," said the employer (we'll call him Harvey Butler). "Shouldn't we all integrate into one culture?"

Which one, I wanted to know. Italian-American? Swedish-American? Irish-American? Integration is not the real goal, I told him. It may become a healthy by-product, but what we want is equality. "In any case," I said, "Willie Lee Jackson can hardly integrate if he's kept outside the factory because you refuse to acknowledge his intelligence and his culture."

Butler allowed as how maybe all that made some sense, but he just couldn't imagine what this black culture could be. And so I began to tell him, not all of it, but part of it, in a big black voice....

Afro-American, popularly known as Soul, is our language and our evolving culture. It is indigenous to this land, but it's separate, too.

Indigenous, because we are not cultural Africans anymore. The 22 million blacks in this country could not move en masse to any nation in Africa and find complete cultural compatibility in terms of food, religion, what-have-you. Separate, because we are not white Americans, and 22 million blacks could not move, in small groups even, into the suburbs and resorts of this nation and find cultural compatibility, not to mention physical safety.

Nevertheless, some individual black men have gone back and are making it in African cultures. Others have moved into the white world and become very popular token participants. But the great majority are not at either extreme. Instead, they are seeking to develop and understand their own black culture. And that's Soul.

The evolving Soul culture is not complete, because we do not yet exercise local control of our institutions of commerce, education and government. We do control our language, customs and traditions—our family, religion and art.

Soul is love, and it's fed by the Southern farm and the big-city ghetto. It's being flexible, spontaneous. The Soul brother is sensitive and frank. He's cool, too—he judges things by what he sees, not just by what the credentials say. Where black people meet, you find a special warmth that you don't find any other place. Soul brothers can communicate by using only the essence of a message—straight to the point. Results are more important than procedures.

When a brother has a car that's falling apart, and he's not

a mechanic, but he turns a screw here and puts a rubber band on there, and the car runs: that car is running on Soulforce.

When a welfare mother with only a fifth-grade education stands up at a public meeting, out-thinks and out-talks a welfare director and puts him down so he knows it and everybody else knows it: that takes Soul.

Soul is everything that happens in the black experience: in church, nightclub or university. It's un-Soulful to try and define Soul, but we can take language as an example of it. Here are some samples of the Afro-American vocabulary:

Big juice—A big-time white racketeer, believed to enjoy police protection.

Burn—To improvise superlatively, in music, in cooking or in life. The phrase "Burn, baby," was shouted at performers long before the riot in Watts. During the riot, it became a pun.

Burner—The tops in his field, whatever his field is.

Changes, going through some—Having difficulties; regularly on the receiving end of bad news.

Chest, trying to get some—Looking for a fight.

Fox—Beautiful female.

Hog—Any large automobile, but especially a Cadillac.

Jive—An unreliable person. A persuasive talker, quick to make commitments, but prone to lie and make excuses for not delivering.

Main man—A woman's boyfriend; a man's closest friend. Feminine form: *main squeeze*.

Pig—A frightened, sadistic and corrupt individual who happens to be a policeman.

Whale—To run very fast, think very clearly, or be in any way a righteous burner.

Then, as another example of Soul, there is the church. White Christianity was the only institution allowed to blacks on this continent during slavery. (The black family as an institution was almost totally destroyed by slave sales and forced "breeding" practices.) So it happens that the white Jesus is very big in the ghetto.

Many sensitive black men have lamented the fact that we are one of the few peoples in history who worship an anthropomorphic god who bears no resemblance to them. Some men have tried to do something about it. Malcolm X abandoned the white Jesus, looked to the East and found Allah. The Rev. Albert B. Cleage, of Detroit, has taught his expanding congregation that Jesus was not white but swarthy or black.

Yet the church, white God and all, has still been vital to the development of the Soul culture. In many small Southern towns there was nothing else to do but go to church and pray, and sing—whether you were down and looking for comfort, or happy and wanted to let everybody know. The extremes of sorrow and joy were something outside the ken of the white church. And the way we express ourselves in the black church, the all-out givingness of the congregation and the minister, is also at the heart of Soul.

The church has given black people more than just songs and sermons. It was the rock from which Dr. Martin Luther King rose to lead the black man into meaningful confrontations with repression and gave him new cause for pride in himself and his people.

The word "Soul" comes out of the church, of course, but jazz and blues brought it out into the non-black world. Soul music embraces a wide variety, but it all has that distinct feeling. For the brother, this is important. He can be moved by Soul music for days. At a theater where, say, rhythm-and-blues singer James Brown is into his act, performer and audience are not separate. They feel as one, and the music is made up to fit the mood then and there. You know this moment will never again happen.

I travel a lot, and wherever I go, if my day has been foul, I can turn on my radio and everything's mellow. Soul music and the black press are my first links to the whole world. Soul music is relevant to this time, and these people. It is a gift from our culture to all of America.

Food is also a part of Soul. Plenty of super-sophisticated whites already know about chitlings—"Soul food" restaurants have sprung up in places like Hollywood and lower Manhattan. So black people started calling chitlings ruffle steaks, out of the need of black privacy; now whites are picking up that term, and the ghetto has started calling them wrinkles.

Of course, privacy is only a part of it because we also know that when white people start making ruffle steaks into a gourmet dish the price will go up. It's all a little funny, too, because Soul food was originally nothing more than leftovers. When the slaveholder on that old Southern plantation ate turnips, slave got greens. When it was ham or bacon for the big house, slave got innards to make chitlings, or the hard end of the nose to make snout (pronounced "snoot"), or the tips of the feet to make trotters.

Soul food traveled in a shopping bag on the train with the big move from farm to city, from South to North. The black man found all kinds of expensive new foods in the new places, but it wasn't strong-flavored and it didn't fill you up the way Soul food does. It still doesn't.

Another part of Soul involves appearance. At present, hair-straightening is giving way to the bush or Afro look—which is more natural to the black man. But both styles are part of our culture. Through the appearance of our hair and bright clothing we are blending the African and American esthetics into "our own thing."

There is much more to Soul, but I didn't have time to tell Harvey Butler there in Watts everything. But I wanted to make just one more point.

What our culture needs, in order to develop in a responsible way, I told him, is an honorable source of income for the male head of a household. People like Willie Lee Jackson, for instance, who don't know about R.S.V.P.

"Okay, okay," Butler said. "Tell you what I'll do. I'll hire Willie Lee Jackson, even though he failed in my white middle-class test. What do you think of that?"

I answered him in a big, black, warm voice: "You're only gonna hire one?"

THE ART OF

PAYING A

COMPLIMENT

by J. Donald Adams

ONE OF the best ways to smooth relations with other people is to be adept at the art of paying a compliment. The sincere, appreciative remark helps the other fellow to realize his own inherent worth. And, what is more, the ability to pay a compliment bolsters our own ego—which is not a bad thing either.

We never forget a compliment that has deeply pleased us, nor do we forget the person who made it. Yet often the luster of praise is needlessly dimmed by awkwardness in the manner of its giving. Like all ventures in human relations, the art of paying a compliment takes thought and practice. We have all experienced the remorse of having our praise fall flat because we chose the wrong time to give it or the wrong language to couch it in.

According to Leonard Lyons, a compliment of the right sort was paid Toscanini by Judith Anderson when she saw him after a concert.

"She didn't say I had conducted well," said the maestro. "I knew that. She said I looked handsome." It is human nature to enjoy praise for something we are not noted for. When someone calls attention to an unadvertised facet of our personality it makes him forever our friend.

We all pride ourselves on our individual distinctions. It is a gross misconception to think you are complimenting a person by telling him he looks exactly like so-and-so, even if so-and-so is a movie idol. I have noticed that nothing pleases us less than to have a double.

The best compliments are those which reinforce our sense of personal identity. A woman acquaintance of mine who is slender to the point of being skinny was sitting on the beach when a friend remarked, "You certainly have a flat stomach!" After the first shock wore off, she felt pleased by this frank tribute to her appearance.

One of the most satisfying kinds of compliment to give or receive is the double, or relayed, compliment—one passed on to you by someone who heard it. Recently, a correspondent enclosed a letter he had received from a friend who happens to be a man of eminence in his field. This man's opinion of a column I had written puffed me up considerably. Relayed to me by my friend, it was a compliment amplified—far more effective than if it had come direct.

The ingenuous compliment may touch us deeply, but it is probably the hardest to pay, for it depends on pure inspiration. I am reminded of an example that Margery Wilson cites in her book *Make Up Your Mind*. She once had a butler who knew a great deal about sculpture. His hero was Gutzon Borglum, the man who carved the massive portraits of Washington, Jefferson, Lincoln and Theodore Roosevelt on a mountainside in the Black Hills of South Dakota. Borglum came to tea and the butler, beside himself with excitement, spilled a glass of wine on him. Swabbing the sculptor desperately with a napkin, the butler said, "I could have served a lesser man perfectly."

To his embarrassed worshiper Borglum replied, "I was never so complimented in my life!"

Among the varieties of compliment is one with a particularly pleasing punch; I should call it a "bonus compliment of recall." It is indeed a heart-warming surprise when a person remembers something you said a long time ago that made a lasting impression on him. That it should have been hoarded and served up to you at an appropriate time is an experience bound to smooth out your kinks of self-doubt.

Urging me to go on a trip, a friend once said, "Memories are the best investment you can make." It was just as casual as that, yet it gave me courage to travel as I might not have, thinking I ought not to invest the money or the time. When I later reminded my friend of his remark, I found he had completely forgotten the incident. But my reminding him nourished his ego anew.

Compliments offered in the kidding vein hit home just as surely as those with a serious-minded approach. And they involve no responsibility on the part of the receiver for a mincing rejoinder. He can laugh with the crowd and happily accept his accolade.

I overheard a remark of this type in a restaurant recently. A group of businessmen were finishing lunch at the table next to mine. Said one of them, "Harry is the best computing machine here; he's a real mathemagician. So he gets stuck with figuring out the check!" They all chuckled; it was obviously a compliment.

A well-turned compliment is never unmindful of what are regarded as the distinguishing characteristics of the sexes. I think most men feel some measure of annoyance at being praised for individual features. Compliments on complexion or eyes, after all, border on what is most prized as a feminine attribute. But men will bask in the sunshine of being told how well built or how strong they are. Women traditionally have preferred to be saluted for their looks, their intuition, their capacity for understanding and sympathy.

Pushed to the point of flattery, the compliment is distasteful to most of us. We have all known people so vain that no syrup is too sweet for their taste, but they are in the minority. If we have any sense of proportion about ourselves, we are at once aware that we are being overpraised. This can be as painful as criticism.

Sometimes in a group of people we get so caught up in our own good words for a person that we overplay a tribute. When we finally stop, the recipient feels called upon to fill the sudden void in conversation with refutation equal in violence.

A compliment casually worked in, so that the threads of general conversation can easily be retrieved, makes less demands on the recipient—and leaves him with more glow than he would have gained from the spotlight. For example, as simple a thing as a question may become a compliment. If, instead of telling Bill that you think he has a wonderful garden, you ask him for advice about yours, you accomplish a number of things. You have indicated that you admire his gardening skill: you have singled him out from the crowd. He can give you advice without any to-do about acknowledging the compliment. And he's likely to feel you are a discerning guy.

When a man by virtue of success comes in for constant personal kudos, we face a dilemma when we want to get across to him our feelings of admiration. We know he must be tired of hearing the same things, of making the same perfunctory acknowledgment. Here is a place where we can use the indirect compliment to great advantage by telling him how much we admire his children, his house, his garden, a picture that hangs in his living room. In effect we are telling him that we admire what he admires. A man may question the truth of what we say about *him,* but he will not question a tribute to the things he loves.

One of the choicest indirect compliments I have heard was a husband's anniversary greeting to his wife: "I love you not only for what you are, but for what I am when I am with you." She prized those words more than the handsome present.

Compliments smooth the paths of social intercourse, help to dispel the recurrent dissatisfaction most of us have with ourselves and encourage us toward new achievement. "Appreciative words," says Dr. George W. Crane, "are the most powerful force for good will on earth."

HOW TO

READ BODY

LANGUAGE

by Flora Davis

ALL OF us communicate with one another nonverbally, as well as with words. Most of the time we're not aware that we're doing it. We gesture with eyebrows or a hand, meet someone else's eyes and look away, shift positions in a chair. These actions we assume are random and incidental. But researchers have discovered in recent years that there is a system to them almost as consistent and comprehensible as language.

Every culture has its own body language, and children absorb its nuances along with spoken language. A Frenchman talks and moves in French. The way an Englishman crosses his legs is nothing like the way a male American does it. In talking, Americans are apt to end a statement with a droop of the head or hand, a lowering of the eyelids. They wind up a question with a lift of the hand, a tilt of the chin or a widening of the eyes. With a future-tense verb they often gesture with a forward movement.

There are regional idioms too: an expert can sometimes pick out a native of Wisconsin just by the way he uses his eyebrows during conversation. Your sex, ethnic background, social class and personal style all influence your body language. Nevertheless, you move and gesture within the American idiom.

The person who is truly bilingual is also bilingual in body language. New York's famous mayor, Fiorello La Guardia, politicked in English, Italian and Yiddish. When films of his speeches are run without sound, it's not too difficult to identify from his gestures the language he was speaking. One of the reasons English-dubbed foreign films often seem flat is that the gestures don't match the language.

Usually, the wordless communication acts to qualify the words. What the nonverbal elements express very often, and very efficiently, is the emotional side of the message. When a person feels liked or disliked, often it's a case of "not what he said but the way he said it." Psychologist Albert Mehrabian has devised this formula: total impact of a message = 7 percent verbal + 38 percent vocal + 55 percent facial. The importance of the voice can be seen when you consider that even the words "I hate you" can be made to sound seductive.

Experts in kinesics—the study of communication through body movement—are not prepared to spell out a precise vocabulary of gestures. When an American rubs his nose, it may mean he is disagreeing with someone or rejecting something. But there are other possible interpretations, too. Another example: when a student in conversation with a professor holds the older man's eyes a little longer than is usual, it can be a sign of respect and affection; it can be a subtle challenge to the professor's authority; or it can be something else entirely. The expert looks for patterns in the context, not for an isolated meaningful gesture.

Kinesics is a young science—about 28 years old—and very much the brainchild of one man, anthropologist Ray L. Birdwhistell. But it already offers a smorgasbord of small observations. (For example: eyebrows have a repertoire of about 23 possible positions; men use their eyebrows more than women do.) Most people find they can shut out conversation and concentrate on watching body language for only about 30 seconds at a time. Anyone can experiment with it, however, simply by turning on the television picture without the sound.

One of the most potent elements in body language is eye behavior. Americans are careful about how and when they meet one another's eyes. In our normal conversation, each eye contact lasts only about a second before one or both individuals look away. When two Americans look searchingly into each other's eyes, emotions are heightened and the relationship tipped toward greater intimacy. Therefore, we scrupulously avoid this, except in appropriate circumstances.

Americans abroad sometimes find local eye behavior hard to interpret. "Tel Aviv was disturbing," one man recalled. "People stared right at me on the street; they looked me up and down. I kept wondering if I was uncombed or unzipped. Finally, a friend explained that Israelis think nothing of staring at others on the street."

Proper street behavior in the United States requires a nice balance of attention and inattention. You are supposed to look at a passerby just enough to show that you're aware of his presence. If you look too little, you appear haughty or furtive; too much and you're inquisitive. Usually what happens is that people eye each other until they are about eight feet apart, at which point both cast down their eyes. Sociologist Erving Goffman describes this as "a kind of dimming of lights." In parts of the Far East it is impolite to look at the other person at all during conversation. In England the polite listener fixes the speaker with an attentive stare and blinks his eyes occasionally as a sign of interest. That eye-blink says nothing to Americans, who expect the listener to nod or to murmur something—such as "mmhmm."

There are times when what a person says with his body gives the lie to what he is saying with his tongue. Sigmund Freud once wrote: "No mortal can keep a secret. If his lips are silent, he chatters with his fingertips; betrayal oozes out of him at every pore."

Thus, a man may successfully control his face, and appear calm, self-controlled—unaware that signs of tension and anxiety are leaking out, that his foot is beating the floor constantly, restlessly, as if it had a life of its own. Rage is another emotion feet and legs may reveal. During arguments the feet often tense up. Fear sometimes produces barely perceptible running motions—a kind of nervous leg jiggle. Then there are the subtle, provocative leg gestures that women use, consciously and unconsciously.

Recent studies by psychologists suggest that posture often reflects a person's attitude toward people he is with. One experiment indicates that when men are with other men whom they dislike, they relax either very little or very much—

depending on whether they see the other man as threatening. Women in this experiment always signaled dislike with very relaxed posture. And men, paired with women they disliked, were never up-tight enough about it to sit rigidly.

Congruent postures sometimes offer a guide to broad relationships within a group. Imagine that at a party, guests have been fired up by an argument over student radicalism. You may be able to spot at a glance the two sides of the argument by postures adopted. Most of the pros, for example, may sit with crossed knees, the cons with legs stretched out and arms folded. A few middle-of-the-roaders may try a little of each—crossing their knees *and* folding their arms. If an individual abruptly shifts his body around in his chair, it may mean that he disagrees with the speaker or even that he is changing sides. None of this, of course, represents an infallible guide, but it is apparently significant enough to be worth watching for.

While children learn spoken and body language—proper postures, eye behaviors, etc.—they also learn a subtler thing: how to react to space around them. Man walks around inside a kind of private bubble, which represents the amount of air space he feels he must have between himself and other people. Anthropologists, working with cameras, have recorded the tremors and minute eye movements that betray the moment the individual's bubble is breached. As adults, however, we hide our feelings behind a screen of polite words.

Anthropologist Edward T. Hall points out that, for two unacquainted adult male North Americans, the comfortable distance to stand for private conversation is from arm's length to about four feet apart. The South American likes to stand much closer, which creates problems when the two meet face to face. For, as the South American moves in, the North American feels he's being pushy; and as the North American backs off, the South American thinks he's being standoffish.

The American and the Arab are even less compatible in their space habits. Arabs thrive on close contact. In some instances, they stand very close together to talk, staring intently into each other's eyes and breathing into each other's face. These are actions the American may associate with sexual intimacy and he may find it disturbing to be subjected to them in a nonsexual context.

The amount of space a man needs is also influenced by his personality—introverts, for example, seem to need more elbow room than extroverts. Situation and mood also affect distance. Moviegoers waiting in line to see a sexy film will queue up much more densely than those waiting to see a family-entertainment movie.

George du Maurier once wrote:

"Language is a poor thing. You fill your lungs with wind and shake a little slit in your throat and make mouths, and that shakes the air; and the air shakes a pair of little drums in my head . . . and my brain seizes your meaning in the rough. What a roundabout way and what a waste of time."

Communication between human beings would be just that dull if it were all done with words. But actually, words are often the smallest part of it.

THE FINE ART OF

COMPLAINING

by George Weinberg

MILLIONS OF people choose not to object to what they consider mistreatment, when objecting would greatly improve their lives. Instead, they remain silent, fearing that making a legitimate complaint will reveal a weakness of which the other person will take advantage. Others mistakenly feel that anyone who complains is automatically a troublemaker or a shrew. (These people are usually the children of dominating, haranguing parents, and they'll do anything to avoid being like those parents.)

Others feel that they are worthwhile to other persons only so long as they act compliantly. Nearly all these people think that they have tried to voice their objections and weren't listened to. Usually it turns out that the expressions of dissatisfaction weren't heard, because they were vague or so loaded with irrelevant insults that the main point was obscured.

In an intimate relationship, when one person suffers as a result of the other's behavior, often the inflicter of pain doesn't realize what he's doing—and may never find out if the sufferer doesn't speak up. Meanwhile, if the sufferer doesn't voice his objection, he predisposes himself to think the worst of the other person—and he may never find out whether the other person *could* control his harmful actions if they were pointed out to him.

Most of us don't want to inflict pain, yet we are all capable of harming the people we love. If a friend or mate belittles you by the way he talks to you or behaves toward you, it's your responsibility to tell him, and give him the opportunity to show good faith. But complaining is an art as well as a responsibility, and to make an objection in a way that is fair and forceful and accurate takes practice. The following principles of making and taking criticism, evolved over years of working with college students and married couples, have helped to maintain constructive communication in many relationships.

Making Criticism

1. Complain to the person you think is harming you, not to anyone else.

2. Try not to object to your mate's behavior in front of someone else. To most people, being criticized seems like being personally attacked. Your indifference to your mate's comfort, displayed by your willingness to criticize him in front of others, will be taken at least as seriously as the content of what you say. In fairness to him, and for your own sake, wait until you are alone with him.

3. Don't compare the person's behavior with that of others. No one wants to be described as inferior to anyone else. Comparisons predispose other people not to listen, even when the complaint is justified. Anyhow, such comparisons always miss the main point.

4. Make your complaint as soon as you can, when you're alone with the other person and can articulate it. Speaking up, like any other task, becomes more difficult when you postpone it. Waiting allows your anger to build, and increases the likelihood that you will make irrelevant comments.

5. Don't repeat a point once you've made it and the other person has carefully considered it. The reward for patiently listening to criticism ought to be exoneration from having to hear the same crime discussed again.

6. Object only to actions that the other person can change. You may ask a person not to shout; but if you ask him not to be angry with you, you're probably expecting too much. I always ask patients who wear sunglasses to take them off in my office, both for their sake and for mine, since I can make better contact with people when I can see their eyes. But though nervousness is often the reason that these people come to my office wearing sunglasses, it would be pointless for me to ask them to relax.

7. Try to make only one complaint at a time. If you make more, you'll demoralize the other person and perhaps obscure your major point. For example, don't quibble about the carpeting in your office when you've stormed in to ask your boss for a well-deserved promotion. If the subject changes to the price of carpet, you'll feel unsatisfied—and your boss may feel he has discharged his obligation by promising to have your carpet changed.

8. Don't preface your complaint. "Listen. There's something I've wanted to tell you for a long time. It may hurt you. Please don't feel offended, but..."

What could be worse? Instead of inoculating your listener against the pain, you are stabbing him to death with your hypodermic needle. By prefaces, you convince both him and yourself that your complaint is to be monstrous, and that probably he won't be capable of receiving it in the same friendly spirit in which you are making it.

9. After making your complaint in good faith, don't apologize for it. Apology will only detract from the merit of your accomplishment, in your own mind, and renew your conflict about whether you had the right to say what you did. Apologizing is asking the other person to brace you so you won't fall down under the stress of disagreeing with him. Doing so imposes an unnecessary burden on him.

10. Avoid sarcasm. Among sarcasm's invariable motivations are contempt and fear. Your contempt will predispose the other person not to heed you, and because you make a choice not to confront him directly, you intensify your fear of him. Being sarcastic is cowardly and sniveling, no matter how clever the turn of phrase.

11. Don't talk about other people's motivations when making an objection. Hardly a man is now alive who doesn't sense the difference between "Please don't interrupt me" and "You never want me to finish what I'm saying."

"You don't *care* how long I wait for you." "Quit *trying* to make me angry." You give the listener reason to disregard your essential complaint if he concludes that your speculation about his motive is wrong. Steer clear of the tendency to confuse consequence and intention.

12. *Avoid words like "always" and "never."* Exaggerations intended for emphasis when making an objection rob you of accuracy and the psychological advantages that go with it.

13. *If you never compliment the other person, don't expect him to remain open to your criticisms.* Complaints ring loud and long when they're the only sounds that are made. If you want to make occasional objections, you have the obligation to compliment the person at other times. Also, I recommend the practice of thanking people for listening to your criticisms.

Taking Criticism

1. *Be quiet while you are being criticized, and make it clear that you are listening.* Whether you agree or not with what is being said is an issue to be discussed later.

2. *Look directly at the person talking to you.* Only in this way can you convey open reception to what he is saying.

3. *Under no condition find fault with the person who has just criticized you.* If he has made a mistake in grammar, for example, wait a half-hour before telling him. It probably won't seem so important then.

4. *Don't create the impression that the other person is destroying your spirit.* The hardest people to deal with are those who are belligerent at first, and who then, when cornered, act as though they were at the edge of despair. Don't be a fragile bully.

5. *Don't jest.* Flippancy is properly perceived as contemptuous by a great number of people, and is hurtful to just about everyone.

6. *Don't caricature the complaint.* If a person says you were *thoughtless,* don't ascribe to him the statement that you were *vicious* and then defend yourself against a charge he didn't make. The deliberate exaggeration of a charge against you amounts to dismissal of the charge.

7. *Don't change the subject.* Use your intelligence to help articulate the objection, not to obscure it.

8. *Don't imply that your critic has some ulterior, hostile motive.* If you are asking *why* he objected, you are not dealing

with his objection. The question about him should come later, if ever.

9. *Convey to the other person that you understand his objection.* Paraphrasing it is one good way of doing this. In effect, you are saying that you have received the message and noted it.

Don't let people carp at you on the pretext that they're giving you constructive criticism. (You can distinguish carping from criticism by whether the person stays within the rules for making a reasonable objection.) I think you have the right at any time to ask for a short suspension of criticism. Refusal to grant it, or inability to tolerate it, betrays the compulsive critic. The ideal path is narrow: you must be open to criticism but not allow yourself to be tyrannized by it.

EXPERIENCE AND
ENCOUNTER

"TOUCHED

BY SOMETHING

DIVINE"

by Richard Selzer, M.D.

I. Smile, Doctor

I INVITED a young diabetic woman to the operating room to amputate her leg. She could not see the great black ulcer upon her foot and ankle that threatened to encroach upon the rest of her body, for she was blind as well. There upon her foot was a Mississippi Delta brimming with corruption, sending its raw tributaries down between her toes. She could not see her wound, but she could feel it. There is no pain like that of the bloodless limb turned rotten and festering.

For over a year I had trimmed away the putrid flesh, cleansed, anointed, and dressed the foot, staving off, delaying. Three times each week, in her darkness, she sat upon my table, rocking back and forth, holding her extended leg by the thigh, gripping it as though it were a rocket that must be steadied lest it explode and scatter her toes about the room. And I would cut away a bit here, a bit there, of the swollen blue leather that was her tissue.

At last we gave up, she and I. We could no longer run ahead of the gangrene. We had not the legs for it. There must be an amputation in order that she might live—and I as well. It was to heal us both that I must take up knife and saw, and cut the leg off. And when I could feel it drop from her body to the table, see the blessed *space* appear between her and that leg, I too would be well.

Now it is the day of the operation. I stand by while the anesthetist administers the drugs, watch as the tense familiar body relaxes into sleep. I turn then to uncover the leg.

And there, upon her kneecap, she has drawn, blindly, upside down for me to see, a face; just a circle with two ears, two eyes, a nose, and a smiling upturned mouth. Under it she has printed SMILE, DOCTOR. Minutes later, I listen to the sound of the saw, until a little crack at the end tells me it is done.

II. A Man of Letters

A man of letters lies in the intensive-care unit. A professor, used to words and students. One day in his classroom he was speaking of Emily Dickinson when suddenly he grew pale, and wonder sprang upon his face, as though he had just, for the first time, *seen* something, understood something, that had eluded him all his life. It was the look of the Wound, the struck blow that makes no noise, but happens in the depths somewhere, unseen. His students could not have known that at that moment his stomach had perforated, that even as he spoke, its contents were issuing forth into his peritoneal cavity like a horde of marauding goblins.

From the blackboard to the desk he reeled, fell across the top of it, and, turning his face to one side, he vomited up his blood, great gouts and gobbets of it, as though having given his class the last of his spirit, he now offered them his fluid and cells.

In time, he was carried to the operating room, this man whom I had known, who had taught me poetry. I took him up, in my hands, and laid him open, and found from where he bled. I stitched it up, and bandaged him, and said later, "Now you are whole."

But it was not so, for he had begun to die. And I could not keep him from it, not with all my earnestness, so sure was his course. From surgery he was taken to the intensive-care unit. His family, his students, were stopped at the electronic door. They could not pass, for he had entered a new state of being, a strange antechamber where they may not go....

For three weeks he has dwelt in that House of Intensive Care, punctured by needles, wearing tubes of many calibers in all of his orifices; irrigated, dialyzed, insufflated, pumped, and drained . . . and feeling every prick and pressure the way a lover feels desire spring acutely to his skin.

In the room a woman moves. She is dressed in white. Lovingly, she measures his hourly flow of urine. With hands familiar, she delivers oxygen to his nostrils and counts his pulse as though she were telling beads. Each bit of his decline she records with her heart full of grief, shaking her head. At last, she turns from her machinery to the simple touch of the flesh. Sighing, she strips back the sheet, and bathes his limbs.

The man of letters did not know this woman before. Preoccupied with dying, he is scarcely aware of her presence now. But this nurse is his wife in his new life of dying. They are close, these two, intimate, depending one upon the other, loving. It is a marriage, for although they own no shared past, they possess this awful, intense present, this matrimonial now, that binds them as strongly as any promise.

A man does not know whose hands will stroke from him the last bubbles of his life. That alone should make him kinder to strangers.

III. Encounter With a God

I stand by the bed where a young woman lies, her face postoperative, her mouth twisted in palsy, clownish. A tiny twig of the facial nerve, the one to the muscles of her mouth, has been severed. She will be thus from now on. The surgeon had followed with religious fervor the curve of her flesh; I promise you that. Nevertheless, to remove the tumor in her cheek, I had cut the little nerve.

Her young husband is in the room. He stands on the opposite side of the bed, and together they seem to dwell in the evening lamplight, isolated from me, private. Who are they, I ask myself, he and this wry-mouth I have made, who gaze at and touch each other so generously, greedily? The young woman speaks.

"Will my mouth always be like this?" she asks.

"Yes," I say, "it will. It is because the nerve was cut."

She nods, and is silent. But the young man smiles.

"I like it," he says. "It is kind of cute."

All at once I *know* who he is. I understand, and I lower my gaze. One is not bold in an encounter with a god. Unmindful, he bends to kiss her crooked mouth, and I so close I can see how he twists his own lips to accommodate to hers, to show her that their kiss still works.

I remember that the gods appeared in ancient Greece as mortals, and I hold my breath and let the wonder in.

I'M A

COMPULSIVE

LIST-MAKER

by Naomi R. Bluestone, M.D.

A FRIEND OF MINE said to me, "You have so many lists, I bet you even keep a *list* of your lists!" I nodded. It is true that I maintain lists and constantly rearrange not only their substance but their order and nature as well. For me, writing down a chore is almost as good as doing it. In fact, it is often such a satisfactory substitute that the need to actually do the chore vanishes.

I used to maintain lists by content, subdivided into things to fix, things to buy, people to call, letters to write. I soon found that this grouping failed to take into account the places in which these functions were to be performed. So I regrouped my lists into things to do around the house, at the office, on Montague Street (my local shopping area). This, of course, meant setting up a cross-reference indexing system—*buy lampshade, see Montague Street.*

There is always some conflict in my mind over whether to use pen or pencil. Notations made in pencil can be easily erased, leaving room for new entries without disturbing the symmetry. However, they may be *too* quickly erased in erroneous anticipation of completion and, thus, lost to recall forever. Notations made in ink, however, can be blotted out only with wild slashes of a felt-tip pen, leaving angry residues on still usable sheets. The inevitable messiness of the paper leads to decisions to start afresh, which gives rise to large numbers of unbound sheets of paper with a tendency to wander.

Perhaps the hardest decision of all is whether to maintain flexibility with blank note-and-tear pads or to incorporate all entries in a notebook. And if so, should this be a ring binder, where sheets can be easily replaced (and easily lost), or a permanently bound blank book? My compromise has been a bound spiral volume covered in leftover red-and-white-checked shelf paper and clearly marked "Personal."

I also find it helpful to supplement my bound lists with loose sheets of paper such as grocery lists. I am free, then, to take with me to the supermarket only the day's list. However, my trusty notebook accompanies me to the office, where I can browse through it at will when the substance of my day starts to pall or while waiting for secretaries to put through their bosses who have telephoned me. In case the volume should be lost, I keep a duplicate, with all entries, locked in my desk at home. (For income-tax purposes, I keep old lists for ten years, along with my checks, receipts and calendars. No one has ever asked to see them, but someday I may get lucky!)

It is important to make entries the moment they come to mind; for, like pieces of inspiration, they may not recur. This includes ideas that come during sleep. For this reason, I keep my lists by my bedside, along with my book of dreams. (I do not keep lists of dreams, since these are not, technically, things to do.) It is also important not to rank items in terms of importance but to record them indiscriminately as they occur. This morning, I entered the following; *sew waistband blue slacks dammit, outline Public Law 93-41 and buy onions!!!* (Note that adjectives and punctuation marks can be effectively utilized to delineate priorities.)

Another helpful device is to break down vague classifications into the most concrete subdivisions possible. I used to write *clean closets*. Now I prepare a meticulous list of clothes to be given away, thrown away, put away, fixed—and so forth, *ad infinitum*.

On occasion I will write down something that has to be done *after* I have done it, only to have the pleasure of immediately crossing it off the list. In any event, acknowledging that an item has to be "entered" can be a definitive gesture in itself. For example, *clean stove* (which I have never done) has been on my list since six years before I moved to my present apartment two years ago. The stove always needs cleaning, so I preserve this entry around which to build if my list gets skimpy. I strive to maintain a hefty list, since this increases my sense of self-worth and importance. I list, therefore I am.

The sum of all the items on my various lists today totals 63, an all-time high. It is an amazing array, ranging from *chop down tree* to *fix stethoscope*. Now such things could easily seem like trivia to another person, but each item is precious to me, a piece of myself.

For example, the *go to watchmaker*. That has a whole personal story to it. You see, I broke one watch, then another, and then I broke the strap on the watch belonging to the fellow next door, and now I suspend it from a long piece of string around my neck and under my blouse where it makes a bulge. I have to go to the ladies' room to tell the time. (This particular item will be speedily checked off my list.)

A number of admirers, and a handful of weirdos who consider my preoccupation a bit bizarre, have asked me when I developed my interest in recording functional data. Actually, there was a precipitating incident, which occurred on the wards when I was a house officer. A young Portuguese sailor was admitted to the hospital with an acute ulcer and not even a defensive knowledge of English. I placed him on a diet that entitled him to cream garnished with atropine sprinkles and not much else.

His improvement was remarkable, and I forgot all about him until I ran into the fellow a few months later while rotating through Physical Medicine and Rehabilitation. His skin was alabaster, his pupils had completely absorbed his irises, and his body had swollen. The story, as I pieced it together, was that after several futile weeks of crying *"faminto,"* he had suffered a bilateral spastic paralysis of the masseter (lower jaw muscle). His chart was reviewed, and it was recognized that someone (me) had forgotten to change the diet order. With solid food and rehab he made an uneventful recovery.

I was traumatized by my thoughtlessness. I vowed I would always carry a checklist of sample orders so that I would be equipped at all times to order whatever a patient's comfort might demand. From organizing my doctor's list to maximize its effectiveness and minimize its tyranny, I graduated to organizing the rest of my life.

Now I fancy that life itself is fueled by lists—to flicker out only when I can find no more entries to make.

GOD BLESS

OUR SHIMMED-UP

HOME

by Joan Mills

AROUND our house, what we can't fix, we shim. We favor matchbooks, rubber wedges, bricks or badly written paperbacks, depending on what's sagging *this* time. If we pulled out every shim, our house would moan once and collapse in a shower of sticks and stones and piano strings.

So it would seem—but in my heart I doubt it. This house has been settling itself down since 1810. When we first moved here, we saw how earlier generations had providently shimmed sags in the foundation. So we thought we'd smooth a multitude of ups and downs by raising the whole back end with jackposts. The effort was an insult to ancient bones: we achieved only disconcerting humps in the floor. A decade has passed. The house still stands—upon spongy sills, strong character, and shims. And time has taught us that the gentle art of shimming also works wonders in other places. In ourselves, for example. More later. Back to the house.

Our floors and walls and ceilings lean whither they will. We prop the lesser stuff—shelves, stair treads, sinks, door stoops, downspouts, dressers, chimneys, cupboards—for when a house is out of plumb, so are all its innards and outards, ornaments and accessories. All, all, *all*. But a well-chosen shim meets every emergency.

As when the oven door fell off. Hollering for help, I

hooked the back of a chair under the handle and propped the door back where it belonged. We—kids, husband, dog and I—crowded the kitchen debating ways to repair the fragmented hinge. There was, we decided, *no* way. For two weeks, on account of the chair, it looked as if I expected burglars to break in via the oven; then my husband figured that we could shim the door in its frame with a length of lathing. Wonderful! I've been shimming the oven shut for ten years now, and I doubt that I'll ever get a new stove. Not unless we run out of shims.

I suppose it was inevitable that when we had lived here awhile and needed another car, we would buy one that was old and, like the house, lopsided. It was a mini-import, stubborn with age in ways that we understood, respected and enjoyed. It puttered us happily about on Sunday drives, the adults remarking on other people's plumb houses, the kids roiling around in the back and writing on the windows with spit.

One such Sunday, the five of us were refreshing ourselves with grape popsicles and the pleasant scenery when the putter of the car turned to putt-putt, cough-cough, *silence*. My husband futilely flicked switches and thumped pedals. Finally, he and I got out and walked around back, where the engine was. We lifted the engine cover and looked inside.

"Hmmm," he said. "I don't *see* anything, do you?"

"Just the engine," I said, sucking earnestly on my popsicle.

Poking around, we discovered a wobbly doohickey that looked, by golly, as if it needed a shim.

"Hurry up and finish your popsicle," my husband said. So I lapped fast, and he took the damp stick and wedged it under the doohickey. Then he got back in the car and started the engine on the first try.

"I'll be damned," he muttered dazedly—and we drove home.

We ran the car four more years on gas, oil and popsicle sticks. One stick was good for about 100 miles, which meant that we had to eat an awful lot of popsicles in season so as to get through the winter months. Whenever the car sputtered to an unscheduled stop, my husband reached in the glove compartment for another stick and trotted around back.

That car had gone 210,000 miles, mostly on popsicle

sticks, when the generator shorted out and set the engine on fire. We gave the charred corpse to a friend. He revived it with a paint job, a new generator and a fresh supply of sticks. Now the car is raced every winter on frozen lakes. The first time out, it won a trophy: "Best in class!" my husband reported.

"What class?" I wondered. But in my mind's eye I saw our little car leaning crazily into the turns, and I felt antic satisfaction tickling my ribs.

For cars, houses and people, solutions are rarely perfect. Perfection is a rarity that makes its own demands. Something less than that is easier to realize, and can be good to live with. Besides, something less is what we're surest of, day by ordinary day—in ourselves, particularly.

We're made, the Bible tells us, less than the angels. That's only suitable, I think. To be human—and imperfect—is ample earthly experience. It grants us the *hope* of perfection, which is the substance of our worthiest dreams. (What in heaven's name do angels dream of, by the way?) I'm happy to be merely human, bumbling hopefully along; improved, if not perfected, by every shim to my spirits that life provides.

There are doodads in my psyche that wobble and stop working unless shimmed. I see few level paths between me and what I think I want to be. But simple pleasures, not perfection, keep me going. I laugh. I take my miracles small (as in snowflakes and the shape of daisies), and I get along.

Small shims to my spirits have sustained me since the very best of Christmas was down at the toe of my stocking, and the best part of school was recess, and the best part of love was a hug. On such as these I grew, shaping whatever dreams I have. So, when I married, I chose me a man with an eye for small blessings. Together, we've counted quite a few.

Time was, we were searching our pockets for pennies, but money was no object when we didn't plan to buy. We window-shopped the most expensive stores, walking the dusk-blue city sidewalks and sighting early stars beyond the city lights. We went home with a pint of chocolate ice cream, saying, "You take the bigger dish." "No, you."

I wept for having overdone the muffins. "They're nice and crisp," he said, testing one with his teeth. ("I'll learn," I thought, and smiled.) We were finding what a lift there can be to moments of sharing and caring.

We said we'd have a boy first—but she wasn't. "I like girls, too," her father said, as her fingers tightened on his thumb. When she was one year old, we gave her a brother in a basket. (She preferred her birthday cupcake with roses on top.) We said we'd have another baby later. And we did.

Children build entire days on the shims of small delights. Ours talked to worms and woofed at dogs and tugged us by the ear, whispering whooshy secrets in big breaths. They demanded of one another that animal crackers be eaten feet-first in tiny nibbles, and gingerbread boys beginning with the buttons. Bored with the world as it was, they stood on their heads to invert it, or dizzied the whole house by whirling around in place.

"Kisses make hurts go away," they told me. (That works for grownups, too.) They wiped their tears on teddy bears, and dragged about rag dolls with tolerant stitched-on smiles. They gave us look for look when, for love, we cupped their faces in our hands.

When, in time, we moved into this old house, we found the kitchen was impossible, but the view from the sink was grand. The furnace was huffy and crotchety, but the pear tree was heavy with fruit. The roof was the worse for weather, but the air smelled of damp earth, fresh hay and phlox. We sighed for the mice in the cellar. But for every depressing fault we discovered a heartening virtue.

"There are lilacs in the hedge," I said. "I've *always* wanted lilacs."

"I found birch and apple wood for fires," my husband said. "Imagine."

So we've lilacs to think of when spring is merely mud, and fires to brood by on black winter nights. My muffins are lighter, and generally admired. We've a house full of flaws that are homey. The view from the sink is consistently grand.

We have lived here long enough for me to have adopted the house's ways as my own. There are days when I sag, and when I am disposed to go wherever gravity leads me, which is down. But I am restored by the lift of laughter, or somebody's shoulder to lean on. They give my spirits a sturdy and steadying shim.

PIED PIPER

OF SEVENTH

AVENUE

by James Comer

IT IS rush hour in a New York City subway station. I careen through the closing doors of a graffiti-laden car to join the fluorescent pallor of 40 fellow robots. Their faces hidden behind newspapers, they seem to plead only for anonymity. "Please don't bother us," they proclaim. "We're not really here."

I spot a space miraculously vacant, plop down and open my newspaper. My eye momentarily strays to the gentleman on my right. *Now* I know why the seat was empty: I am installed beside a certifiable weirdo.

Physically he is unassuming—a portly, middle-aged man sporting an open shirt that shouldn't be and baggy pants long overdue for laundering. His garb is not the threat, though; it's what he's *doing*. He is grasping what appears to be an ordinary gray typewriter case. Painstakingly, he places it between his knees, balancing this apparent treasure with great deliberation. Finally satisfied as to the perfection of its placement, he pulls out an aging pair of drumsticks and gets to work.

Eyes focused on an unseen maestro, he plays that typewriter case with an enthusiasm rarely reserved for portable luggage. My initial reaction is to flee. (I long ago learned that it is easier to read about eccentricity than to sit next to it.) Besides, how dare he interrupt my gloom? Yet he holds me by his commitment and wins me by his style.

Not a student of percussion, but a confirmed pencil-thumper since birth, I quickly realize that he is good. Not just interestingly incongruous, but *good*. Rhythms fly. Tempos alter abruptly. Those thin sticks mercilessly flail that unassuming Samsonite. A stick is dropped. He picks it up, scrupulously searches for a structural defect. Finding none, he resumes the concert unperturbed.

What showmanship! A poor man's Liberace, with taste. Pounding away furiously, eyes closed, he sends first one stick and then the other high above his head. Surely this time he has overreached himself. No, he retrieves them both with indolent ease, never missing a beat.

He is an artist, never questioning his gift, never acknowledging the presence of his captive audience. He solicits no money and receives none. This is understandable. Would you tip Leonard Bernstein?

Finally, I notice my fellow passengers. Robots redeemed! I see about me a carful of radiant, beaming human beings. Smiles on New Yorkers such as I've never known. Teeth for miles. *Grins!* Feet tapping, heads keeping time, we have become a community if only for a few stops.

Our nameless drummer has accomplished this transformation in less than five minutes. At 72nd Street he quietly gathers his possessions and departs, accepting my meager accolade with a dignified nod.

Eccentric? Crazy? A frustrated genius too poor to buy a drum? I don't know. I prefer to remember him as the Pied Piper of Seventh Avenue.

And my smile lasted all the way to 86th Street.

UNDER THE SKIN

YOU ARE

EXTRAORDINARY

by Roger J. Williams

IN DEALING with people, statistics should be used with care. A group of people is something like a collection of marbles of all sizes and compositions, and all colors of the rainbow. Try to "average" these marbles, and you come out with nonsense. You can "average" their color by mounting them on a circular disk and rotating it rapidly. The color comes back a dirty gray. But there isn't a dirty-gray marble in the lot! People are as distinctive as marbles, and when we attempt to average them we come up with dirty-gray "man." Averaging when applied in this careless way to people can be vicious, for we are all unique specimens.

During my years as a biochemist, noting different people's reactions to drugs and other such "idiosyncrasies," I became convinced that each of us is built in a highly distinctive way *in every particular,* and that this is the basis of individuality. It is well known, for example, that a person has distinctive fingerprints and a natural perfume distinctive enough that a bloodhound can trail him. These differences are trivial. If we could look at our "insides," we would be startled at the even greater variations.

Stomachs, for example, vary in size, shape and contour—perhaps far more than do our noses or mouths. They also vary in operation. Digestion takes place largely because of the enzyme pepsin. A Mayo Foundation study of about 5000 people who had no known stomach ailment showed that the gastric juices varied at least a thousandfold in pepsin content. The hydrochloric-acid content varies similarly, and a substantial percentage of normal people have none at all. Such differences are partly responsible for the fact that we tend not to eat with equal frequency or in equal amounts, nor to choose the same foods.

Normal people also have large differences in their hearts. The study of autopsy specimens shows that the inner construction does not by any means follow a single pattern: an auricle in one heart may bear little resemblance to an auricle in another. There is similar variation in arteries and circulatory system.

In fact, marked variations in normal anatomy are found wherever we look for them. Some of the most far-reaching internal differences involve the endocrine glands—thyroids, parathyroids, adrenals, sex glands, pituitaries—which release different hormones into the blood. These, in turn, affect our metabolic health, our appetites for food, drink, amusement and sex, our emotions, instincts and psychological well-being.

Our nervous systems also show distinctiveness. For example, on human skin there are tiny areas sensitive to cold, other areas sensitive to warmth, still others sensitive to pain. A simple experiment shows that these spots—nerve endings—are widely unequal in number, and distributed differently in different individuals. Twenty-one pairs of normal hands were tested for sensitivity to pain by pricking comparable, marked squares with a needle. Every single hand was different. Out of 49 spots in a square inch, one hand had 25 spots that were insensitive to pain; another had only one. Similar observations have been made of spots on the skin that are sensitive to cold and to heat. Indeed, we know this to be true of nerve endings of all kinds—in eyes, ears, nose and mouth, as well as skin. Since our nerve endings are our *only* source of information from the outside world, this means that the world is different for each of us.

And the brain? The famous neurologist Dr. Karl S. Lashley wrote: "The brain is extremely variable in every character that has been subjected to measurement. Its diversities of structure within the species are of the same general character as are the differences between related species, or even between orders of animals." Your brain probably differs from your neighbor's far more than your facial features vary from his. The result is that each of us has a highly distinctive mind.

Think then of this world as made up of *individuals,* each with different inborn characteristics that influence every minute of each life. Every facet of human life is altered by such a view.

That children are innately different has been observed by parents for thousands of years. At the Menninger Foundation a few years ago, two investigators found abundant evidence of individual differences in 128 babies that they observed, 16 at each four-week age level from four weeks to 32 weeks. Some babies were bold, others shy; some reacted quickly to outside stimuli, some slowly. Some were very regular in their feeding-sleeping-playing-crying patterns, others irregular. Some could tolerate tension and frustration readily; others couldn't take it. Marked personality differences show up from the very start of life. Education must take on a new dimension when we consider these facts.

Mutual knowledge about the differences can help greatly in relationships between husbands and wives. Some "little things" that help tear people apart involve distinctive reactions to temperature: coffee, food or soup may be too hot or not hot enough; rooms may be too hot or too cold or too stuffy; bed covering may be too warm or too light. Sense of timing is often individual; one person may have a keen sense of time, while to another ten minutes may seem about the same as 60. One may get sleepy at the wrong time or be "raring to go" at the wrong time. One may fail to remember and be continually losing things; another may remember things well that should be forgotten.

Knowledge of one's biochemical individuality is most important in matters of health and nutrition, too. Some people say, "The caffeine in coffee doesn't keep me awake; I'm sure it can't keep others awake—it must be in their minds." This overlooks the fact that the amount of a drug necessary to bring about the same effect in different individuals may vary as much as tenfold. Alcohol is a real danger to some people, while others have almost no chance of becoming addicted to it.

Again, take as simple a thing as sleep patterns. That these have a biological basis is shown by animals. Chickens, for example, are monophasic in their sleep behavior; that is, they fill their daily sleep quota in one stretch. Other animals such as cats (or lions) are polyphasic in that they indulge in "cat naps."

In human beings we see these animal patterns mimicked with variations. Some individuals would never think of taking a daytime nap. Others cannot resist them. Most people are monophasic sleepers, and they often assume that those who are constitutionally different are simply indulging themselves. Yet such outstanding figures as Napoleon and Edison tended to have polyphasic sleep patterns. Both required very little sleep, but took short naps during the day.

All of this information about individuality is good news, with far-reaching implications. It gives us a basis for realizing our own individual worth. It opens the door to a real and appreciative understanding of ourselves *and others,* and of how people individually can make the most of the equipment they have.

HOW TO LIVE

365 DAYS A YEAR

by John A. Schindler, M.D.

How MANY of your last 365 days were ones in which you felt that you were truly alive? If you are like most of us, you had at least a few such days—enough to make you wish there were more.

Most people, as a doctor knows all too well, put in many days when they feel too tired, too worried or too disagreeable to get the full zest out of the adventure of living. The purpose of this book is to show beyond question that most such "lost" days are unnecessary, and to show that it is possible to make each of the next 365 days one of your "good" days. To do this, however, we must first understand what causes the unnecessary "bad" days.

A patient almost always comes to the doctor because of some physical pain. He is seldom aware how often these physical symptoms are caused by his failure to control his emotions. But doctors now know that the problems of more than 50 percent of those seeking medical aid have their roots in badly handled emotions.

For instance, the Ochsner Clinic in New Orleans found that 74 percent of 500 consecutive patients admitted for gastro-intestinal diseases were actually suffering from illness caused by the emotions. The Yale University Out-Patient Medical Department has reported that emotional stress contributed to the ills of 76 percent of all the patients coming to that clinic.

How Do Emotions Affect Our Health?

William James has defined emotion as "a state of mind that manifests itself by sensible changes in the body." With every emotion changes are taking place in muscles, in blood vessels, in the viscera, in the endocrine glands. These changes and the mental state that accompanies them *are* the emotion. Without these bodily changes, there would be no emotion.

With minor exceptions, all emotions belong in one of two groups: the *unpleasant* emotions, which harmfully *overstimulate* any organ or muscle or one of the endocrine glands. (These emotions include anger, anxiety, fear, discouragement, grief, dissatisfaction.) Opposed to them are *pleasant* emotions which create an *optimal stimulation* in the body, one neither too extreme nor too weak. Among these are hope, joy, courage, equanimity, affection, agreeableness.

When we have learned to control the unpleasant emotions and to encourage the pleasant ones, we have come a long way toward learning how to live a happier and probably a longer life.

The unpleasant emotions have definite physical effects on the body. The moment you become angry, for example, the muscles at the outlet of the stomach squeeze down so tightly that nothing leaves the stomach, and the entire digestive tract becomes spastic; many people have severe abdominal pains either during or after a fit of anger. At the same time the number of blood cells increases greatly, and the blood clots more quickly than usual. The heart rate goes up markedly, often to 180 or 220, or higher, and stays there until the anger has passed. The blood pressure rises steeply, from a normal of 130 or so to 230 or more, often with dire results. More than one person has developed a stroke during a fit of anger because his blood pressure rose so high that he "blew" a blood vessel in his brain. Also, in anger, the coronary arteries in the heart squeeze down hard enough to produce angina pectoris, or, as happens fairly frequently, a fatal coronary occlusion.

The great English physiologist John Hunter, who had the uncomfortable combination of a ready temper and a bad set of coronary arteries, always said that the first rascal who got him really mad would kill him. The "rascal" finally appeared at a medical meeting and made him so angry he dropped dead of a heart attack.

Most emotionally induced illness, however, does not come as the result of one large emotion. Far more often it is the result of the monotonous drip, drip of seemingly unimportant emotions, the everyday run of anxieties, fears, discouragements, longings.

A few years ago two Cornell psychologists, H. S. Liddell and A. U. Moore, tried an interesting experiment on sheep. They tied a small wire to a sheep's leg and, as the animal dragged it about the field, sent slight electric shocks through it. The sheep merely twitched its leg and went right on eating, no matter how often the shocks were repeated.

The two investigators then tried ringing a bell for ten seconds before they gave the shock. The jolt was no stronger than before, but now when the sheep heard the bell it stopped eating and waited apprehensively for the coming shock. Monotonous repetition of this bell-shock apprehension soon induced functional illness in every sheep on which it was tried. The sheep would first quit eating, then stop walking. Next it would fail to stay on its feet and finally would begin to have difficulty in breathing. Then the experiment was stopped or the sheep might have died. An important finding of the experiment—for it bears on our own need for regular relaxation—was the discovery that if the monotonous repetition of apprehension was interrupted at intervals, the sheep would not develop functional illness so often or so seriously.

Muscle Tension as a Cause of Pain

Unpleasant emotions are commonly accompanied by tightness in the skeletal muscles and the muscles of the internal organs. If these muscle-tensing emotions are continued long enough, or if they are monotonously repeated, the muscles involved begin to hurt, causing what we have called *muscular rheumatism* or *fibrositis*. Tense muscles are one of the most common sources of the general aches and pains we experience more or less constantly.

Only in the 1940s did we learn the extent to which emotional tension can bring on muscular pains. During World War I, a certain percentage of the boys in the trenches developed fibrositis. It was thought to be due to the wet and miserable living conditions. But in World War II, almost exactly the same percentage of men in combat developed fibrositis. And the percentage was the same whether they were fighting in the cold, wet Aleutian Islands or in hot, dry North Africa.

It was found, furthermore, that the incidence of fibrositis increased steadily as the boys moved toward the front. Eventually it was determined that an emotion was often responsible—the emotion a person has when he is called upon to do something he would much rather avoid.

In this situation he involuntarily steels himself and tightens certain muscles—very often those of the neck and shoulders. This tension also occurs, of course, in individuals in civilian life who must constantly meet situations they would rather avoid. If such situations are acute enough, or if they are of long enough duration, pain is eventually produced. Eighty-five percent of the patients complaining of a pain in the back of the head, radiating down the neck, have such pain as a result of emotional tension. Another site of such pain is the pectoral muscles of the chest. If the pain is in the left chest a person may become alarmed; and if some uncertain doctor then murmurs, "You might have a little heart trouble," he is apt to be off on a long, emotionally induced illness.

Fibrositis is an exceedingly common cause of pain. Most people will have it at some time or other, and *some* people are subject to it all the time. Many of them fear they have cancer, or a crippling rheumatism. But fibrositis never becomes crippling; it becomes incapacitating only if you let it. It is not serious; merely a confounded nuisance.

The stomach is one of the organs *par excellence* for the manifestation of emotions. When our world is going along well, we have a good appetite. However, when things do not go well, we suddenly find that we have lost our appetite. If, then, something good should happen, our appetite is back right away.

When the stomach muscles tighten because of certain emotions, the feeling is that of a lump in the upper abdomen; some people describe it as a "stone." When the stomach muscles squeeze down *really hard,* a pain is produced, sometimes a very severe one which resembles the pain produced by an ulcer. For even if one *has* an ulcer, many experts believe it is not the ulcer that hurts but the painful contraction of muscles next to it. Fully

50 percent of the patients who complain of an ulcerlike pain are found to have merely an emotional muscle pain of the stomach.

The same kind of painful spasm occurs in the 28 feet of intestine that lie beyond the stomach, but most especially in the part known as the colon. If this spasm happens in the colon in the upper right-hand portion of the abdomen, it will produce a pain very similar to a gallstone colic. Fifty percent of the people we see with fairly typical "gall bladder attacks" turn out to have normal gall bladders.

If the emotional spasm occurs in the right lower quadrant of the abdomen, it will look for all the world like an attack of appendicitis. Even a very smart doctor may be unable to make a positive diagnosis, especially in children (in whom this kind of thing is apt to occur). Very often, to be safe, the surgeon will open the abdomen, only to find a normal appendix and a bowel squeezed down so tight that it is blanched white.

There are so many emotional disturbances of the colon that all sorts of terms have been evolved for them like "spastic colon," "irritable colon," "nonspecific ulcerative colitis," and many others, all of them merely synonyms for "emotional colon."

Every muscle in the body is influenced by the emotions, especially those in the walls of the blood vessels. All but the very smallest vessels have such muscles, and the moderate-sized ones lying inside or outside the skull are highly sensitive to emotional stimuli. As these vessels contract emotionally, headache is often produced, both the common headache and the more severe type we know as migraine. The emotional excitant may be some deepseated trouble which the person may try to hide even from himself. But the emotions behind most headaches are easy enough to spot.

Blood vessels manifesting emotions do even more remarkable things. Fully 30 percent of the skin trouble in these United States is what the dermatologists call *neurodermatitis*. A neurodermatitis can occur anywhere on the body. In the skin involved, the small blood vessels in the second layer are constantly squeezing down in emotional manifestation. Every time they do so a small amount of serum is extruded through the thin walls of the vessel. As this continues, an appreciable amount of serum accumulates in the tissues. First, the skin gets slightly brawny, then red. Soon there is enough serum under pressure to force its way to the surface, and one has the weeping, scaling, crusting and itching of a full-blown case of neurodermatitis.

How Emotional Overbreathing Affects You

There is another set of symptoms, emotionally induced, that is especially common, and that produces severe apprehension, usually groundless, in the people who experience it. This set of symptoms is known medically as *hyperventilation*. The chance is that you have experienced it some time or other. It comes from breathing too deeply, or breathing too fast, or both.

You have noticed that if you become acutely disturbed you will breathe faster than usual. Normally, most of us breathe between 16 and 18 times a minute at rest. If we were to increase our rate to 22 or 23 times a minute, we ourselves, or those near us, would probably not notice the difference, but our *bodies* would soon notice the increase. For when we breathe fast the lungs take more carbon dioxide from the blood than the body creates. And as the level of carbon dioxide in the blood drops, things begin to happen. First there is a crawling sensation under the skin; next comes a numbness of the fingers and hands; gradually the numbness becomes more pronounced, until there is a sensation of needles pricking the skin all over. Meanwhile other symptoms appear. The heart starts to race; there is a trembling feeling, and lightheadedness, or even fainting, occurs.

One of the most interesting things about hyperventilation is that it occurs most commonly in our sleep. If you watch a sleeping person, especially someone who is in a troublesome life situation, you will see him breathe more rapidly and deeply for a time, and then lapse into quiet breathing, only to repeat the whole cycle over again.

Our minds are never at rest; we are dreaming all through the night; and when we sleep, the usual censor—common sense—is not around. If someone says something nasty to disturb us during the day, that person may turn up in our dreams at the head of a band of Indians chasing us toward a precipitous cliff. In our sleep, we react emotionally as though we really were being driven toward catastrophe. We roll and toss—and we hyperventilate. (This is a common cause of leg cramps at night.)

About once every week during my years of medical practice, I have had to see someone, usually about 2 a.m., who woke up during hyperventilation—probably just at the point where he was about to be hurled over the cliff. His heart is racing and his hands are numb. Naturally, he thinks he is dying of heart failure.

Maybe It's Not Your Nerves

Everyone knew for a long time that the nervous system had, in some way, a great deal to do with emotionally induced illness. Then along came Dr. Hans Selye of Montreal, and today a tremendous and amazing new chapter—a new understanding—is being written on the subject. We know today that the endocrine glands have as much to do with emotional symptoms as the nervous system has. What is more important, the endocrine effects of the emotions far outweigh the nerve effects. So much so that it would be closer to the truth to say, "It's my endocrines," rather than, "It's my nerves."

Dr. Selye started with investigations of the pituitary gland.

Located inside the cranium, on the underside of the brain, the pituitary is cradled in a complete bowl of bone, protected against almost any conceivable injury. One might surmise from this that the pituitary is about the most important organ we have. And it is.

The pituitary is only about the size and shape of an overgrown pea. Yet it is the master regulator of the entire body. It produces an amazing variety of hormones—substances which are carried in the blood and which act on other parts of the body. There is one pituitary hormone that raises blood pressure, another that makes smooth muscles contract, one that inhibits the kidneys from producing urine, one that stimulates the kidneys to make more urine. Then there is a whole group of pituitary hormones that regulate the other endocrine glands of the body. These other glands produce many more hormones to regulate just about everything that goes on in our bodies.

The pituitary is like a key industry that works quietly but efficiently night and day making certain commodities that are absolutely essential to the well-being of our body. Not only does it control our physiology in time of peace and quiet but it becomes the key defense plant if the body is threatened in any way.

All threats to the body—from bacterial invasion to emotional strain—Dr. Selye called "stressors." He found that unpleasant emotions, which can stimulate any or all of the many hormones, are particularly effective stressors.

By his experiments Dr. Selye has shown that prolonged bad emotions can produce a sickness such as is produced by a low-grade, chronic infection in the tonsils or in the infected root of a tooth. We have learned to snip out infected tonsils; the trick is to get rid of our equally harmful emotions. Fortunately nature has given us an ally.

The Healing Power of Good Emotions

Each of us has in his own system the greatest known power for good health. This is the power of good emotions. The only medicines whose healing ability is comparable to that of good emotions are the antibiotics such as penicillin, and ACTH and cortisone.

The body knows the secret of optimal hormone balance. We do not. But there is one way you have of achieving optimal hormone balance. That is to provide your body with the stimulus of the pleasant and cheerful group of emotions. For the "medicinal" value of the good emotions cannot be overestimated. They have two general effects. First, they replace the bad emotions which were producing stress effects; and secondly, they produce their own pituitary effect, which is an optimal balance of endocrine function. It is this optimal balance which produces the state which makes us say, "Gee, I feel good!"

Once we know that healthful living is largely a matter of having the right kind of emotions, it becomes clear how important it is to train and handle them properly. A cheerful and pleasant disposition—that is to say, happy fundamental emotions—should be the central aim in the raising of children. Give them this, and they will have more than they can ever get in any other way.

If you've grown up without a naturally happy disposition, it is not too late to cultivate one. It calls for the constant practice of these simple principles:

1. *Keep Yourself Responsive to Simple Things*. They are always near at hand and readily accessible. Don't get in the habit of requiring the *unusual* for your pleasure. Life becomes a tremendously interesting adventure if you learn to live, for instance, like the great naturalists W. C. English, John Muir or Henry Thoreau, occupied with the constant, wonderful world of color, sound, smell and sight that is available every single instant. If you tune yourself to it as these men did, your every moment is a walk down an avenue of ready-made enjoyment.

I met W. C. English when I was in college; he was already in his 60's, and he enjoyed everything around him. He needed no automobile to travel. He could see more afoot. And in a mile afoot, he found infinitely more wonder than most people find in 10,000 miles on wheels. He knew every plant, every bush, every tree. He knew the places where the pink lady's-slipper grew, where to find the fringed avens, and how to trick a fox into showing where he lived. He knew about geology, fossils and caves.

He was not a pedant, he was just a happy man, enjoying a world in which *everything* interested him. I have seen him spend a whole afternoon watching a jumping spider. When he needed money he lectured or wrote an article. But he had no great need for money, because he was richer than Henry Ford and John D. Rockefeller combined. We can't all be W. C. Englishes. But we *can* cultivate the ability to find our major and constant enjoyments in the common things which are always at hand.

2. *Avoid Watching for a Knock in Your Motor*. Among the world's most miserable people are those who can't get over the idea that something is terribly wrong with their health. They are forever listening for a possible knock in their motors, a grinding in their differentials. They belong to a huge organization, the "Symptom-a-Day Club," in which it is required that the members start the day by waking up and immediately asking themselves, "Where am I sick today?"

It is an interesting physiological fact that if any of us stop to ask, "Where do I hurt?" we can by self-examination find some place where we do hurt. All one needs to do to turn one of these insignificant, unimportant pains into something genuinely severe is to keep one's attention on the pain. It soon grows ten times as severe.

One of my patients, an executive who was always under terrific pressure, frequently felt a tightness in his chest. As long as he was intent on his job, he paid no attention to it. But during a routine physical examination he mentioned the tightness to the company doctor, who told him that he probably had early coronary heart disease. From then on the poor fellow was licked; he thought of his heart all the time and became apprehensive whenever the tightness appeared. He became unable to work and was a complete invalid for a year. It took numerous examinations by the best heart specialists in the country, and very intensive assurative therapy, to get him back to his work. Finally, he could again evaluate the tightness for what it was—a manifestation of the harrying and worrying that were a part of his job.

To avoid such morbid concern with health, have a sensible doctor make a thorough physical examination every year—or oftener, if something turns up to cast any doubt in your mind. Then, having assured yourself that you are reasonably sound, make nothing further of it.

The group in my part of the country who have emotionally induced illness *least* often are the farmers' wives with families of nine or ten who, in addition to their housework, also help out on the farm. Their minds are too occupied with work to allow them to worry, and they are too busy taking care of other people to think of themselves. One of these wonderful human beings told me one time when I asked her whether she ever got tired (one of the most common functional symptoms), "Son, 25 years ago I taught myself never to ask myself that question." And that, incidentally, is the best cure for that kind of tiredness.

3. *Learn to Like Work*. The chances are that, like most of the rest of us, you have to work for a living. As with every other necessary factor in your life, you might just as well like it and avoid making trouble for yourself by not liking it.

A person who has convinced himself that he doesn't like work has a monotonous repetition of unpleasant emotions while he is working, and he is well on the way to an emotionally induced illness. I used to suggest to a person who didn't like the type of work he was doing that he find himself a job he did like. But I found that often such a person didn't like the second job any better than the first. The root of the matter was that he just didn't like work.

If a person likes to work, and has learned the simple joy of doing something well, if he feels pleased at producing something of value to society, he will be generating pleasant emotions all the time he is working. Furthermore, the man who has more than enough work to keep himself occupied doesn't have time to "think." "Thinking" usually means thumbing mentally over troubles. Work is therapy. Liking it is a wonderful guard against emotional ills.

4. *Like People and Join the Human Enterprise.* It is surprising how many people with emotionally induced illness dislike practically everyone, from the President, whom they have never met, to their next-door neighbor, whom they wish they had never met. Their immaturity has isolated them; the extent of their cooperation in human society is limited to what they can get out of it. Next, on finding themselves isolated, they begin to pity themselves and to feel persecuted. They become hypochondriacal, develop deep-seated inferiorities and lead an unnecessarily miserable life.

One of the finest sides to living is wanting to share actively in the human enterprise, to add a bit to the sum total of the effort the human race is making to get out of the jungle. Entering consciously into this human enterprise, feeling oneself a part of the community, is an important element in maturity and in general good health.

5. *Get the Habit of Cheerfulness.* There are few moments that won't benefit from a sally of humor or a cheerful lift. Yet, some people regularly complain about everything, griping at the taxes and the political opposition and lambasting everyone under them. Frequently the gripers wind up in the doctor's office. But I know many executives who carry on under tremendous pressure as affably and kindly as a girl skipping down the street. They are the boys who get along and stay out of the hospitals.

It is particularly important in family life to develop the habit of pleasant conversation. Do not, for your own, your children's or your digestion's sake, make the family meal a recitation of troubles, anxieties, fears, warnings, accusations. And what is more important, don't let the feeling pervade your family that everyone is so taken for granted that a pleasantness or kind word is unnecessary. The crabbed note that clangs daily in so many families is a good foundation for many of the neurotic characteristics of later life.

6. *Meet Your Problems With Decision.* In the multitude of practical problems you must meet every day, you cannot always be right. So it is better to allow yourself a few mistakes than to keep milling and turning every little problem over and over. Such indecisive stewing will certainly create emotionally induced illness. The best rule to follow, therefore, is to make your decisions without a long huffing and puffing. Decide what you are going to do about a problem and then quit thinking about it.

7. *Make the Present Moment an Emotional Success.* Some people live on an expectancy basis, always looking for something in the future, completely losing the only value they have—that which is in the present moment. The boy in high school anticipates college; in college, he anticipates the joy that will be his when he gets an engineering job. When he gets his engineering job, he believes that joy will come when he marries Mary and has a home; and so he goes on...anticipating.

There finally comes a time when anticipation is no longer rosy. That point is accompanied by a tremendous readjustment of thinking, values and motives. That is the point where the individual begins to look old and beaten. Anticipation is shifted into thinking about the glories of the past (which *are* past).

Actually, the only moment we ever live is the present moment. It is the only time we ever have to be happy. Naturally, we have to plan for the future, but too much looking ahead entails fear and apprehension. The best insurance for a satisfactory future is to handle the present hour properly, do a good job of living now, be effective in your work, your thinking, your helpfulness to other people. The future will turn out to be as good as your present if you keep on handling the present moments correctly. That's an important way to be sure that you are living the full 365 days of the year.

HEARING IS

A WAY OF

TOUCHING

by John Kord Lagemann

OUR WORLD is filled with sounds we never hear. The human auditory range is limited to begin with: if we could hear sounds lower than 20 vibrations per second, we would be driven mad by the rumblings and creakings of our muscles, intestines and heartbeats; every step we take would sound like an explosion. But even within our auditory range we select, focus, pay attention to a few sounds and blot out the rest. We are so assaulted by sound that we continually "turn off." But in the process we shut out the glorious symphony of sound in which the living world is bathed.

Everything that moves makes a sound, so all sounds are witnesses to events. Thus sound is a kind of fourth dimension, telling us what is going on, revealing nuances and complexities opaque to vision alone. If touch is the most personal of senses, then hearing—an outgrowth of the sense of touch, a highly specialized way of touching at a distance—is the most *social* of the senses.

The sound-tormented city dweller who habitually "turns off his audio" loses a dimension of social reality. Some people, for example, possess the ability to enter a crowded room and from the sounds encountered know immediately the mood, pace and direction of the group assembled. Everything becomes more real when heard as well as seen. It is, in fact, quite hard really to know a person by sight alone, without hearing his voice. And it is not just the sound of the voice that informs. Even the rhythm of footsteps reveals age and variations of mood—elation, depression, anger, joy.

For these reasons, hearing has a kind of primacy for the social being called man. A baby responds to sound before he does to sight, smell or taste. There is good evidence that the human fetus listens to its mother's heartbeats weeks before birth. This may explain why babies are easily lulled to sleep by rhythm, and why their first words are repeated syllables—*da-da, ma-ma, gee-gee*—that sound like the *lub-dub* of the heartbeat.

All through life, hearing is a major channel of experience, a more vital stimulus than vision. It is also the watchdog sense. Since there is no sound without movement of some kind taking place, sounds warn us of happenings. When we go to sleep, our perception of sound seems to be the last door to close, and the first to reopen as we awaken. Even as we sleep, the brain is alerted by certain key sounds. A mother wakes at the whimper of her baby. The average person is quickly roused by the sound of his own name.

Watchdog, stimulator, arouser—it is not surprising that modern urban man has turned down and even crippled this most stressful of senses. But hearing can also soothe and comfort. The snapping of logs in the fireplace, the gossipy whisper of a broom, the inquisitive wheeze of a drawer opening—all are savored sounds that make us feel at home. In a well-loved home, every chair produces a different, recognizable creak, every window a different click, groan or squeak. The kitchen by itself is a source of many pleasing sounds—the clop-clop of batter stirred in a crockery bowl, the chortle of simmering soup, the conversational maundering of an electric percolator on the breakfast table. Every place, every event has a sound dimension.

The sense of hearing can perhaps be restored to modern man if he better understands its worth and how it works. Most people would be surprised to discover how far the sense can be pushed by cultivation. At a friend's house recently, my wife opened her purse and some coins spilled out, one after another, onto the bare floor. "Three quarters, two dimes, a nickel and three pennies," said our host as he came in from the next room.

And, as an afterthought: "One of the quarters is silver." He was right, down to the last penny.

"How did you do it?" we asked.

"Try it yourself," he said. We did, and with a little practice we found it easy.

On the way home, my wife and I took turns closing our eyes and listening to the sound of our taxi on the wet street as it reflected from cars parked along the curb. Just from the sound we were able to tell small foreign cars from larger American cars. Such games are one of the best ways to open up new realms of hearing experience.

An allied beneficence of hearing is that "extrasensory" faculty of the blind called facial vision. Doctors have long marveled at this sensitivity to reflected sound. About 200 years ago, Erasmus Darwin, grandfather of Charles Darwin, reported a visit by a blind friend, one Justice Fielding. "He walked into my room for the first time and, after speaking a few words, said, 'This room is about 22 feet long, 18 wide and 12 high'—all of which he guessed by the ear with great accuracy."

Sound engineers call it "ambience," the impression we all get in some degree from sound waves bouncing off walls, trees, even people. For a blind person to interpret the echoes effectively, he uses a tapping cane, preferably with a tip of metal, nylon or other substance that produces a distinct, consistent sound. (Wood gives a different sound wet than dry.) The metal noisemaker called a "cricket" is equally effective. Animals, both terrestrial and nonterrestrial, also use "echo-location." The bat, for example, emits a very high-pitched sound and picks up echoes from any obstacle, even as thin as a human hair.

The human ear is an amazing mechanism. Though its inner operating parts occupy less than a cubic inch, it can distinguish from 300,000 to 400,000 variations of tone and intensity. The loudest sound it can tolerate is a trillion times more intense than the faintest sounds it can pick up—the dropping of the proverbial pin, the soft thud of falling snowflakes. When the eardrums vibrate in response to sound, the tiny piston-like stirrup bones of the middle ear amplify the vibrations. This motion is passed along to the snail-like chamber of the inner ear, which is filled with liquid and contains some 30,000 fibers. These fibers are made to bend, depending on the frequency of the vibration—shorter strands respond to higher wavelengths, longer strands to lower—and this movement is translated into nerve impulses and sent to the brain, which then, somehow, "hears."

While we are still under age 30, most of us can hear tones as high as 20,000 cycles per second (c.p.s.), about five times as high as the highest C on a piano. With age, the inner ear loses its elasticity. It is unusual for a person over 40 to hear well above 10,000 c.p.s. He can still function, of course, since most conversation is carried on within an octave or two of middle C, or about 260 c.p.s.

Curiously, evidence indicates that people *need* sound. When we are lost in thought, we involuntarily drum with our fingers or tap with a pencil—a reminder that we are still surrounded by a world outside ourselves. Just cutting down *reflected* sound can produce some odd results. The nearest thing on earth to the silence of outer space, for example, is the "anechoic chamber" at the Bell Telephone Laboratories in Murray Hills, N.J., which is lined with material that absorbs 99.98 percent of all reflected sound. Men who have remained in the room for more than an hour report that they feel jittery and out of touch with reality.

One remarkable quality of the human ear is its ability to pick out a specific sound or voice from a surrounding welter of sound, and to locate its position. Toscanini, rehearsing a symphony orchestra of almost 100 musicians, unerringly singled out the oboist who slurred a phrase. "I hear a mute somewhere on one of the second violins," he said another time in stopping a rehearsal. Sure enough, a second violinist far back on the stage discovered that he had failed to remove his mute.

We owe our ability to zero in on a particular sound to the fact that we have two ears. A sound to the right of us reaches the right ear perhaps .0001 second before it reaches the left. This tiny time lag is unconsciously perceived and allows us to localize the object in the direction of the ear stimulated first. If you turn your head until the sound strikes both ears at once, the source is directly ahead. Primitives, to pinpoint the source of a sound, slowly shake the head back and forth. Try it sometime when you hear the distant approach of a car.

The sound you hear most often and with greatest interest

is the sound of your own voice. You hear it not only through air vibrations which strike your eardrums but through vibrations transmitted directly to the inner ear through your skull. When you chew on a stalk of celery, the loud crunching noise comes mainly through bone conduction. Such bone conduction explains why we hardly recognize a recording of our speech. Many of the low-frequency tones which seem to us to give our voices resonance and power are conducted to our ears through the skull; in a recording they are missing, and so our voices often strike us as thin and weak.

Perhaps hearing will atrophy in a civilization where, increasingly, too much is going on. As a result of this overload, we learn to ignore most of the sound around us, and miss much that could give us pleasure and information. Too bad—because there is a wisdom in hearing which we need.

...LISTEN!

by Alison Wyrley Birch

THERE ARE sounds to seasons. There are sounds to places, and there are sounds to every time in one's life. So many of us tune them out, missing one of life's greatest experiences.

In the spring there is the sound of the peepers; in fall, the katydids. Summer is tuned up with every conceivable insect and bird pouring out its amazement at its own existence and the existence of the world. Winter is deep with the grandest sound of them all—silence.

The sound of children is one of the greatest of all sounds. Children calling to one another; mothers calling to children. It's an ageless, deep, abiding sound of love and caring.

Some sounds are sad: the wind howling in the night; the drifting, lingering, hooting sound of a railroad locomotive. In the sadness of sound there is most likely a remembered nostalgia, singularly sweet—something promised but undone about the past. Conversely there is maximum joy in sound. The gathering, strident sound of a jet on takeoff. The *clop-clop* of a horse's hoofs. The rushing, rising, lifting sound of a giant waterfall. The wind in the trees before a storm. The telephone voice of a long unseen friend. The homecoming voice of the family.

Some sounds are gentle—like the breathing of a sleeping

baby. The soft sound of a light rain outside while a fire burns brightly within. The upstairs sound of a father's voice as he reads aloud to his children. The fragile *click* of knitting needles in the act of creating a gift.

Listen, also, to the relaxing sound of the ocean, as its waves beat out their rhythms against a craggy coast. And to the sound of the dip of paddles in a lake, as a canoe glides by.

The sources of sound are magnificently unlimited. There is the raucous caw of a crow against the November sky; despite its harshness, it has the sound of harvest and comfort in it. There are the domestic sounds of dishes clattering in the kitchen with a promise before the meal, and remembrance and comfort after. There is the dry, indulgent sound of pages turning in a book.

What adults don't do, children do do. They really listen. Hundreds of generations of children have sat on the top step of the staircase listening to adult conversations floating up from the rooms below. They listen, totally lost and involved, when someone reads to them. They are caught up in the essence of sound and in the total activity of absorbing the wonderful flavor of words. And then it happens. Somewhere along the trail to adulthood, the child tunes out and the emerging adult loses the art of listening—unless he refuses to surrender it.

HOW TO

RELAX

by Joseph A. Kennedy

MOST OF US, in practically all our everyday activities, are driving with the brake on. That brake is unconscious tension. We have worked and played in a tense condition for so long that we regard it as more or less normal. We do not notice the clenched jaw, the tight abdomen, the constricted muscles. Yet the resulting fatigue burns up our energy, impairs our skills and even dulls our appreciation of the world about us.

Tension is excess effort: trying too hard to do things that should be done automatically. It causes muscles to jam and contract. Make a conscious effort to speak correctly and you stutter or become tongue-tied. Let the accomplished pianist think about his fingers and he is likely to make a mistake.

Most of us put forth too much effort for the task at hand. Our muscles work better when we speak our orders quietly than when we shout at them. In order to see perfectly, for example, the eyes must make numerous minute movements, scanning the object under observation. This scanning is an automatic reflex; it is no more subject to your will than is your heartbeat. But when you stare—make a conscious effort to see—the eyes become tense. They do not scan as they should and sight suffers.

Nor is the damage done by tension limited to the body. When muscles are tense, contracting without purpose, a feeling of confusion is relayed back to the brain. Why is it that a poised man whose ideas reel out effortlessly when he is in his own study suddenly finds his mind a blank when he is attending an important board meeting? Because tenseness, resulting from making too much effort, has jammed his psychomotor mechanisms.

Tension tends to become an unconscious habit; muscles tend to stay constricted. How, then, can you become conscious of unconscious tension? How can you relax?

First, by locating the tension in your muscles. For example, you are probably unaware of any tension in your forehead at this moment, but there is a good chance that some is there. In order to recognize it, consciously produce more tension: wrinkle your forehead into a frown and notice the feeling in the muscles. Practice sensing the tension that you thus consciously produce. Then, tomorrow, stop working for a moment and ask yourself, "Am I aware of any tension in my forehead?" You can probably detect the faint sensation already there. One student told me, "When I started to relax, I discovered layer after layer of tension of which I had been totally unaware."

Once you learn to recognize tension, you can learn to relax. The way to do this is first to produce *more* tension in your muscles. Don't *try* to relax! A muscle tends to relax itself. Consciously tense a particular muscle; then stop. The muscle relaxes and will continue to relax automatically if it is not interfered with.

The muscles of the brow and forehead need special attention, for they are closely associated with anxiety and confusion. With the brow relaxed it is practically impossible to feel worried. The next time you have a problem to solve, make it a point to keep your brow relaxed and see if the problem does not seem less difficult.

The jaw is one of the most expressive parts of the human body. We grit our teeth in rage, clench our jaws in determination. When your jaw is tensed, your brain, which is constantly receiving nerve messages from your muscles, reasons something like this: "We must be in difficulty, we must have a terrible job to do." You then become conscious of a feeling of pressure.

As soon as you relax your jaw muscles, however, your brain says, "Ah, we are out of difficulty now," and you get a feeling of confidence. So, every time you feel anxious or experience self-doubt, notice that you are contracting your jaws. Then stop.

The hands are the main executive instrument of the body. They are involved in almost everything we do or feel. We throw up our hands in hopelessness, shake our fist when we are angry. When hands are kept tense, the whole body is geared for action. Learn to relax your hands when you find yourself in a tight spot or when something irritates you. It will take the pressure off and give you a feeling that you are master of the situation.

If you were expecting a blow in the pit of the stomach, you would instinctively tense the abdominal muscles for defense. And if you habitually live on the defensive, your subconscious keeps your stomach muscles continually tensed. Thus, another vicious circle is set up. The brain receives defensive messages from the abdominal muscles and this keeps you feeling insecure. Learn to break the circle. When you feel anxious or worried, stop and relax your abdomen.

If you try to control your anxieties mentally, you will probably only make yourself more nervous. But you *can* control your key muscles. Learn to relax them at midmorning, just before lunch and in midafternoon. Sit down and "jelly" yourself into the most comfortable position. Or lie on your back on a bed with your arms at your sides. Then check your key points for tension: brow, abdomen, jaw, hands, and so on. Tighten each, and then let go, allowing the muscle to relax by itself.

Breathing furnishes a valuable control for toning down the degree of excitement throughout the entire body. When we are emotionally tense, we say we have something on our chest. When a crisis is past, we say that we can breathe easier. But it works both ways. If we can learn to breathe easier in the first place, we won't get so tense.

It will help you to learn to breathe correctly if you recognize that the body has two separate breathing patterns. Nervous breathers breathe high in the chest by expanding and contracting the rib box. They also breathe too fast and too deeply. This particular breathing pattern was engineered for emergencies. It is the way you breathe when you are out of breath from running a race. Your chest heaves as you take in great gulps of air. Your muscles need oxygen fast, and this is the way to get it. Nervous people are so used to reacting with emergency behavior to simple, ordinary tasks that they use this emergency-breathing mechanism all the time.

Non-emergency breathing is belly breathing. It is done more from the diaphragm; most of the movement is in the lower chest wall and the upper abdomen. As the diaphragm smoothly contracts and lets go, a gentle massage is applied to the whole abdominal area. The abdominal muscles relax. It is virtually impossible to feel tense when you breathe habitually from your belly.

If you find yourself breathing nervously and fast, keep right on—but breathe that way because you *want* to. Take as many as 50 to 100 of these deliberate nervous breaths, thus bringing your breathing under control of your will. This conscious control will in itself cause the feeling of nervousness to diminish. After a time you will find that it is an effort to keep breathing fast, and a relief to let yourself breathe more slowly.

One of the most malicious causes of tension is hurry. You can hurry while sitting down, apparently doing nothing, or while waiting for a bus. Many people feel hurried because they think there just isn't enough time. They would do well to heed Sir William Osler's advice to his students when he told them to think of how much time there is to use, rather than of how little.

Whenever you feel a sense of hurry, deliberately slow down. Everyone has his own best pace or tempo for doing things, and when we give in to hurry we allow external things and situations to set our pace for us. The great Finnish runner, Paavo Nurmi, always carried a watch with him in his races. He referred to it, not to the other runners. He ran his own race, keeping his own tempo, regardless of competition.

A basic cause of tension is putting too much emphasis on the ultimate goal, trying too hard to win. It is good to have a clear mental picture of your objective; but your attention should be concentrated on the specific job at hand.

And when that job is done, remember there will be something else to do tomorrow. So relax! Life is not a 100-yard dash, but more in the nature of a cross-country run. And no one can sprint all the time.

PUT YOUR

BEST VOICE FORWARD

by Stephen S. Price, Ed.D.

HAVE YOU ever heard how your voice sounds to others? If not, go to a corner of the room. Face closely into the corner, cup your ears and speak a few words. That stranger you hear talking is you.

It is this voice which has been labeling you in people's minds. It labels you every time you meet someone at a party, greet a new customer, express an opinion at a meeting or talk on the telephone.

Is it a voice that gives warmth and assurance, that helps you make the right impression?

There is no one who cannot make his or her voice more appealing. In acting as voice counselor to thousands of people, I have found five major vocal shortcomings. To check up on them in yourself, ask yourself these questions:

"Is my speech slurred rather than clear?"

Do people frequently misunderstand you or ask you to repeat? Say this sentence aloud several times: "Leaves, frost crisped, break from the trees and fall." If it makes you feel a little tongue-tied you are probably lip lazy. Vowels are easy to say, but we get power and clarity into our speech with consonants. To pronounce these properly you must use the tongue, lips and teeth energetically.

A father asked me to help his 19-year-old daughter, whose speech was listless and mumbling. She was moody and unhappy. I encouraged her to spend 30 minutes each day in front of a mirror energetically repeating the alphabet, and five minutes whistling. Whistling is a good corrective for lip laziness. Within two months people began noticing a change in her.

If you need to make your enunciation clearer, practice talking like Gary Cooper, through clenched teeth. This makes you work your tongue and lips harder. With teeth closed tightly, read aloud, slowly at first, then rapidly. Repeat such phrases as, "He thrust three thousand thistles through the thick of his thumb." You'll find you have to exert more power in your breath, and your speech will be more energetic.

"Is my voice harsh rather than agreeable?"

Shrill, grating or brassy voices stem from tension in the throat and jaw. Foreigners often comment on the harsh voices of American women. (Tension shows up more in a woman's voice.)

To relax your throat muscles, slump forward in your chair. Let your head drop, your jaw sag and your arms flop. Slowly and gently roll your head in a circle. Continue circling three minutes. Then yawn a few times, opening your mouth wide and then say such words as "clock," "squaw," "gong," "claw."

For at least a few minutes every day concentrate on talking slowly and gently to people—as if talking to a baby or a puppy. Gradually, gentleness will pervade all your talk.

"Is my voice weak?"

Your diaphragm, the band of muscle a few inches above your midriff, is the bellows that blows fire into your speech and adds oomph to your personality. If your diaphragm is weak you probably have a thin, uncertain, shy voice. People don't pay much attention when you talk.

A young research expert with a wispy voice said to me, "In a group I rarely get a chance to finish a sentence. Someone always butts in." I put my hand on his diaphragm and asked him to say loudly, "Boomlay, boomlay, boomlay, boom!" His diaphragm muscle barely fluttered. A well-developed diaphragm will really bounce when you say "boom."

To give him a vigorous diaphragm I prescribed boxing lessons and daily "deep-breathing walks." I also told him to lie on the floor breathing deeply, with a heavy book on his diaphragm. Then to shout several times, "Hay! he! ha! hi! ho! who!" Then to sit up, inhale and blow out through a tiny hole formed by pursed lips. After these exercises he was to pick up a newspaper and see how long he could read aloud with one breath. As his diaphragm strengthened he was able to read for 15, and later 20, seconds in one breath (25 is excellent).

But it is breath control, not mere lung capacity, that gives you an outstanding voice. To check your breath control, hold a lighted candle four inches from your mouth and say, "Peter Piper picked a peck of pickled peppers." If you blow out the flame you have poor breath control.

Whispering aloud is an excellent way to develop breath control and voice power. Have a friend stand across the room, then whisper loudly to him. As soon as he can hear you clearly, have him move into another room, and then go as far away as your whisper can reach him.

"Is my voice flat rather than colorful?"

Many persons talk in a droning, boring monotone. A prim New England woman with a cold, listless voice once came to me. I asked her if she knew anyone who got a big kick out of life. She said, "Yes, the Italian who helps with our gardening." She envied his exuberance. To help bring warmth to her voice, I suggested she spend a few hours each week working along with him. I also instructed her to laugh out loud, up and down the musical scale—first using "ho," then "ha," "he" and "hoo." She was to do it slowly at first and then faster and faster. In two months her voice took on warmth and feeling.

A widespread cause of flatness is "talking through the nose" in a twangy manner, a common quality in American speech. To check for this defect, hold your nose and say "meaning." Notice how strangely muffled it sounds. Feel the vibration. That is because the sounds, "m," "n," and "ng" (and only those three basic sounds) are resonated mainly in the nose. Say, "Father Manning." You should feel vibration in your nose only when you say "Manning." If any other letters sound muffled, you are probably nasal in your speech.

To stop talking through your nose and add richness to your voice, use your mouth, throat and chest. The farther you open your mouth, the richer, fuller and lower your tones will be. Try saying "olive" by opening your lips only slightly. Now repeat it while really opening your mouth and see the difference. To add vibrance to your voice, hum your favorite songs at odd moments every day.

"*Is my voice high-pitched?*"

You cannot actually "lower" your voice, but you can increase the use of your lower register by practicing sounds that can be resonated in the chest, such as, "Alone, alone, all, all alone. Alone, alone on a wide, wide sea."

Say, "Hello, how are you?" The first time, put your hand on your forehead and pitch your voice toward your hand. Now put your hand on your chest and low-pitch your words to the chest. Notice the greater depth and richness? You also can develop the warm lower tones of your voice by breathing more deeply as you talk and striving to speak softly, even when under stress.

A few general suggestions: Join in group singing. Read aloud classics such as the Bible. This will challenge and improve your articulation and rhythm. After a month or so of regular practice, your new way of speaking will begin to be automatic. When you sound better you can't help feeling better, and you will not only enjoy increased self-respect but people will look at you in a new way.

STATE OF MIND

THE ONE

SURE WAY TO

HAPPINESS

by June Callwood

HAPPINESS IS the rarest, most prized and most misunderstood state of man. Actually, lasting happiness depends on how much maturity a man has been able to assemble—some of it derived from being desperately unhappy. It is a consequence of at least a moderate amount of education or training, because happiness requires a decently stocked mind. It is bound up with the ability to work, and to be readily interested in the world around you. It also is part of an unembarrassed appreciation of leisure and of solitude.

The relationship between happiness and maturity defeats the rationalization of many aging adults—that happiness is youth and naturally diminishes with time. Happy people can be any age, past 20. Children are rarely happy: they have *flights* of joy, but their helplessness in a restrictive adult world keeps them close to despondency. Until their personalities stabilize, a process generally completed after the age of 35, they are likely to be wretched with self-doubts and dismay at their inner muddle.

Younger adults may describe themselves as "happy"; it's a serviceable word to protect privacy. But many of them are frantic at the acceleration of time they are beginning to feel. They can sense the years wheeling by without any substantial or satisfying accomplishment. Grieving over their mistakes and wrong choices, they don paper hats for laughs, give anxious parties, drink too much, talk too much and say too little. They see old age as a catastrophe, a final bad joke on the false dream of being happy.

Yet all over the world, men and women, most of them in their 30s, are turning a corner that they didn't see, and stand transfixed by the miracle of finding themselves happy. Nothing has changed in the room, in the family; nothing is different—but everything seems so. The personality has put together enough experience to make sane judgments, enough vitality to love, a few fragments of clarity and courage, and a great deal of self-appraisal. There is a soundless *click*, and a steady state of happiness ensues.

True happiness is unmistakable. One woman compared it with the unequivocal quality of a genuine labor pain. "When you're carrying your first baby," she explained, "you keep wondering what a labor pain is like. Every time you have a cramp or twinge you wonder if this is it. Then eventually you have a whopper of a labor pain. There is no question in your mind about it; you *know* that this positively is the real thing. Well, becoming happy is just the same. You think you are, from time to time in your life, but when it really arrives you recognize it immediately."

No one is born happy. "Happiness is not," says psychoanalyst Erich Fromm, "a gift of the gods." It is an achievement, brought about by inner productiveness. People succeed at being happy in the same way they succeed at loving, by building a liking for themselves for true reasons. Hollow people, lacking any conviction of their worth and without self-respect, have nothing to give—a profoundly unhappy state. They must connive to secure love and admiration for themselves, and they can't depend on keeping it.

Unhappy people rarely blame themselves for their condition. Their jobs are at fault, or their marriages, or the vileness of parents, or the meanness of fate. The real cause is the incoherency of their lives. Sterile and confused, they have no warmth to give, in work, play or love. They wait in apathy for a visit from the fairy godmother, and in the meantime try to distract their attention from the abyss of barrenness and boredom within them. The furthest notion from their minds is to improve their lot by tackling some self-reconstruction.

"The happiest person," said Timothy Dwight, when he was president of Yale University, "is the person who thinks the most interesting thoughts." One of the world's most respected psychologists, William McDougall, had a parallel comment: "The richer, the more highly developed, the more completely unified or integrated is the personality, the more capable it is of sustained happiness, in spite of intercurrent pains of all sorts." Aristotle believed that happiness was to be found in use of the intellect, an occupation characterized by self-sufficiency, unweariedness and capacity for rest. The self-sufficiency theme was echoed with a mathematician's spareness by Benedict Spinoza, who wrote 300 years ago, "Happiness consists in this: that man can preserve his own being."

Nothing on earth renders happiness less approachable than trying to find it. Historian Will Durant described how he looked for happiness in knowledge, and found only disillusionment. He then sought happiness in travel, and found weariness; in wealth, and found discord and worry. He looked for happiness in his writing and was only fatigued. One day he saw a woman waiting in a tiny car with a sleeping child in her arms. A man descended from a train and came over and gently kissed the woman and then the baby, very softly so as not to waken him. The family drove off and left Durant with a stunning realization of the real nature of happiness. He relaxed and discovered that "every normal function of life holds some delight."

When Adm. Richard E. Byrd believed himself to be dying in the ice of the Ross Barrier, he wrote some thoughts on happiness. "I realized I had failed to see that the simple, homely, unpretentious things of life are the most important. When a man achieves a fair measure of harmony within himself and his family circle, he achieves peace. At the end only two things really matter to a man, regardless of who he is: the affection and understanding of his family."

One American writer announced that he had been a happy man every day of his adult life. Of course, he admitted, there had been days when he was jobless and hungry, days of grief, days of nausea and illness. But on each one of them he had been able to contact the deepest part of himself which was operating steadily, soundly and happily. A permeating, permanent state of happiness is rare—but the world abounds in people who are achieving ever-larger fragments of it.

A psychologist who questioned 500 young men to determine their degree of happiness made the not-unexpected discovery that happiness and health generally go together. Happy people tend to be ill less often, recover more quickly, even seem to have bones and tissue that heal better. And happy people often seem to age more slowly. They have better color, glossier skins, more erect carriage than their contemporaries who suffer the graying atrophy of depression and anxiety. "Increased circulation brightens the eye," said Darwin; "color rises, lively ideas pass rapidly through the mind, affections are warmed."

Oddly, laughter has little or no relationship to the state of happiness. Calm, serene happiness rarely laughs or cries. It has too much stability to need the tools of the tense. It is embodied in the private conquest of self-dislike and the honesty of self-definition.

A Frenchman once said that wise men are happy with trifles but nothing pleases fools. All wise men, however, have been fools. There is a trick to their conversion:

Count your blessings—only numskulls are tormented by regrets and recriminations. *Pause to enjoy*—Goethe, a craftsman at happiness, explained that happiness is not transitory joy but a longevity of secret power. *Sharpen your wits when you observe man and nature*—because understanding the unique strength and beauty within all living things is the heart of happiness. *Never fear to use yourself up*—the great elixir of life, according to George Bernard Shaw, is to be thoroughly worn out before being discarded on the scrap heap—"a force of nature, instead of a feverish, selfish clod of ailments and grievances." *Never delay*—unhappiness is nurtured by the habit of putting off living until some fictional future day.

Fromm proclaimed, "Happiness is proof of partial or total success in the art of living." There are few total successes but it is not an impossible art. Never, ever, impossible.

THE WISDOM

OF TEARS

by Morton M. Hunt

TEARS ARE much more than the outpouring of sorrow, for they may also start forth in the presence of beauty, in moments of great joy, at times of sudden relief from worry. In such situations, they seem unreasonable and inappropriate. Yet a significant lesson of contemporary psychology is that such unexpected actions stem from the most powerful but best-hidden needs and secrets of our own hearts. Unaccountable tears can therefore be a means of self-revelation, personal wisdom and deeper happiness.

Not long ago, my wife was leafing through our photograph album—a vivid reminder of our life when we were a poor young couple clinging to each other in the big city, full of fears and hopes. When I came into the living room I found her brokenheartedly crying for the lean and frightening days that are no more. We are happier and better off today in every way than we were then; yet she cried for those days all the same.

Illogical? No, for behind her tears there lurked an important truth. She wept not only because a part of life and youth were gone but also because deep down she realized that no one lives as intensely and as warmly as he would if he were only aware of the pathetic shortness of our years, of the dreadful finality of the past.

My wife was crying for the days—no matter that they were hard and anxious—in which we were in such a hurry to get on with life that we neglected to suck the full sweetness out of each blessed hour. And to realize this, it seems to me, is a very high form of wisdom. The unreasonable tears of nostalgia can teach each of us that truth, if we but use them as a stimulus to reflection.

So, too, with other kinds of tears. One afternoon when the people in an old folks' home were treated to ice-cream cones, a palsied old man in a wheel chair dropped his ice cream on the floor. His smile of anticipation faded, and big soundless tears rolled down his cheeks. A volunteer aide stared at him for a moment, and then fled to an anteroom where she bawled like a baby. When I asked her why, she told me: "Because he was so old, so pathetic—oh, you know!"

But I think there was more to her tears, if she could only have found words for it. Man is a fragile thing, she might have said, and death hovers over him; let us have compassion for one another. But alas, most of the time we fear our own impulse toward sympathy, and clear our throats gruffly and laugh at what we call "sentimentality." Only when tears burst forth in spite of ourselves do we realize the universal need of all human beings to pity and sympathize with each other.

An army colonel I once knew was riding through southern Germany in a staff car shortly after V-E Day. Along the sides of the dusty road he saw long lines of ragged German soldiers who had just been released by our own forces, plodding homeward across the land with their packs on their backs.

"I hated their guts," he told me. "A few weeks earlier they had been shooting at us, and I presumed that many of them were confirmed Nazis. Yet suddenly I saw them there in the sunshine and the dust as human beings, hopefully hurrying back after long years of absence to the job of mating, rearing children, tilling the soil, living out their own joys and sorrows. And I found myself crying before I could help it."

In one astonishing moment, tears had let him glimpse the universality of human desires and feelings, and had begun to wipe out in his own heart the bitterness of war.

Insights like this lie waiting for us behind the tears that mysteriously catch us by surprise at the unlikeliest times. A visit to a great medieval cathedral has left many a sensitive traveler moist-eyed and choked with unnamed emotion. Why tears? Why not simply smiles of pleasure and appreciation for the cathedral's majesty and rich detail?

The answer, I would venture to guess, lies in a dazzling vision of the kinship of all men, a momentary revelation of the labors, hopes and achievements of unknown men who lived long ago. The traveler looks at the incredible detail of the mighty carved façade, or gazes up at the soaring buttresses with their exquisite carving; and he thinks of the millions of careful blows of hammer upon chisel, the calloused and aching hands that held the tools, the weary muscles and tired backs, the satisfied proud faces of the craftsmen and the designers. And so he weeps, because if man is often little and mean, he is also occasionally lofty and noble.

Like these tears of sympathy or identification, tears of joy can teach us much about our hidden selves. Can such weeping come from pure happiness? Psychiatrists think not. In one study, Dr. Sandor Feldman, associate professor of psychiatry at the University of Rochester, concluded that no one ever weeps for unalloyed joy; such tears always tell of a hidden element of sadness. At a wedding, the purely happy bride does not cry. But her mother, who is also happy, weeps for the sorrow that may come to one who until that moment was her child—and also, perhaps, because she, the mother, feels she has lost part of her function in life.

Some of us are moved to tears by the purely beautiful. Once when Charles Laughton visited the University of North Carolina to do a reading, he went walking through the Chapel Hill flower gardens. Coming suddenly upon a bank of massed daffodils and narcissuses, he promptly burst into tears. Other people have wept at the first sight of the Rocky Mountains, or a blue lake nestled in the hills, or the perfection of a Mozart sonata.

If you study the physiology of weeping, you discover that it seldom occurs during a state of complete tension, or one of complete relaxation—but during the *transition* from the tense toward the pleasant. I suspect the principal reason beauty can bring forth tears lies within the nature of the one who so weeps. He may be one who is more easily hurt than most, or more bottled up, or more tense. In the course of everyday living he is bound to gather many a minor wound and unexpressed sadness. Then the sudden sight of beauty brings pleasure, release and the flooding forth of gentle emotions—and with the barriers down, there spill forth the accumulated tears of mingled joy and sadness.

Anger, fear or the shock of sudden sorrow brings physical changes in our bodies. The digestion is shut down, the blood pressure is raised, the heart speeds up and the skin becomes cold. Maintained over a prolonged period, this emergency status makes the body—and the personality—tight, dry and rigid. In people who are afraid to let themselves pour forth their painful emotions, doctors find the suppressed tears can trigger such ailments as asthma, migraine headache and many others.

Weeping, on the other hand, comes as part of the reversal of conditions of alarm, shock and anger. Tears do not, therefore, mark a breakdown or low point, but a transition to warmth and hope and health.

This shows up clearly in bereavement. Dr. Erich Lindemann, psychiatrist-in-chief of the Massachusetts General Hospital and a pioneering investigator of human grief reactions, cited this remarkable case: A young nurse tended her father, to whom she was deeply devoted, through the long months of his terminal illness, always fighting back her tears. When he died, a well-meaning person sternly forbade her to show any grief, so as to spare her mother's feelings and weak heart. Within a few hours she began to suffer from intestinal distress, and after a few days had a raging case of ulcerative colitis. Her body, denied its native access to relief, was slowly corroded away from within by the disordered impulses of her nervous system. She eventually died, killed by an emotion she would not permit herself to express.

In contrast, many a patient with complaints as dissimilar as a painful shoulder or recurrent nightmares has been dramatically relieved of them by the beginning of real weeping. Lucy Freeman in her book, *Fight Against Fears*, tells how she suffered for years from chronic colds and sinus trouble; when she learned to vent her feelings by crying, the colds and sinusitis disappeared.

Philosophers once thought that our emotions interfered

with the ability to think, and that one had to eliminate his emotions before he could attain understanding. Modern medical science holds that the *repression* of our feelings may be more damaging to our ability to think clearly than anything else.

So there *is* a genuine wisdom in tears: in the tears of grief, or remembrance, of sympathy, or esthetic pleasure, of the appreciation of grandeur, of poignant joy. They all express deep-seated needs—the need to love and be loved, the need to cast out anger and hate, the need to wash away trouble and tension. In permitting ourselves to weep instead of manfully repressing the impulse, we help ourselves to health. And wisdom; for in the state of physical release which tears bring, our thoughts can flow freely, and bring us insight and understanding we never knew were within our grasp.

HAPPINESS DOESN'T

COME IN PILLS

by Arthur Gordon

NOT LONG ago a magazine reported that Americans are now spending more than one billion dollars a year on tranquilizers, sometimes known as "mood" or "happiness" pills. Although doctors differ about their value, even their safety, these little packages of synthetic bliss are being gobbled at an ever-increasing rate by people fleeing from "anxiety" and "nervous tension." Astonishingly, nowhere did the article ask *why?* Why are these pills in such demand? Why are so many people in such a jet-propelled swivet?

Is it "the pace of modern living?" This is a phrase dear to our hearts, yet never before have people had so much leisure, so much time to take things easy. What is it then? Here in the land of the free and the home of the brave, with more security than any other nation, with the highest standard of living in the world, we spend a billion dollars a year trying to run away from something. From what?

From normalcy, that's what! From stresses and strains that the human animal was designed to stand, and is perfectly capable of standing.

Consider some of the uses one manufacturer recommends that his tranquilizer be taken for:

Financial worries.

Family tensions caused by sickness, weddings, funerals. Trouble stemming from differences of opinion.

Apprehension connected with approaching parenthood.

Tension in children, resulting from arrival of a new baby or a move to a new home.

Tension among adolescents caused by social competition, increased responsibility, first jobs.

The list might be funny if it were not frightening. All these "crises" are the normal problems of living. Everyone has financial worries. There will always be differences of opinion—I hope. As for the tension-ridden moppets and adolescents, it never seems to occur to the happiness monger that by separating youngsters from their normal small anxieties we may be damaging a vital attribute—the capacity to adjust to new situations and circumstances.

The whole incredible business is based on a misconception of the nature and purpose of anxiety—or, to use a less fancy term, fear. Fear is an uncomfortable emotion, certainly, and too much of it can be disastrous. But there is a good reason for our capacity to feel it: self-preservation. I don't mean just the kind of fear that keeps you from petting a rattlesnake. I mean the steady anxiety that keeps you doing your best from day to day and makes you rise to an emergency when one comes along.

The error of the mood-pill eaters lies in thinking that, since too much fear is bad, *all* anxiety is to be avoided. They ignore the fact that anxiety is usually caused by something specific, and that swallowing a pill will not make that something go away. It will still be there in the morning—and so will the temptation to reach for another pill.

So far, the mass consumption of happiness drugs seems to be an American phenomenon. This is partly because no other nation is rich enough to spend a billion dollars on such nonsense. But it may also reflect the disturbing fact that a lot of Americans can't endure normal stresses of living because they haven't been trained to face trouble.

Learning to face trouble calls for progressive exposure to inconvenience and minor difficulties, starting in childhood. And in this department many American parents are falling flat on their responsibilities.

One fall, for example, there was great consternation in our neighborhood when the school bus service was discontinued, although the school was less than two miles away. A chorus of anguished wails arose from the younger generation. And the parents were so appalled at the prospect of having their offspring use their legs (or bicycles) that they rose up en masse and forced the school to restore the buses. The school designated a pick-up point some three blocks away, whereupon, so help me, some of the neighbors organized a car pool to transport the youngsters the three blocks.

The manufacturers of happiness pills should be delighted. The small individual who is not permitted to face the minor discipline of walking to school, whose life is overprotected, later on may well be the first to reach for the pills when the going gets rough. Parents who insulate their children from any sort of discomfort or disappointment are cheating them of the chance to acquire the flexibility and toughness they are going to need. True, small children need a lot of security, but they cannot remain small children forever. Somewhere along the line they have to acquire stability and stamina.

What is called for is straighter thinking on the closely related subjects of happiness, fear, nervous tension, emotional stress and so on. And the reorientation might well begin in the schools. It would not be impossible, I should think, to teach children that anxiety is not something to be avoided at all costs, but part of an elaborate and necessary built-in warning system.

Furthermore, it might do no harm to dust off a few old copybook maxims about duty, obligation and responsibility, and interpret them so that the growing mind of a child could grasp *why* they are valid and valuable to him.

The central point is simply that a certain amount of tension is an unavoidable part of living, and a certain amount of anxiety is a sign of life. Moreover, happiness has to be earned. It doesn't come in pills.

THE SECRET

OF

HAVING FUN

by Eda J. LeShan

STUDYING FOR his doctor's degree in psychology some years ago, my husband decided that he needed relaxation, and tried to teach himself to play the recorder. He struggled grimly for several evenings with scales and "Three Blind Mice." Then he gave up. "Too much like work," he said, and went back to his books. Our four-year-old daughter discovered the instrument one morning on his study bookshelf. Holding it up expectantly, she put it to her lips and blew a high, quavering toot. Delighted, she skipped out into the sunshine, improvising a melody as she went along. My husband said to me later, "The moment she made that ridiculous sound, I knew she was playing the recorder as I had longed to—just playing it and having fun!"

All too often we adults work so hard at our "fun" that we really don't enjoy ourselves at all. In fact, couldn't the real cause of much of our fatigue, tension and anxiety be as simple as this—we've forgotten how to play? As a psychologist and consultant on family-living problems, time and again I've heard the unhappy questions: Where did the magic go? What happened to the joy in life? How can I recapture the thrill of being alive? And after years of studying and observing young children—children at play—I'm convinced that they have the answers.

What's the secret? Part of it is that a child doesn't ask if what he's doing is worthwhile. He plays for the sake of play, as an end in itself. Take a four-year-old to a playground, and with a leap and a bound he is hanging by his knees from the highest bar on the Jungle-gym, absolutely enthralled with the way the world looks upside down. No thoughts of muscle development or losing weight—just sheer pleasure in the playground's riches and in life itself.

When we adults want to enjoy ourselves, we almost always seek to be entertained by others—on television, at the theater, at a baseball game. Or we fall back on things that provide us with a kind of programmed play: cards, dominoes, bowling balls, golf clubs. We let places and objects tell us what to do, how we should react.

When a child plays, *he* is the manipulator; he makes do with whatever is at hand. His imagination transforms the commonplace into the priceless. A wooden clothespin, rescued from under the kitchen table and wrapped in a dishcloth, becomes a baby; a penny thrust under a cushion becomes a buried treasure. As we grow older and "wiser," we lose this talent. I think of this sometimes in New York City as I walk across Central Park at 72nd Street. Here, when I was a little girl, we played Tarzan. To us as children, it was an exotic place, full of thrills and adventures, home of lions and gorillas—a piece of Africa. Today, as I pass the spot, all I see is a small hill and a few low rock formations.

What can we do to regain this lost capacity for play, for make-believe? Here are some of the things that children teach us:

Be alive to the moment. Study the absorption on a child's face as he sails a feather through the air, or rolls a potato across the floor into a dustpan. For him the moment is everything. Without conscious thought or plan, he brings to whatever he is doing spontaneous—and infectious—joy.

There is in children's play a fresh and quite lovely quality of freedom, of "letting themselves go." And we adults will find that something wonderful happens to us when we "let go" of our grown-up self-consciousness. A father of four told me recently how one night, after a frustrating day at work, he found himself becoming increasingly annoyed by the playful antics of his children's dog, who wouldn't let him alone. He tried to relax, but it was hopeless. Finally he took the dog outdoors. "The air was fresh and cool, and suddenly something snapped! Before I realized what I was doing, I was playing with that dog like some kind of a nut. We chased each other around the lawn; I'd throw sticks and then we'd race to see who could pick them up first. Afterward it took me 20 minutes to catch my breath—but it was the first night in months that I didn't feel half-dead when I went to bed."

Children know instinctively that when you are being spontaneous you have the most fun. When friends of ours bought a house not long ago, they planned to have it redecorated before they moved in. The day the papers were signed, they sent out invitations to a "Paint-In," telling the guests to wear old clothes. When we arrived, the husband announced that we could draw, write or paint anything we wanted on the interior walls. What a wonderful, relaxing evening that was! Some wrote jokes and limericks, some painted enormous murals, some played ticktacktoe. It was marvelous: having fun without any thought for the demands of the future. It was the moment that was important, and our direct participation in it.

Be flexible. Don't be rigid about what seems sensible. A child feels no compulsion to continue an activity beyond the moment when it ceases to give him pleasure. He's ready for any new adventure, anytime. We, however, grow ashamed of being spontaneous. If we are at home doing the family wash or at the office writing the monthly sales report, and suddenly a warm breeze through the window makes us dizzy with the thought of spring, what do we do? We tell ourselves that the schedule must be kept. Grimly we go on with our work—then wonder later why we have a headache or a backache. If only we had taken ten minutes off for a walk, to listen to a bird sing or watch a squirrel, to sit on a bench in the sun!

Giving in to one's impulses for a few minutes does *not* automatically lead to lazy irresponsibility. Quite the reverse: it can lead to greater efficiency and productivity, for it refills the reservoir of self and nurtures an inner core of being that needs to be lovingly refreshed. Even dedicated scholars, in their wisdom, know when to yield to an impulse. Philosopher George Santayana was lecturing a class at Harvard one early-spring day when suddenly he broke off, saying: "Gentlemen, I'm afraid that sentence will never be completed. I have an appointment with April." With that, he left the classroom.

Whenever our daughter is feeling especially exasperated with us, she reminds herself of one of the happiest evenings of our lives. About midnight of a school night my husband and I ended a discouraging discussion about money. It had had its usual effect—we were ravenous, not for anything ordinary, but for chicken supreme at Sardi's. We awakened Wendy, age 12, from a sound sleep, something we'd never done on impulse before. She wasn't a bit surprised. "I'd love it! Can I wear my velvet party dress?" So the three of us piled into a cab, drove to the restaurant and blew the last of our bankroll.

Renew your ties with nature. Caught as many of us are in concrete boxes on concrete streets, we lose contact with our roots in nature. We need to find and invent ways to keep in touch with sky and sun and sea. Children understand the sacredness of these things. They are absolutely sure that the world is full of remarkable and exciting things to see and do, to taste, touch and feel. They respond with their senses to the miracles of the natural world. When they tug you outside by the sleeve, give in. Follow them. I know one father who insists that walking in puddles in a summer rain is one of the better things he's learned from his sons. Take them to a farm, a zoo, a botanical garden. Join them for a walk in the woods; lie down with them in an open field, look up at the sky and chew on a piece of grass. For a moment, see the world through their eyes.

A friend told me how one gray and cheerless day, when she was feeling depressed after a severe attack of flu, she got into her car and drove alone to a beach. "I wrapped myself up in an old blanket and sat on the sand and listened to the surf. I became fascinated watching sandpipers running in and out of the waves. When I finally looked at my watch, I realized that I had been sitting there for *three hours!* I felt fully refreshed when I got home—it was like having been on a vacation." She had given to herself of the deeper rhythms of life around us.

Reach back for the child within you. It is not by accident that stories of young lovers describe them going on picnics, running barefoot down a beach, visiting a zoo or eating ice cream cones on a carrousel. When we begin to fall in love, we know instinctively that somehow we find our truest selves in the playful games of childhood. Maurice Sendak, who writes children's stories, was asked how he was able to communicate so sensitively. "First," he said, "I have to reach and keep hold of the child in me." This is true not only for the creative artist but also for the rest of us, if we are to get close to what is unique in ourselves—our own personal identity.

About a year ago I happened to notice a toy horn in a music store, each note hole marked in a different color. With it came a booklet of tunes in which all the notes were written in the corresponding colors. My husband's favorite Christmas carol was in the book. *Eureka!* I thought. *Here is an instrument that he can play without work.*

It was the best present I ever gave him. Now, in the hallowed halls of a great university, one can sometimes hear the high, squeaky sounds of "Good King Wenceslas" as a psychology professor, resting from his teaching and research, fills his office with the only music he can make—on a toy horn, with colored notes. He is one of the rare and fortunate grownups who have watched a child play and learned a precious lesson about living.

THAT VITAL SPARK

—HOPE

by Ardis Whitman

"EVERYTHING THAT is done in the world is done by hope," said Martin Luther. "Hope is, perhaps, the chief happiness this world affords," said Samuel Johnson.

One thing is sure. Neither individuals nor society can survive without it. Hope is the mechanism that keeps the human race tenaciously alive and dreaming, planning, building. Hope is not the opposite of realism. It is the opposite of cynicism and despair. The best of humanity has always hoped when there was no way; lived what was unlivable; and managed to build when there was little to build on.

This is the natural and healthy attitude for living beings. "A merry heart doeth good like a medicine," says the Book of Proverbs. This ancient knowledge has gained new confirmation in our time. It was found after World War II, for example, that American prisoners of war who had been convinced they would come out alive, whose mind and spirit were focused on life as it was to be lived in the future, emerged with much less damage than those who felt they would never go home again.

Psychiatrist Flanders Dunbar once wrote of two cardio-vascular patients equally ill. One said, "It's up to you now, doctor." The other said, "I've got to do something to get well." The first died; the second recovered.

Dr. Martin E. P. Seligman, of the University of Pennsylvania, has performed experiments on the causes of depression, the disorder that affects millions every year. He has found that depressed people regard every minor obstacle as an impassable barrier. Responding to anything is felt to be useless because "nothing I do matters." Successful therapy, he told me, starts when we begin to believe again that we can be effective human beings and can control our lives.

Also, how much we dare hope about ourselves affects how we behave toward other people. We've all encountered the kind of person that poet A. E. Housman meant when he wrote of "the mortal sickness of a mind too unhappy to be kind." The man who hopes sees other human beings as they *could* be, and so helps *them*.

A man I knew had an alcoholic wife. Again and again she disappointed him. But he never lost hope. One night, she shamed him in front of old friends. Afterward, she broke into tears. "Why don't you leave me?" she cried. "Because I remember a very beautiful person," he answered. "And I believe she's still there." Ultimately, she did recover.

But doesn't hope betray us every day? Isn't hope for most people just whistling in the dark? To answer such questions is only to say what we have always known. Hope is *against* odds. Damon Runyon, the writer, once said, "Life is six to five against." It has always been so. All life is a contest of light against darkness, joy against despair. Yet, most of us *do* hope, most of the time.

Why? Perhaps because hope is natural to man. We are new people every morning, because somehow, on this side of the night, we spring out of the dreaming darkness and start over again. I recall a man who was so distracted by his griefs—a wife who had run off with another man, a child in reform school, a crippling illness and, finally, a fire which nearly destroyed his house—that he tried to commit suicide. Yet, on the morning after the attempt, he woke and said to the friend who had been sitting with him, "What a pretty day this is! You know, I think I could build my house again." Life itself had quickened within him.

We hope again as naturally as the seeds sprout and the sun rises, and perhaps for the same reasons. Hope's signature seems to be written on earth and sky and sea and on all that lives. Cells divide; flowers grow; trees put out leaves; animals breed and protect their young—all in a kind of cosmic expectation, the same expectation, the same call toward the future, which dreamed the light and the starry meadows of the sky.

But, natural and vital as hope may be, we can lose it. With many of us, hope simply grows tired as our lives grow tired. Can we be told *how* to hope, or helped to regain it?

Of course we can. Precisely because hope is in the natural flow of life, it is unleashed naturally by removing the abnormal impediments that block it. Here are some suggestions.

Hope for the moment. There are times when it is hard to believe in the future, when we are temporarily just not brave enough. When this happens, concentrate on the present. Just as alcoholics must learn to stay sober one day at a time, despairing people must learn to hope for one day's mercy at a time. Cultivate *le petit bonheur* ("the little happiness") until courage returns. Look forward to the beauty of the next moment, the next hour, the promise of a good meal, sleep, a book, a movie, the immediate likelihood that tonight the stars will shine and tomorrow the sun will rise. Sink roots into the present until the strength grows to think about tomorrow.

Take action. "When I can't see any way out," a stranger wrote me some years ago, "I do something anyway." This is good advice to anyone paralyzed by despair; it helps him get off dead center. "The only real sin in the world," wrote Charles McCabe in his column in the San Francisco *Chronicle*, "is not to fight, not to realize the fullness of your own nature." If all else is paralyzed, remember, we can at least change *ourselves*.

Believe in hope. Don't be persuaded that the pessimists have a corner on truth. These people would rather live in a fog of skepticism than chance disappointment. Besides, the minute one says there is no hope, there is nothing one has to do; it's the world's best alibi against action. It is the adult in us, not the child, which, knocked down, gets up again and says, against the odds, "Tomorrow will be better."

Hope is not a lie but the truth itself. It is true that man aspires and builds his hope into institutions that move forward even when he wearies. The Tom Dooleys and Albert Schweitzers of the world are as real as the Hitlers. Average people, strengthened by faith, do perform saintly deeds—and heroic ones.

So, summon hope. It is as right as spring sunlight. But, even if it were not, it would work its magic, since hope is a goal in itself. It is an exercise in gallantry, a frame of mind, a style of life, a climate of the heart.

Even if we are not going to win, even if death and disaster are finally going to catch up with us, hope is worthwhile, for it enables us to drain the last drop of joy from whatever time we have left. If joy is coming, hope will have proved itself right; if disaster, hope will have strengthened us to meet it.

PARENT—CHILD

THE DAY

WE FLEW

THE KITES

by Frances Fowler

"STRING!" SHOUTED Brother, bursting into the kitchen. "We need lots more string."

It was Saturday. As always, it was a busy one, for "Six days shalt thou labor and do all thy work" was taken seriously then.

Outside, Father and Mr. Patrick next door were doing chores. Inside the two houses, Mother and Mrs. Patrick were engaged in spring-cleaning. Such a windy March day was ideal for "turning out" clothes closets. Already woolens flapped on back-yard clotheslines.

Somehow the boys had slipped away to the back lot with their kites. Now, even at the risk of having Brother impounded to beat carpets, they had sent him for more string. Apparently there was no limit to the heights to which kites would soar today.

My mother looked out the window. The sky was piercingly blue, the breeze fresh and exciting. Up in all that blueness sailed great puffy billows of clouds. It had been a long, hard winter, but today was spring. Mother looked at the sitting room, its furniture disordered for a Spartan sweeping. Again her eyes wavered toward the window. "Come on, girls! Let's take string to the boys and watch them fly the kites a minute."

On the way we met Mrs. Patrick, laughing guiltily, escorted by her girls.

There never was such a day for flying kites! God doesn't make two such days in a century. We played all our fresh twine into the boys' kites and still they soared. We could hardly distinguish the tiny, orange-colored specks. Now and then we slowly reeled one in, finally bringing it dipping and tugging to earth, for the sheer joy of sending it up again. What a thrill to run with them, to the right, to the left, and see our poor, earth-bound movements reflected minutes later in their majestic sky dance! We wrote wishes on pieces of paper and slipped them over the string. Slowly, irresistibly, they climbed up until they reached the kites. Surely all such wishes would be granted!

Even our fathers dropped hoe and hammer and joined us. Our mothers took their turns, laughing like schoolgirls. Their hair blew out of their pompadours and curled loose about their cheeks; their gingham aprons whipped about their legs. Mingled with our fun was something akin to awe. The grownups were really playing with us! Once I looked at Mother and thought she was actually pretty. And her over 40!

We never knew where the hours went on that day. There were no hours, just a golden, breezy Now. I think we were all a little beyond ourselves. Parents forgot their duty and their dignity; children forgot their combativeness and small spites. "Perhaps it's like this in the Kingdom of Heaven," I thought confusedly.

It was growing dark before, drunk with sun and air, we all stumbled sleepily back to the houses. I suppose we had some sort of supper. I suppose there must have been a surface tidying up, for the house on Sunday looked decorous enough.

The strange thing was, we didn't mention that day afterward. I felt a little embarrassed. Surely none of the others had thrilled to it as deeply as I had. I locked the memory up in that deepest part of me where we keep the "things that cannot be and yet are."

The years went on; then one day I was scurrying about my own kitchen in a city apartment, trying to get some work out of the way while my three-year-old insistently cried her desire to "go park and see ducks."

"I *can't* go!" I said. "I have this and this to do, and when I'm through I'll be too tired to walk that far."

My mother, who was visiting us, looked up from the peas

she was shelling. "It's a wonderful day," she offered, "really warm, yet there's a fine, fresh breeze. It reminds me of that day we flew the kites."

I stopped in my dash between stove and sink. The locked door flew open, and with it a gush of memories. I pulled off my apron. "Come on," I told my little girl. "It's too good a day to miss."

Another decade passed. We were in the aftermath of a great war. All evening we had been asking our returned soldier, the youngest Patrick boy, about his experiences as a prisoner of war. He had talked freely, but now for a long time he had been silent. What was he thinking of—what dark and dreadful things?

"Say!" A smile twitched his lips. "Do you remember . . . no, of course you wouldn't. It probably didn't make the impression on you it did on me."

I hardly dared speak. "Remember what?"

"I used to think of that day a lot in PW camp, when things weren't too good. Do you remember the day we flew the kites?"

Winter came, and the sad duty of a call of condolence on Mrs. Patrick, recently widowed. I dreaded the call. I couldn't imagine how Mrs. Patrick would face life alone.

We talked a little of my family and her grandchildren and the changes in the town. Then she was silent, looking down at her lap. I cleared my throat. Now I must say something about her loss, and she would begin to cry.

When Mrs. Patrick looked up, she was smiling. "I was just sitting here thinking," she said. "Henry had such fun that day. Frances, do you remember the day we flew the kites?"

DIARY

OF A NEW

MOTHER

by Judith Geissler

"Before the reality of the delivery room, I was certain that the ultimate extension of my career as a teacher would be my involvement in my own child's quest for identity. I felt that that experience would reveal to me the meaning of my own existence. I entered motherhood searching for the new dimension that would make my womanhood complete. Here, then, are the thoughts and feelings of the first six months recorded in my journal as I began my new life."

In one moment of undrugged physical release, our baby is thrust into the world, uniting us, husband and wife, in the communion of birth. We join hands as we watch his tiny face crumple in protest. My own body, so recently reaching into unknown reserves of energy, relaxes beneath a reviving flood of undiluted emotion. I share with women throughout the centuries the joy of bearing my husband a son.

The baby, a startling fragile-looking creature, is handed to me for a moment and then to his father. I refuse to acknowledge my own awkwardness. Will I not somehow be endowed with the accumulated wisdom of mothers before me?

I am wheeled from the delivery room and permitted to watch my son's first bathing. Feeling entirely satisfied to let the nurse handle him, I dismiss as fantasy the notion that the process of giving birth mystically transforms a woman into a mother.

And later, in my hospital room, I bask in the lingering glow of achievement, content to rest. Not until a few hours later does an instinctive hunger to cuddle my child and nourish him rise within me.

The nurse helps me prepare for this first nursing. Then she hands me a nest of soft wrappings that holds a tiny red face, mouth stretched wide. Instinct bobs his head back in a body-quivering search for the warm nipple. He is so trusting and I am so clumsy. And already he's asleep, his mouth open against my breast. Now motherhood is creeping over my old self like a long-awaited tomorrow that finally is today. I have lived it all again and again in my mind, but without the intoxication.

Even while he's asleep, his lips are remembering milk. His chin trembles unexpectedly; his body jerks without waking; his muscles respond to unwilled urges. I could spend half of each day just watching him.

Already, in his third day of life, the sound of my voice seems to have meaning for him. Milk will soothe him back into the sleep he never fully woke from. This newly discovered pleasure causes him to call out with impatience. To me his cry sounds rich and strong.

It seems so simple to put your baby on your shoulder and wait for a burp, but little knees used to being curled up to the chin leave you with a round baby ball that rolls down into your lap.

Carefully choosing from the travel case the exact baby clothes to suit the weather, I am aware that my husband and I are acting worse than newlyweds. We have that almost embarrassing pride gleaming in our eyes and the awkward meticulousness of our own just-assumed roles. The nurse removes our son's hospital garments and wraps his strangely long and straggly body in the oversized going-home outfit that once looked so unbelievably small. Understanding nurses call good-by, and the elevator takes us down, a family now.

Out in the parking lot my husband dashes around in the fall drizzle, solicitously opening car doors, undoubtedly trying to stay in motion lest the nurse decide to hand him the baby. It's a little scary taking this helpless creature and driving off with him. What if he starts crying and I can't figure out how to stop him? I can't explain things to him—that he can trust me to feed him, change him, burp him or just hold him. And babies cry so loud. He won't understand that he doesn't have to let *everyone* know he's unhappy. Just me.

Our son is one week old. There he lies, flushed from yelling, his bowlegs attached below his abdomen where his hips will be, his softly curved arms attached below his ears where his shoulders will be.

He dominates my life. My days are a whirl of diapers and false-alarm hunger cries to be eased with a pacifier. My nights are a daze of half-heard wails answered with half-remembered feedings and a midnight rendezvous with the diaper pail. My former routines no longer serve me. I must concentrate on every movement and every minute until the mechanics are a part of me and motherhood allows me to resume my role as wife, sharing with my husband the wonder of being a parent.

We reflect upon our new status and decide there's nothing unusual about a new father's feeling terribly masculine and also terribly uninvolved in the three-ring circus his home has become.

Our son looks like a relic from a miniature monastery, with his long gown and smooth scalp. He fits the part of a tiny old holy man toothlessly wise. The only bits of world that penetrate into his hazy awareness are sudden bursts of light let in at random by his eyes. At times his whole being seems concentrated unblinkingly on a beam of light. Perhaps he's struggling with an idea too complex to absorb.

To have my baby take nourishment from my body, to see his eyes drift shut, to hear his purring contentment, is painfully exquisite. How many mothers spend their children's lives trying to satisfy their own urge to give and protect and be needed? *Now* is the time to give myself over to the cuddling and crooning, so that as his need diminishes I can loose my hold without regret.

Now at three months, I am suddenly faced with a crisis. As he sucks on his pacifier his grabbing fingers accidentally pull it out, leaving his mouth naked. Instinctively he plugs up the space between his lips with the built-in pacifier—his little mouth closes around his thumb. I watch apprehensively like a parent seeing her son sampling his first cigarette, envisioning him hooked on the habit but fearing to interfere. Fending off the warnings left by psychologists in my memory, I finally force myself to let my natural reactions guide me.

These newly acquired responsibilities are awesome. My gaze, voice, touch, have the power to bring about rewarding smiles, happy sounds and hearty eating, or they can encourage tears and fussy meals and frustrated thumb-sucking. I see motherhood ahead of me like an overgrown path that disappears into a dark woods. On one side is the fear of forcing a child into a mold not his own; on the other, the danger of leaving him to be molded by indifferent circumstances. Who am I to decide which behavior shall bring rewards and which reproof?

I am his mother.

Our son is four months old. The center of his world, the source of all pleasure and all unhappiness, is oral sensation. If he could fit the whole world into his mouth, he would understand all there is to know. He tries frantically to stretch his lips to admit both fists into the inner sanctum, the better to comprehend their purpose. His sausage feet loom before his eyes—within grabbing distance, but inaccessible to his waiting mouth.

And when he finally makes it over from his back to his belly, my husband and I realize that our own muscles have tensed, urging him on.

Secure within his hazy aura of mother love, he reaches out to his father. His eyes reveal the moment when indifference to this other familiar figure changes to recognition.

The baby's concentration is intense as he studies our eating movements. He mimics our simplest gestures. But also he has his own style of table manners: eagerly he dumps his peaches in my lap, slurps from his cup before plunking it to the floor, smears a handful of beets onto his high-chair tray, gleefully sneezes cereal in my face.

The half-year mark approaches, and the novelty of my breast as the milk machine is gone. His lips lose their hold on the nipple in the fascination of discovering a button or stroking my sweater's softness. I am prepared to surrender the lifeline of milk, knowing that his needs and mine must be one.

I watch our son perform award-winning roles, unconcerned about audience acclaim. He is a turtle accidentally stranded on a rock, frantically projecting head and limbs high in the air, but unable to budge; a victorious boxer, clasping hands overhead in triumph. He is The Thinker, scratching pensively behind his ear; a Lilliputian superman with his bib flung over the shoulders.

I nurse him for the last time, savoring the ritual about-to-be-memory. My thoughts go back to when he emerged from the womb, clothed only in innocence, skilled only in searching. Soon he will unlock the mysteries of self-propulsion. One dare not think of the terrible void that will be left by the absence of this tiny, incredibly lovable being.

But motherhood sweeps away all thoughts of the impermanence of the human body in a wild exhilaration of love and dreams, and the bearable ache of letting go little by little, day by day. As my child struggles to sit, to search out the sounds and feel of the world, I sense that my role these six months has been beneath him, supporting. From now on my role will be from above, lifting.

Motherhood feels comfortable.

HOW TO

BE A BETTER

PARENT

by William E. Homan, M.D.

No OTHER task in the world is so complicated and challenging as that of raising children. Yet a career spent with youngsters and their problems has led me to this haunting conclusion: each set of new parents approaches the formidable assignment of raising humans with the least imaginable training and preparation. For the relatively simple roles of doctor, lawyer, pilot, plumber, it is taken for granted that years of preparation will be necessary to attain even mediocrity. But one is apparently assumed to come to the job of being a parent divinely endowed with knowledge and experience. And when we stumble along the path, and the resulting product is less than perfect, the world feels free to point an accusing finger at us.

How, then, does the perplexed parent avoid stumbling? What guidelines will help make him a *good* parent?

To me, the good parent is simply one who *more than half the time* does the right thing instead of the wrong. He knows that thousands of factors contribute to and shape the final personality of a growing human being. But he realizes that in the long run only three basic needs are absolutely essential: love, discipline, independence.

Love. Of the three fundamental requirements, the first—love—is the most important. And it is unique in that there

187

can never be too much. An excess of discipline, or too much independence, can be harmful. But of love, the more the merrier.

The type of love a child needs is the kind that says, "I love you, Joe, not for what you do or don't do, but just because you're you." This is the uncritical kind of love that builds self-confidence, creates a strong self-image, leads to a willingness to try without fear of the consequences of failing. There is no doubt that most parents feel this sort of affection for their children, but don't know how to express it effectively. Three precepts may prove helpful:

● *Disapprove of what a child does, not of who he is.* There is no inconsistency in paddling a child for misbehavior, and then putting your arms around him and telling him what a fine boy he is and how much you love him. Indeed, you bother to discipline only because you love—a concept that children readily perceive.

● *Praise a child more for being than for doing.* Parents generally react favorably to a good report card or to a thoughtful act on a child's part. This is all well and good—as long as these accomplishments are not the child's major or sole source of praise and love. In fact, a child should receive a greater share of cuddling or praise when he is producing nothing, is daydreaming, or in fact has recently done something that had to be criticized.

● *Communicate your love.* It is not enough to feel love; you must make the recipient aware of your feeling. This can be done by a thousand little acts and gestures:

Tucking a child into bed at night, while forbearing to review his misdeeds of the day.

Offering a comforting arm or a lap even though he's not hurt badly.

Being visibly proud of him when he has given you no earthly reason even to admit that he's yours.

Perhaps the most elegant way of all to communicate your love is to praise a child out loud to strangers, to relatives, to your mate, in the child's presence.

Discipline. Discipline is important simply because we live in an organized society where, if you have not learned life's requirements at an early age, you will be taught them later, not by those whose love tempers the lesson but by strangers who couldn't care less about the harm they do to your personality.

"Discipline" and "punishment" are not synonymous. Punishment suggests hurting, paying someone back for a wrong committed. Discipline implies an action directed toward a goal. You discipline with the intention of helping the recipient to improve himself.

The basic rules of discipline apply equally to any teaching situation:

● *Establish authority*. The first step in the discipline of a child must be the lesson that his parents are correct, and are to be trusted and obeyed at all times.

Now, don't panic, Mom and Dad. Though you may know very well that you are not absolute authorities, you must assume the *disguise* of authority. Here is the key: an authority is only a fellow who knows more about a subject than the person he is addressing. Therefore, until the pupil's confidence in the discipliner is established, the subject must always be chosen so that the teacher can prove his point if challenged. The child is not scolded, not reasoned with, not nagged, not punished. He is simply *made* to comply! The spoken command coincides with physical enforcement. The creeper headed for the lamp cord is called back only as he is being bodily carried back. The toddler is summoned to lunch only as his mother grasps his hand and leads him to the table.

Thus, by concentrating early discipline on lessons which can be promptly backed up by physical means, the parent begins to establish infallibility as an authority. And the converse must also be observed: Avoid disciplining in matters which you cannot enforce. For example, it is unwise to instruct a young child to "Eat your food," "Go to sleep," "Stop that crying," because you cannot possibly enforce the lesson.

● *Be consistent*. Unpredictable discipline on the part of a single parent, or inconsistency between parents, produces a sense of confusion and panic within the child, so that he ultimately says, "The heck with it," and gives up trying to follow *any* teaching. Thus parents who constantly disagree about how to teach their children had best compromise their differences— or match their child's college fund with a child-psychiatrist fund. The same is true of "well-meaning" outside persons— grandparents, older siblings, servants—who are equally capable of disrupting discipline. Parents must decide early whether their first allegiance is to the child or to the outsider, however closely related.

• *Criticize the act, not the child.* There is a mountain of difference between "You are a bad boy for kicking me in the shins," and "Kicking in the shins is bad, and I won't tolerate it." If this seems like hairsplitting, let me emphasize that this difference represents one of the major mistakes that parents make in raising children. It is relatively harmless to attack another person's actions; after all, these he can always learn to change. But it is disastrous to attack his self-esteem.

• *Don't explain or bribe.* Much nonsense has gone into the myth that one should explain to a child as one disciplines. The familiar refrain—"Anita, come in for dinner." "Why?" "Because I say to."—may seem hard for the child to accept. But—"Anita, come in for dinner." "Why?" "Because I want to get dinner over with and go to a show."—is terrifying. It thrusts upon Anita the burden of deciding whether it is more important to play or to consider the happiness of her mother. And she does not yet have the knowledge to make a valid decision. Such "explanations" should come only after Anita has long since mastered the fact that when Mother calls her, she had better come.

Bribery is equally dangerous. When you say, "Bob, I am proud of the way you behaved in front of Aunt Agatha today," you are rewarding Bob. When you say, "Bob, *if* you behave well in front of Aunt Agatha today, I'll be proud of you," you are offering a bribe. The first is legitimate; the latter, destructive. For a bribe, like an explanation, thrusts upon the child the necessity of choosing.

Independence. The third factor indispensable to the development of the normal personality is the emergence of independence. The nature of independence is such that:

• *It cannot be forced.* A child will automatically learn to make decisions on his own when he is ready, provided that the opportunity to do so is not kept from him. It is not possible to push him into acting independently before he feels ready without making him fearful of the consequences, desirous of clinging to the nest. Thus, an infant will feed himself when he is capable of doing so, if given the opportunity, and not because he is urged or forced.

• *It should not be smothered.* Its emergence should be tolerated in all permissible forms. Minor hurts, physical and mental, are pretty much essential to the development of independence. The toddler must stumble and fall a number of times before he masters walking. The first-grader must suffer the scorn of his colleagues when he chooses to dress inappropriately for school.

• *In an area that would result in permanent, serious harm to the child, it must be prohibited.* Allowing a child to make decisions of thought or action *before* he is capable of understanding the consequences, if the consequences could be dangerous, is not realistic. For example, the need for the development of independence should not lead to the toddler falling down the cellar stairs. Perhaps the best way to put it is that the child should be permitted to make minor errors of judgment—but not allowed to exterminate himself.

So there it is: the triad of requirements necessary for the development of emotional health. Give away your love to your children, and you will receive back more love than you can encompass. Discipline your children to recognize reality, and in the doing you will enrich your own understanding. Welcome their evolving independence, and you will be supported by the strength you have helped them attain.

BIRTHDAY PRESENT

by Mavis Burton Ferguson

A WEEK after my son started first grade he came home with the news that Roger, the only Negro in the class, was his playground partner. I swallowed and said, "That's nice. How long before someone else gets him for a partner?" "Oh, I've got him for good," replied Bill. In another week I had the news that Bill had asked if Roger could be his desk partner.

Unless you were born and reared years ago in a white-supremacy state as I was, you cannot know what this means. I went for an appointment with the teacher.

She met me with tired, cynical eyes. "Well, I suppose *you* want a new desk partner for your child, too," she said. "Can you wait a few minutes? I have another mother coming in right now."

I looked up to see a woman my age. My heart raced as I realized she must be Roger's mother. She had a quiet dignity and much poise, but neither could cover the anxiety I heard in her questions. "How's Roger doing? I hope he is keeping up with the other children? If he isn't, just let me know."

She hesitated as she made herself ask, "Is he giving you any trouble of any kind? I mean, what with his having to change desks so much?"

I could feel the terrible tension in her, for she knew the answer. But I was proud of that first-grade teacher for her gentle answer: "No, Roger is not giving me any trouble. I try to move all the children around the first few weeks until each has just the right partner."

I introduced myself and said that my son was to be Roger's new partner and I hoped they would like each other. Even then I knew it was only a surface wish, not a deep-felt one. But it helped her, I could see.

Twice Roger invited Bill to come home with him, but I found excuses. Then came the heartache that I will always suffer.

On my birthday Bill came home from school with a grimy piece of paper folded into a very small square. Unfolding it, I found three flowers and "Happy Birthday" crayoned on the paper—and a nickel.

"That's from Roger," said Bill. "It's his milk money. When I said today was your birthday he made me bring it to you. He said you are his friend, 'cause you're the only mother that didn't make him get another desk partner."

THE WORK WORLD

FIVE WAYS

TO IMPROVE

YOUR LUCK

by Max Gunther

OVER THE past 20 years, I have asked more than a thousand men and women this question: What do lucky people do that unlucky people don't do?

Their answers have led me to conclude that five major characteristics distinguish the lucky from the unlucky. Furthermore, I am convinced that most people can improve their luck simply by incorporating these characteristics into their daily life. Here's what you can do:

1. Form Many Friendships. In general, the luckiest people are those who have many friends and acquaintances. O. William Battalia, an executive "headhunter" who brings luck to people in the form of lucrative job offers, has analyzed the chains of circumstance that led him to winning job candidates. The majority of such chains turned out to be those of acquaintanceship.

"Lucky people," says Battalia, "are gregarious. They go out of their way to be friendly. They talk to strangers. They're joiners, meeters, greeters. If they sit next to somebody on an airplane, they start a conversation. The man who sells them their morning newspaper is more than just a face. They know his name and how many kids he has and where he went on his vacation."

Dr. Stephen Barrett, a Pennsylvania psychiatrist, finds that not only do lucky people have the knack of initiating friendly contacts but they also have a certain magnetism that makes them the targets of *others'* friendly approaches. Barrett calls this a "communication field." He believes that facial expressions, body positions, voice tones, choice of words, ways of using the eyes form a communication field clearly visible to other people.

"We usually know instinctively whether somebody likes us or not," he says. "We can meet a total stranger and know in seconds if he or she wants to spend more time with us. Lucky people communicate inviting and comfortable signals."

The bigger your web of friendly contacts, the better your odds of finding some pot-of-gold opportunity. Actor Kirk Douglas, for one example, got his first big break through an earlier contact with a then-unknown actress, Lauren Bacall. She was only one of many people whom the gregarious young Douglas had befriended. But by befriending many, he increased the chances that a helpful Bacall would turn up.

2. *Honor Your Hunches.* A hunch is a conclusion based on facts that your mind has accurately observed, stored and processed. But they are facts that you don't consciously know because they are stored on some unconscious level of awareness.

Hotel man Conrad Hilton owed his monumental success partly to a finely tuned hunching skill. Once he was trying to buy an old hotel in Chicago whose owner was selling to the highest bidder. All the sealed bids were to be opened on a certain date, and several days before the deadline Hilton submitted a $165,000 bid. He went to bed that night feeling vaguely disturbed and woke with a strong hunch that his bid was not going to win. "It just didn't feel right," he said later. Acting on this strange intuition, he submitted another bid: $180,000. It was the highest bid. The next one down was $179,800.

Hilton's hunch could have welled up from stores of facts in the recesses of his mind. Ever since he bought his first hotel as a young man in Texas, he had been gathering knowledge about the business. Moreover, in bidding on that Chicago hotel, he undoubtedly knew much about the likely competing bidders— knew it without being able specifically to articulate it. When his conscious brain assembled known data and produced a bid, his subconscious was rummaging in a huge dark warehouse of other facts and concluded that the bid was too low. He trusted the hunch, and it was magnificently right.

How do you know whether to trust a hunch? Says one successful huncher, a retired stockbroker, "I ask myself: Is it conceivable that I've gathered data on this situation without realizing it? Have I found out all I can about it, done all the work I can? If the answers are yes **and** if the hunch feels strong, I tend to go with it."

Two warnings: One, **never** trust hunches about such things as lotteries and slot machines. There is no possibility that such a hunch can well up from some hidden pool of facts inside you, because there *are* no facts. And two, never confuse a hunch with a hope. A lot of bad hunches are just strong wishes in disguise.

3. Be Bold. Lucky people tend to be bold, and the most timid, with exceptions, the least lucky. Luck probably creates boldness, but boldness also helps create good luck. To act boldly, follow these rules:

• Be ready to zigzag, to jump off in a new direction, when a good opportunity comes your way.

• Know the difference between boldness and rashness. If you bet your life savings on a spectacular venture in which you stand to lose everything, that is rash. If you accept an exciting new job opportunity even though you are scared by the thought of stepping into the unknown, that is bold.

J. Paul Getty, the oil billionaire and a supremely lucky man, zigzagged in his early years. He went to college thinking he wanted to be a writer. Then he decided he wanted to enter diplomatic service. Out of college, however, he found himself attracted by the Oklahoma oil boom, in which his father was then enriching himself. The oil business was off Getty's main route, but he felt compelled to postpone his diplomatic career for a year and try his hand as an oil wildcatter.

Getty raised money by working around other wildcatters' rigs and occasionally by borrowing from his father. (His father's stern principles forbade coddling his son; he would lend the young man money but give him only trivial cash gifts.) Young Getty was bold, not rash. He never entered a venture whose cash requirements, in the event of a loss, were big enough to cause him serious hardship. His first few ventures were flops. But in 1916 he hit his first major producing well. It founded his fortune—when he was but 23!

Lucky? Of course. But Getty deserved to be lucky. He had done everything right. How did Getty know the well would produce? He didn't, although he had gathered all the facts he could. "There is always an element of chance," he said, "and you must be willing to live with that element. If you insist on certainty, you will paralyze yourself."

4. *Limit Your Losses.* Lucky people discard bad luck before it becomes worse luck. This sounds like a simple trick, but many people—the essentially unlucky—never seem to master it. There is almost always a time at the start of any souring venture when you can get out with a minor loss or none. But that time may pass very quickly. After it has gone, the glue of circumstance rapidly hardens around your feet. You are stuck, perhaps for life.

Bill Battalia tells a story of avoidable bad luck. A young chemist left a small mining company to take a higher-paying job with a large organization near New York City. His wife thought he was making a mistake and would be miserable in an urban environment. His old boss also doubted that the young man would adapt well to life in a big company. "When you want to come back," he said, "just let me know."

Within a few months of moving, the chemist knew his wife and former boss were right. He didn't like life in the metropolis. Moreover, his job and prospects were both quite different from what he had signed up for. This would have been the time to cut his losses, but the chemist kept hoping the bad beginning would evolve into a happy ending. By the time he finally determined that his problems weren't temporary, he was stuck.

It's hard to say, "I was wrong." Hard to abandon an investment of money, love, time, effort or commitment. Yet, as the late Gerald M. Loeb, one of the brightest and luckiest stock-market speculators in recent times, put it, "Knowing when to sell out and having the guts to do it is an essential technique of successful living."

A Swiss banker and self-made millionaire summed it up this way: "If you are losing a tug-of-war with a tiger, give him the rope before he gets to your arm. You can always buy a new rope."

5. *Prepare for Problems.* Most lucky people nurture pessimism, guarding it against assaults, exercising it daily to keep it lean and hard. Said J. Paul Getty, "When I go into any business deal, my chief thoughts are on how I'm going to save myself if things go wrong."

The uses of pessimism among the lucky can be articulated in terms of Murphy's Law: "If something can go wrong, it will." Never, never assume that you are fortune's darling. Never drop your guard.

A study of accidents among bus drivers in South Africa concluded that among "bad-risk" drivers—those involved in more than a normal share of accidents—an outstanding personality trait turned out to be over-optimism. The bad-risk driver had too much faith in his own skills, in other drivers' good sense and ability, and in luck.

Lucky men and women, notably more than the unlucky, are aware that no life is ever totally under the control of its owner. If you cling to an illusion of control, you won't build defenses against bad luck and, when bad luck does strike, you will be too demoralized to react in useful ways.

People who are lucky are by definition those whom fortune has favored—but one reason they are favored is that they never assume they will be. They know fortune is fickle.

THE SUMMER

I WRAPPED

CABBAGE HEADS

by Maggie Smith

THE MAN said, "This job requires patience. Not skill.
Just patience. You sit on this low stool surrounded by hundreds
  of cabbages. You wrap each head in a piece of cellophane.
  People don't usually stay at this job more than a month."
When I went home and told I had a summer job wrapping
  cabbages, my father said, "One of two things will happen.
  You'll love your work and think back on it with joy or you
  will hate your work and never want to see another cabbage."
"She'll never want to see another cabbage!" promised my
  brother Harry.
My father mused, "A cabbage is a marvelous creation. After its
  seed matures it takes up a square foot of space on earth.
"Cabbages live in the country and travel to town. Often they
  travel by jet. I doubt if you could find anyone taking his
  cabbages to market in a cart these days.
"Out there in the country cabbages see the lights of the city wink
  on at night. They see the stars and the moon and the satellites
  in orbit. They witness considerable.
"No other vegetable is quite so similar to the human head as the
  cabbage with its bold-interlocking veining system. Some
  smooth-veined...some veined...some protruding...all
  with character. They have a most refined and civilized
  appearance.

"Some cabbage leaves are blue-green...some yellow-green...some leaves are highly curled...some prim stiff and proper...erect and sprawling.

"You'll even see red cabbages. Lucky the day you handle a red cabbage...."

He said it all softly, but I heard every word my father said.

And all that summer while I wrapped the cabbage heads his words and the cabbages sustained me. I lasted three months and left only because it was time to go back to school.

I was sorry to see that summer's work come to an end.

OBEY THAT IMPULSE

by William Moulton Marston

FOR YEARS as a psychologist I have sought in the careers of great and of everyday people the inner springs that make for successful living. There are two which seem to me of prime importance: The first is hard work, governed by cool, logical thoughtfulness. The other is sudden, warm, impulsive action.

Admitting that I can't name a single person of true accomplishment who hasn't forged success out of brains and hard work, I still hazard the sweeping assertion that most of the high spots and many of the lesser successes in their careers stem from *impulses* promptly turned into action.

Most of us actually stifle enough good impulses during the course of a day to change the current of our lives. These inner flashes of impulse light up the mind for an instant; then, contented in their afterglow, we lapse back into routine, feeling vaguely that sometime we might do something about it or that at least our intentions were good. In this we sin against the inner self, for impulses set up the lines of communication between the unconscious mind and daily action. Said William James, "Every time a resolve or fine glow of feeling evaporates without bearing fruit, it is worse than a chance lost; it works to hinder future emotions from taking the normal path of discharge." Thus we fail to build up the power to act in a prompt and definite way upon the principal emergencies of life.

Once, in Hollywood, where story supervisor Walter B. Pitkin and I were retained by a motion-picture studio, a young promoter presented an ambitious production idea to us. The plan was appealing and, I thought, distinctly worth considering; we could think it over, discuss it and decide later what to do. But even while I was fumbling with the idea, Pitkin abruptly reached for the phone and began dictating a telegram to a Wall Street man he knew. It presented the idea in the enthusiasm of the moment. (As delivered it was almost a yard long.) It cost money, but it carried conviction.

To my amazement, a ten-million-dollar underwriting of the picture project came as a result of that telegram. Had we delayed to talk it over we might have cautiously talked ourselves out of the whole idea. But Pitkin knew how to act on the spur of the moment. All his life he had learned to trust his impulses as the best confidential advisers he had.

Behind many an imposing executive desk sits a man who is there because he learned the same lesson. You've probably seen him in action more than once. Somebody is presenting to him a new idea, say in employee relations. It calls for extensive changes in office routine. And, deciding instantly, he calls an associate and gives instructions to make the change—then and there, not next week or next month.

We envy such men the ease with which they make up their minds and swing into action. But this ease is acquired over a long period of years. Rather than being, as we sometimes think, a privilege of their position, it is a practice that has led to their success. First in small matters and then in larger ones, they have acquired the do-it-now habit.

Calvin Coolidge was an enigma to political commentators because the reasons for his actions were seldom apparent and the source of his astuteness could not be traced. No one could seem less impulsive than Coolidge, yet all his life he trained himself to rely on "hunches." He was not afraid of his impulses, and the celebrated Coolidge luck followed a pattern of action based on them. As a young attorney in a country law firm Coolidge was interviewing an important client one day when a telephone message informed him that the county political boss was in town. It occurred to Coolidge that he ought to see the local big-wig at once and propose himself as a candidate for the legislature. Without hesitation, this usually shy young lawyer cut his legal conference short, left the office and hunted up the county leader. That impulse bore fruit, and from then on the inner urges of Coolidge led him consistently to political success.

It should be clear from Coolidge's case that the person who follows his impulses is not necessarily flighty. The timid soul, however, is fearful lest impulse lead him into all manner of mistakes. But mistakes are inevitable—we are bound to make them no matter which course we take. Some of the worst mistakes in history have followed consciously reasoned decisions. If we're right 51 percent of the time in our impulsive actions we aren't doing badly by any standard.

The mistakes of inaction, flanked by heavy reasoning, are likely to be worse than the mistakes of genuine impulse. For one thing, they make our inertia worse day by day. Not long ago a woman whose husband had left her came to seek my advice. The difficulty between them appeared to be one of temperament which could be easily adjusted. And the woman told me that what she really wanted to do was simply to call her husband up and talk with him. I told her to follow that inclination. She left me somewhat at peace. But she didn't make the call; and in a few days she was back again. Once more she left with the impulse to call her husband. Unhappily, she never did. And a domestic rift that a few impulsive words on the phone might have healed ended in divorce. From childhood she had made time after time the mistake of letting her impulses die a-borning, and when the time came for a simple, direct decision in a situation that mattered, she was unable to act.

We all know people who go through agonies of indecision before taking any important step. There are always arguments for and against, and the more we think about them the more they seem to offset each other, until we wind up in a fretful state of paralysis. Impulsive action which originates in a swift subconscious appraisal of the situation might have saved all that worry. And when a painfully thought-out decision proves wrong, how often we remember an original hunch that would have been right!

The way to get things done is to bring mind and muscle and voice into play at the very second a good impulse starts within us. I know a writer who was once engaged on a major project and was resolved that nothing could divert him from it. But he saw an announcement of a contest for the ten best rules for safe driving. The announcement flashed a light on the panel of his mind. Here was something he knew about. He interrupted his job long enough to get to a library and study up. He wrote 250 words. He turned in his entry in his own typing, not wanting to stop his stenographer from the bigger job. Months later that obeyed impulse netted him an award of $25,000. The project from which he turned aside for a moment finally brought him $600.

Or consider the young college instructor who sat listening one day to a commencement address by Woodrow Wilson, then governor of New Jersey. The instructor had written a book on political science, but had sought a publisher in vain. It embodied his innermost convictions and its apparent failure had caused him to despair of the future of his teaching.

Something Mr. Wilson said made the instructor feel that he ought to seek the governor's advice. He had heard that Wilson was cold and hard to approach; but at the end of the address he let his impulse carry him forward through the crowd; he grasped Mr. Wilson's hand, and said rapidly, "Your speech was wonderful! I've written a book maintaining that..." In a few pithy sentences he stated his theory.

Wilson shook his head. "No," he said. "You're wrong. I'll tell you why. See me after lunch at the Faculty Club." There for two hours Wilson talked earnestly. And under the inspiration Wilson gave him, the instructor wrote a new book. It sold more than 100,000 copies and launched him on a distinguished educational career. The first vital impulse, half-hesitantly obeyed, was the starting point.

The life stories of successful people are chock-full of such episodes that have marked major turning points in their careers. True impulses are intelligent. They show the path we can most successfully follow because they reveal the basic interests of the unconscious mind.

There is in all of us an unceasing urge toward self-fulfillment. We know the kind of person we want to be because our impulses, even when enfeebled by disuse, tell us. Impulsive action is not to be substituted for reason but used as a means of showing the direction reason is to take. Obviously the path is not without pitfalls. To start suddenly throwing ourselves around on impulse might be hazardous. But at least we can begin responding oftener to inner urges that we know we can trust.

We *know* that in the midst of reading we ought to stop and look up a word if the meaning is not clear. We know that we ought to speak more words of unpremeditated praise where they are due. We know that we ought to wriggle out of selfish routine and take part in civic activities, that we ought to contribute not merely money but time to the well-being of the neighborhood.

Such separate moments of achievement are cumulative and result in enriched living, a consciousness of daily adventure, a long-term sense that life is not blocked out and cut-and-dried but may be managed from within. The man whose philosophy is summed up in the feeble and indecisive motto, "Well, we'll see about it," misses the savory moments of experience, the bounce and gusto of life.

Thumb back over the pages of your own experience and note how many of your happiest moments and greatest successes have followed spur-of-the-moment actions and decisions. They are reminders that only from the depths of your inner self can you hope for an invincible urge toward accomplishment. So, obey your best impulses and watch yourself go!

BUT WHAT

USE IS IT?

by Isaac Asimov

IN THE 1840s, the English physicist and chemist Michael Faraday, in one of his enormously popular lectures, illustrated a peculiar phenomenon. He thrust a magnet into the hollow center of a spiral coil of wire connected to a galvanometer that would record the presence of an electric current. There was no current in the wire to begin with, but as the magnet was inserted, the needle of the galvanometer moved to one side of the scale, showing that an electric current was flowing. As the magnet was withdrawn, the needle flipped in the other direction, showing that the current was now flowing the other way. When the magnet was held motionless within the coil, no current flowed at all.

After the lecture, a member of the audience approached Faraday and asked, "But of what practical use can this be?" Faraday answered, "Sir, of what use is a newborn baby?"

It was precisely this phenomenon that Faraday made use of to develop the electric generator, which, for the first time, made it possible to produce electricity cheaply and in quantity. That, in turn, made it possible to build the electrified technology without which modern life would be inconceivable. Faraday's newborn baby grew into a giant.

Even the shrewdest of men cannot always judge what is useful and what is not. Thomas Alva Edison was surely one of the greatest inventors who ever lived. In 1868 he patented his first invention, a mechanical device that would record and total votes at the push of a button. A Congressman whom Edison consulted, however, told him that there wasn't a chance of its being accepted. A slow vote, it seemed, was sometimes a political necessity, since opinions might change as a count was being taken, whereas a quick vote might, in a moment of emotion, commit Congress to something undesirable.

Edison, chagrined, decided never again to invent anything unless he was sure it would be needed.* He stuck to that. Before he died, he had obtained nearly 1300 patents—including one for the first practical electric light, perhaps the most useful of all his inventions.

Over the years, Edison labored to improve the electric light, mainly by making the glowing filament last longer before breaking. One of his hit-or-miss efforts was to seal a metal wire into an evacuated light bulb, near the filament but not touching it. Edison then turned on the electric current to see if the metal wire might somehow preserve the life of the glowing filament.

It didn't, but he could not help noticing that an electric current seemed to flow from the filament to the wire across that vacuum gap. Nothing in Edison's knowledge explained the phenomenon. He wrote it up in his notebooks and, in 1884, being Edison, patented it. The phenomenon, called the "Edison effect," was his only discovery in pure science. Since he could see no use for it, he pursued the matter no further.

Later, however, scientists who pursued "useless" knowledge for its own sake discovered that electric current was accompanied by a flow of sub-atomic particles (eventually called "electrons"). The Edison effect was the result of the ability of these electrons, under certain conditions, to travel through a vacuum. In 1906, American inventor Lee De Forest made use of this new understanding when he devised an evacuated glass bulb with a filament, a wire and a metal plate that enabled it to amplify an electric current. The result is called a radio tube. It

---

*Numerous legislatures, including the U.S. House of Representatives, now use vote-tallying machines.

made possible all of our modern electronic equipment—
including radio and television,

The Edison effect, then, which the practical Edison
shrugged off as useless, turned out to have more astonishing
results than any of his practical devices. In fact, it is difficult to
find a branch of science that *isn't* useful. Between 1900 and 1930,
for instance, theoretical physics underwent a revolution. The
theory of relativity and the development of quantum mechanics
led to a new understanding of the basic laws of the universe and
of the behavior of the inner components of the atom. None of it
seemed to have the slightest use for mankind, and the brilliant
young scientists involved apparently had found an ivory tower
for themselves that nothing could disturb. But out of that
abstract work came, unexpectedly, the nuclear bomb, and a
world that now lives in terror of a war that could destroy
mankind in a day.

It did not bring only terror, however. Out of that research
also came radioisotopes, which have made it possible to probe
the workings of living tissue with a delicacy otherwise quite
impossible, and whose findings have revolutionized medicine in
a thousand ways. Nuclear power stations also offer mankind the
brightest hope of ample energy during all his future existence on
earth.

The point is that we cannot foresee consequences in detail.
Faraday did not foresee a television set when he puzzled over his
magnet-induced electric current. Einstein, as he worked out the
equation $e = mc^2$, did not sense the mushroom cloud.

We now stand in the closing decades of the 20th century,
with science advancing as never before. We've discovered
quasars and pulsars in the distant heavens. Of what use are they
to the average man? Astronauts have brought back rocks from
the moon at great expense. So what? Scientists discover new
compounds, develop new theories, work out new mathematical
complexities. What for?

No one knows right now. But *you* will know if you live
long enough; and if not, your children or grandchildren will
know. And they will smile at those who say, "But what is the use
of sending rockets into space?" just as we now smile at the person
who asked Faraday the use of his demonstration.

In fact, unless we continue with science and gather

knowledge—whether or not it seems useful on the spot—we will be buried under our problems and find no way out. Today's science is tomorrow's solution—and, most of all, it is mankind's greatest adventure.

IN DEFENSE OF

THE OLD RAT RACE

by Howard Upton

A MELANCHOLY portrait has been drawn of Modern American Man. With only one life to live, his critics say, he is spending it not in the pursuit of happiness, but in pursuit of the district managership of the Federated Iron Fittings Co., Inc. With magnificent mountains to be climbed and serenely beautiful lakes to be sailed, he spends his precious early years developing such shoddy skills as are delineated in *How to Become a Tremendously Successful Sales Executive*. With millions of lonely women languishing in their loveliness, he spends his evenings working out a correspondence course in Hard-Goods Distribution, Principles of. While blue waters lap at sunwashed beaches from Acapulco to Nice, demanding his presence, he is busy figuring out a sales approach which will sack up that big double-threaded-pipe order in Houston.

This situation is popularly referred to as the Old Rat Race, and its theme has been repeated so often that a person today cannot avoid the nagging notion that there is something terribly wrong with his involvement in going after the Big Job. Even the fellow who enjoys his work at Federated Fittings and likes living in Suburban Acres senses that he is somehow missing "the important things of life."

Against this dismal background the time has come for

someone to raise his voice in defense of the Old Rat Race.

Let us begin by suggesting that it is one thing for a man to recognize the annoyances and inadequacies of his mode of existence, but it is something else for him to assume that these defects render the whole fabric of his life worthless. Life has never been, for anyone anywhere, a serene uninterrupted flow of ecstasy. Happiness comes, at best, in infrequent periods of contentment or bursts of triumph. And it comes just as often, I strongly suspect, to the commuter from Stamford, Conn., as it does to the beachcombers of Capri.

In the next place, please observe that distress is relative. Human anguish comes in a variety of forms. Boredom is one. A gnawing sense of futility is another. But hunger, fear, poverty and abject despair are also on the list. The American system of social and economic activity, with its incessant emphasis on competition and the importance of money, certainly invokes a feeling of futility in us now and then. Even so, the system holds these other forms of human agony to a tolerable minimum.

When a person can spend eight hours a day in an air-conditioned office for approximately 220 days out of each 365, and manage in the process to provide himself and family with food, a house, medical care, entertainment and other creature comforts, he has reached a plateau of human existence beyond the most extravagant dreams of other times and places. If you doubt this, check the U.S. immigration figures. One man's rat race is another man's paradise.

So what if the Old Rat Race is not so glum as depicted? There are still more noble and gratifying ways in which to spend one's life, you say, than in riding commuter buses and selling plumbing fixtures or writing advertising copy. Perhaps. But let us look closely.

Take the individual who is dissatisfied with the way things are going for him. His soul aches, he tells you, to do something with his life other than pursue the district managership and ultimately possess the biggest car in the neighborhood. All right, if this fellow does not like his present existence it is entirely fair to ask what alternative he would select for himself.

He may, in an offhand way, mention travel: Mexico, Sweden, France, the Caribbean. Or he may mention something nebulous about getting away from the hypocrisy of business, the commuting, the scrounging to pay month-end bills. Don't let him stop there. Pin him down.

If he tells you that what he would really like is a nice home with maybe a 30-foot pool in the back yard and a good chunk of money stashed away, and a nice boat up on the lake, and the kids' education paid for and.... If he tells you this, he does not propose to escape from the Old Rat Race at all. He merely wishes to take a short cut. He desires the ultimate rewards of a system which he ostensibly despises, but he does not wish to earn the rewards by conforming to the rules.

Suppose, on the other hand, the fellow tells you he has something more specific in mind. Such as going back to his old home town and publishing the weekly newspaper. Or moving to Florida and opening up a little camera shop. Or getting a job in the Foreign Service. Or writing a novel. Or running for Congress.

Now these are all commendable alternatives to the Old Rat Race. But his protest will be that they are unobtainable:

"I can't just quit. The way things are, if I missed even one pay check we'd be sunk. Car payments to meet. The boy's teeth need braces. Furniture to pay for. I would like nothing better than to get out of the office and open up a nice little cabinet shop, say in San Mateo. Work with my hands. Make things out of wood. But what can I do?"

The answer is very simple. He can quit his job, sell his house, ignore the fact that little Johnny may have crooked teeth when he grows up, move his family to a modest place in San Mateo and open up a little cabinet shop. That's what he can do!

But wait, you say. Won't that be pretty rough? It will, indeed! And now we are approaching the core of this whole matter. The alternatives to the Old Rat Race usually are rough, relatively speaking. But other men choose them every day. The fact that most of us reject them means this: we conclude that being in the Old Rat Race, with all its defects, is preferable to being out of it.

In this world, which is a good deal less than perfect, the mature man is the one who takes such opportunities and talents as he finds available to him and does with them what he can. If he makes a decision, for example, not to open a cabinet shop in

San Mateo, he is simply recognizing reality. The fellow who acknowledges to himself that he can make the best use of his talents by selling toilet seats is not being ignoble. He is merely exercising his intelligence.

The most recurrent criticism of the man in the Rat Race is that he gives too much of himself to his job. But it should be noted that the satisfaction derived from almost any form of human activity varies in direct ratio to the degree of intensity with which one approaches it. This is true whether the activity is playing tennis, performing surgery, writing a book, making love or selling life insurance. The people who perform best in any human activity are those who "give it all they've got." They are also the ones who derive the most satisfaction from the activity.

We cannot all paint. We cannot all write. We cannot all spend our lives contemplating beauty. In any advanced order of civilization someone has to manufacture and sell doorknobs, gasoline, umbrellas, picture frames, screw drivers and all the other assorted miscellany which distinguishes our society from that of, let us say, the Eskimo. Without the complex commercial activity which makes these things available, the lives of all of us—poets included—would not only be uncomfortable; they would be deathly dull.

This being true, is it not better for a man to be a reasonably good accountant than a mediocre sculptor? Isn't the net contribution—to himself, his family, his society—of a dedicated nuts-and-bolts salesman superior to that of an inept philosopher?

When you look at the total picture, it is not the militant nonconformist who is the hero of our age. The real hero is the fellow you see with the brief case, waiting to catch the night plane to Houston to see what he can do about sacking up that big double-threaded-pipe order.

CHANGING CUSTOM

BETTER WAYS TO

STOP SMOKING

by Walter S. Ross

"IT'S LIKE ending a love affair: at first you can't live without your lover—but then you meet someone new. That's the way it is with quitting cigarettes; after a while you think of them as an old flame."

This nugget of wisdom is from the "Stop Smoking Program Guide," a manual put out by the American Cancer Society (ACS). A gold mine of practical help for smokers who would like to kick the habit, it contains the latest do-it-yourself psychological techniques, plus instructions on how to start and run a kind of Smokers Anonymous group. Records show that about 30 percent of those who try the method quit cigarettes altogether, and another 25 percent cut their smoking by at least half. People who have been helped range from a 77-year-old man who'd smoked for upward of 60 years, to a 12-year-old girl; from four-pack-a-day chain smokers to four-cigarette-a-day tenderthroats.

Of the 54 million U.S. cigarette smokers, an estimated 48 million—54 percent—want to quit. As a public-health expert with the California Interagency Council on Smoking and Health, George M. Saunders used to get four or five phone calls a day from smokers pleading for assistance. Frustrated by the lack of any simple, effective program he could refer them to, he set out to create one. Perhaps group therapy would work. It helps alcoholics, drug addicts, compulsive gamblers and overeaters kick *their* habits—why not smokers?

So in January 1969, Saunders started a quit-smoking clinic as part of the Mount Diablo, Calif., school district's adult-education program: two-hour sessions, two evenings a week for four weeks. He drew up an outline for the "course," collected all the films on smoking and health he could find, and lined up several doctors to deliver lectures.

The first meeting wiped out his agenda. "We don't want films or doctors," said Mrs. Marie Lenz, a blond housewife. "We want to talk to each other about smoking." From then on, the group practically ran itself—and at the end of the four weeks, 33 of the 35 had quit smoking.

Saunders' method has since been picked up as a national priority of the American Cancer Society. All that's needed to start a group of 8 to 18 people is a place to meet, and an ex-smoker willing to act as "facilitator" (since nobody really "leads" a group). This person need not be a professional counselor. Engineers, teachers, scout leaders and high-school students have all been successful.

Often referred by doctors, or under family pressure, group members may come in with a chip on their shoulder. They are told: "What we offer you is the chance to work out in your own mind if you really want to stop smoking. You'll never be asked to quit, or even to cut down. We want you to smoke as much as you've been smoking, during the next two weeks."

Says Saunders: "Each person has to find his own individual reason for quitting. And you have to break that vicious circle of failure and guilt. In our groups, nobody fails, whether he quits or not—because it remains a personal choice. So he can always try quitting later, if he wants to."

Members are given a self-test on "Why I Smoke." On a sheet listing 18 statements such as "I smoke when I feel blue," "Smoking cigarettes is pleasant and relaxing," they circle a number, from one (never) to five (always), next to each. A scoring system translates answers into the underlying reasons: Habit, Stress, Craving, Stimulation, Handling, Relaxation. Usually about 30 percent are primarily stress smokers; craving accounts for another 25 percent; relaxation 15 percent; and 10 percent for each of the other three reasons mentioned.

Once a smoker identifies his hangup, he may get practical help to deal with it from the booklet and from his group. For example, people with a craving for cigarettes are urged to smoke more than they really want for a couple of days, to spoil the taste. A stress smoker is advised never to try to quit during a crisis. It's better to try when he's relaxed, perhaps on a vacation.

Those who use tobacco as a crutch are encouraged to try facing a stressful (smoking) situation without a cigarette. Like 32-year-old Nicole, who could not enter a room full of strangers without her personal smokescreen. "I went to a party without my cigarettes," she reported to her group, "and, you know, nothing bad happened at all."

The smoker who uses cigarettes to relax is counseled to try a pleasing substitute—perhaps eating, drinking, or some kind of social activity.

Groups urge the buddy system. Members are asked to converse generally until they find a partner with whom they can talk comfortably. Having a buddy helps particularly in overcoming any withdrawal symptoms.

After the first session, homework is given out. Each member gets an eight-by-ten piece of ruled paper to wrap around his pack of cigarettes with two rubber bands. On this "wrap sheet" he is to note the day, date, number of that day's pack, and to rate each cigarette by its importance, on a scale of one to five. He also notes the time, his activity, how he feels, and a reason for quitting. Finally, under the statement "I decide to smoke/not smoke this cigarette," he checks one or the other. In one day of wrapping and unwrapping, this simple device makes a smoker realize how many cigarettes he consumes unconsciously. "I was shocked," says Bob, a 35-year-old lab technician, "to find out I was smoking 15 cigarettes a day just after coffee. I quickly eliminated most of those, and cut way down on coffee, too."

Tony, a 43-year-old stockbroker, said, "I was smoking four packs a day, but the wrap sheet proved to me that more than half were just automatic." He dropped the unconscious smokes, and soon quit completely.

The other homework is a "Cigarette Mad Money" envelope, with instructions to put in it the exact sum needed to buy cigarettes—his usual number of packs smoked per day—over the whole four-week course the clinic will run. This money is then used to buy the cigarettes, one pack at a time. If at any point the smoker decides to quit, he seals the envelope. And when the clinic ends, the facilitator suggests he spend the money on a present for himself—a reminder of success. Many ex-smokers continue to tape 50 or 75 cents to a calendar each day they don't smoke, as cash proof of saving.

These gimmicks help—sometimes even in a negative way. After his first session, Jack, a 45-year-old engineer, said disgustedly, "I can't be bothered with these childish tricks." And he quit smoking on the spot.

As the fourth group session is ending, the facilitator suggests that now that they know one another, and recognize their own motives, this might be a good time to try going without cigarettes—but only for the 48 hours just preceding the fifth meeting. It is not put on a make-or-break basis, and at the next session the facilitator doesn't quiz anyone. Most group members do manage the two days without cigarettes, however. And often the entire group gives up smoking, not just for 48 hours but right through the remaining four sessions.

This doesn't mean they've completely conquered the habit. "But even if a person lapses," says Saunders, "he'll be able to quit again because he won't feel guilty about it. In fact we often suggest not quitting 'permanently': just for today and tomorrow. Many people become terror-stricken if they have to think of an endless future without smoking. Some even carry a pack of cigarettes so they know they can have one anytime they're really desperate."

Adds David Witti, a behavior therapist: "One thing these groups *don't* discuss is willpower. We don't know what that is. We just help retrain habits, until new ones take over."

To find a smoking clinic in your area, check with your county medical society, the American Cancer Society, American Heart Association, or American Lung Association. (See phone book for nearest office.)

THERE IS A SAFE WAY

TO DRINK

by Morris Chafetz, M.D.

I HAVE devoted most of my professional life to the problems of alcohol and its abuse, most recently as director of the National Institute on Alcohol Abuse and Alcoholism. So I've spent much of my time trumpeting the fact that alcohol is a drug and that alcohol abuse is the most serious drug problem this nation faces. Nonetheless, I believe firmly that alcohol can do more good than harm. For there *is* a safe way to drink.

Pharmacologically, alcohol is an anesthetic, not a stimulant. In moderate amounts, it *appears* to stimulate, because it inhibits those brain centers which restrict "less civilized" outbursts, as well as those which make us aware of exhaustion. Then we feel physically abler and emotionally freer. But with increasing doses alcohol puts to sleep the brain centers which affect judgment, knowledge and social controls. Sufficient dosage can put us to sleep for keeps, by anesthetizing those centers which control breathing and heartbeat.

Responsible people, therefore, must choose rather carefully the time, place and circumstances of drinking. Obviously, if you are to engage in complex mental or physical activities—writing, driving, business—it is scarcely appropriate to be under the influence of an anesthetic drug. On the other hand, if you're going to be sharing a meal, or some other human

223

interchange, in a relaxed way, alcohol can be a rewarding adjunct to the experience—a true servant of man.

An essential point is that there is a *known* safe level of drinking. In preparing the second report to the Congress on Alcohol and Health, we found that researchers all over the world were independently using the same level to define safe or moderate drinking: 1 1/2 ounces of pure alcohol per day—the equivalent of three one-ounce drinks of 100-proof whiskey (which is 50-percent alcohol), four eight-ounce glasses of beer, or half a bottle of wine.

This limit, of course, is only a statistical average. For some people, even one drop of alcohol is too much. Nor do our findings permit saving up one day's ration in order to drink more the next day. At no time should any individual wishing to remain within the safe limits consume more than 1 1/2 ounces of pure alcohol in a single day.

Studies show that the driver who has consumed an amount of alcohol within this limit is no more likely to have an automobile accident than the driver who does not take any alcohol. But beyond this limit, when the blood-alcohol level (the concentration of alcohol in the blood) begins to creep over the .05 percent "sober" level, the risk of a traffic accident jumps eormously. By the time the blood-alcohol level reaches 0.2 percent—the level of most drunk drivers who are arrested—the risk of an accident is 100 times that of the non-drinking driver.

The *manner* of drinking is also crucial. One should always sip, slowly. Alcohol is a highly unusual foodstuff in that at least 20 percent of it is absorbed directly from the stomach into the bloodstream without going through any digestive processes. Therefore, gulping alcohol produces a sudden, marked rise in the alcohol level in the blood and hence in the brain. Once alcohol is in the bloodstream, nothing, with the exception of a kidney-dialysis machine, can clear it from the blood more quickly than the body's own steady metabolic rate of three quarters of an ounce of pure alcohol per hour.

Another rule of safe drinking is that food in the stomach, preferably protein or fatty products, effectively delays alcohol's invasion of our systems. Food covers the stomach wall, making capillaries less accessible. It also sponges up the alcohol and carries it gradually through the digestive process, slowing absorption and allowing the metabolism and brain to adapt. So, as any experienced drinker knows, the same dose taken with food in the stomach will provide a more pleasant outcome than alcohol on an empty stomach.

A number of other factors also influence our response to a drink. It's best not to take alcohol when physically or emotionally upset, lonely or in need of solace. It is true that alcohol's anesthetic effect will dull the pain of loneliness. But alcohol is no substitute for another person. In other words, do not drink alone.

It's also best to drink in a relaxed setting. If I had to come up with an unhealthy drinking situation, I would have created the American cocktail party. Standing around uncomfortably in a crush of people, most of whom one does not know, one tends to gulp that first drink. People like to think that the alcohol at cocktail parties makes it easier to get acquainted, and cite the fact that strangers frequently pour out intimate details of their lives. In my judgment, a stranger sharing intimacies so freely is not relating to you—he is relating to himself. A medical colleague once tested this at a cocktail party when a woman was pouring out her heart to him. "I have just murdered my grandmother," he said. The woman smiled sweetly, said, "Isn't that nice," and babbled on.

Regardless of where and how you drink, what you expect from alcohol is what you get. As with almost all drugs expectation is strongly related to outcome. If you're part of a group that wants to act drunk, even with small doses you'll feel drunk.

It's best, then, to drink with people who set expectations that are socially useful and not destructive. Too many Americans, preoccupied with drinking, fail in this regard. We spend a good deal of time thinking about drinking, or talking about it. Our liquor advertisements imply that alcohol is proof of sophistication and worldliness. Or else it's funny. Just think about how we laugh when a comedian acts drunk. Thinking something is funny is a society's way of giving it social sanction. It is also a sign of discomfort—for jokes are a "safe" way to ventilate deeper worries. Study after study has shown that Americans are uncomfortable, ambivalent, almost guilt-ridden about their use of alcohol.

Why is this country so uptight about drinking? In my opinion, one major reason is that our society places a great deal of stock in order and control. And being overdosed with a drug—drunk—means being out of control. When we see someone who has lost control, it threatens *our* sense of control. Alcoholism is threatening because so many of us use alcohol. When we see an alcoholic, we are afraid that we could become alcoholics, too.

If our culture were more open and less guilty about alcohol, I think we could do more for people with alcohol problems. We might also do more for our children. Surveys completed in 1975 show that children in this country between the ages of 12 and 17 are already manifesting severe alcohol abuse; in fact, five percent of these "kids" get drunk at least once a week.

What can parents do? For one thing, they can alter the use of alcohol in the home. I contend that we teach our children about alcohol very early. Toddlers notice that when Mommy and Daddy drink this particular liquid they behave differently. The children can't miss the fact that it's something special—especially when we tell them they can't have it "because it's not good for you."

I see no harm in becoming more relaxed about alcohol in the home, even giving your child a taste if you're drinking and he wants it. Why not? Other cultures do, in a matter-of-fact way. Chinese, Lebanese, Spanish, Jewish and Italian people do not think there is anything special about giving alcohol to their young. Nobody makes a fuss about it, and these cultures use alcohol without appreciable problems.

Indeed, always to focus on alcohol in the context of alcoholism is, I think, to miss the point. If you are preoccupied with alcohol, if you or others in your environment are discomfited by this preoccupation, if alcohol interferes with your ability to function in other necessary ways, then you have an alcohol problem.

Our country is very concerned these days with safety and health. We have to remind ourselves that *anything* that affects human beings has a potential for harm. In too great a quantity, even oxygen and water, those essentials of life, can harm or kill.

So life is a risk, and I suspect the only sure way to be safe from disease and dying is to be dead.

But there *are* safe limits that people can use in making their decisions about risk-taking, such as choosing to drink or not to drink or how much to drink. We ought to share with young and old alike the best available knowledge on such subjects. And then let each individual make up his or her own mind.

THE

RIGHT DIET FOR

YOU

by Fredrick J. Stare, M.D., with Mary McSherry

EVERY DIET promises to be *the* quick and painless way to lose weight. And each recommends a different route. Small wonder if by now you've decided that there isn't any diet that is right for you. But there is. Best of all, it is one that fits your life, and it works!

The most important part of any diet is "you." You must be able to live your normal life with it. You have to be able to stay with it comfortably so you can take weight off and keep it off. This means that the diet has to keep you nourished with food you like, and let you eat that food on a schedule that suits you.

If this sounds like a personalized, tailor-made diet, you are right. If you think this diet will be hard to locate or expensive, you are wrong. You begin the diet the way a tailor starts on a suit—with the taking of measurements. To measure yourself, write down the answers to three questions: What kind of person am I? What kinds of foods do I like? What kind of life do I lead?

Under *Kind of Person* jot down characteristics that will affect your dieting. Are you determined? Well-disciplined? Or have past tries at dieting suggested that you—like most of us—are self-indulgent or easily discouraged? Play fair. There's no point in describing a paragon and then being disappointed when plain old you sneaks a piece of cake.

If the cake-sneaking sounds all too likely, figure out the times when you are most apt to give in to temptation. Do you stick to a diet when you're alone? Or maybe with you, it's when you're with people. Do you nibble while you read or watch television? Are you a bedtime snacker? Tell the truth.

Under the same heading write down how much weight you want to lose, what your goal is. Be realistic. If you're a short, stocky person who comes from a family of short, stocky persons, no diet will make you tall and slender. Success for you is being the most attractive *you*.

Now move to *Kinds of Foods I Like*. Divide this list into four parts: 1) meats, fish and poultry; 2) dairy products; 3) fruits and vegetables; 4) potatoes, cereals and all things made of flour. Nutritionists call these the basic four food groups—the kinds of food we must have to stay healthy and to feel well fed. They feel a good daily rule is two helpings of meat, fish, poultry or allied proteins (like dried peas or beans or nuts); two helpings of fruit and two of vegetables; two helpings of milk or milk-based foods—cheese, for instance; four helpings of potatoes or enriched cereals or cereal-based foods—bread, pancakes, spaghetti, anything like that.

List your favorites in all four groups. If too many items fall into the rich-and-gooey, super-fattening class, think a little and list plenty of less-fattening things that you also like.

Finally, on to *Kind of Life I Lead*. What is your daily pattern? Your weekend activities? Note meals you eat away from home. Think back over the past few days and jot down all the times you ate or drank anything. For example, do you take a coffee break every morning at ten? What about the cocktail or two before dinner and after-dinner drinks?

Keep in mind that you're chiefly concerned with your schedule as it affects your food intake and your need for energy. If you take in more food calories than you spend, you'll gain weight. If you take in fewer than you spend, you'll lose weight—because you will use up calories from your stored body fat.

Most adult women need 2000–2200 calories a day; men need 2200–2600. But an adult who wants to lose weight steadily should limit himself to 1200–1400 calories a day. A person who is more active or willing to lose weight more slowly can take in a bit more. Consult your *Kind of Person* and *Kind of Life* lists and decide how active you are, how rapidly you want to lose weight and how determined you are. Then settle on the number of calories you are going to give yourself each day.

Now get in mind the jigsaw pieces you are going to work with to build your diet picture:

1. The calorie content of the foods you like. You already have a list divided into the basic four food groups. Buy a pocket-size calorie chart, and learn their calorie content.

2. The number of helpings of the basic four you are going to include each day. Your calorie chart figures helpings in terms of so many ounces of food or so much of a cupful. Train your eye to be your measuring device. Weigh four ounces of cooked meat or fish, measure out a cup of spinach or peas, a half-cup of cooked rice or cereal. Then put the food on a plate, take a good look at it, and remember.

3. Your own eating pattern. Go over your *Kind of Life* notes and make your schedule—the times of day and night when you are used to eating or drinking something. Note what you've been having at each time—a meal, a snack, a drink or sweet. Put a check mark beside the times which are most important. Now fill in the schedule. Select foods you like and check to make sure you've included the proper helpings. Portion size is critical! Write down meals and snacks for one ideal day. Include everything—the cream in your coffee, the icing on the cake, the works.

Next, add up all the calories. Don't be surprised because the total is considerably higher than the 1400 or so you were aiming at. This sample menu tells you *not* where you are going, but where you have been.

Trimming down your over-caloried menu isn't too hard when you stick to the eating schedule you are used to. For most, the hardest thing about dieting is being locked into a breakfast-lunch-dinner-and-*that's-it* routine. On a tailor-made diet, the snack times continue as before. The only thing that changes is the kind or amount of snack food.

For instance, look at the calories of the snacks of your ideal menu. What did you have? Apple pie? 330 calories. A small candy bar? 155. A bedtime sandwich and a glass of milk? 610.

Can snacks like this stay? Certainly not all of them. You're planning a diet, not a miracle.

If your *Kind of Person* list says that you are self-indulgent and *must* have a daily piece of pie or a cocktail or two, go right ahead. You will have, of course, that many fewer calories to spread over the rest of the day—but it's your day; they are your calories. However, there are many ways to snack without overspending calories. Wheat Thins, for example, are only nine calories each. Animal crackers are 12. Raw fruits and vegetables make good snacks. A peach is only 35 calories. There are low-calorie diet candies and artificially sweetened diet drinks that count very little.

With your eyes sharpened by the low-calorie possibilities in snacks, shift them over to that ideal menu. Even without snacks, the three meals a day probably cost too many calories to fit your diet. Or maybe they are costing calories you'd rather spend for special treats—a weekend party or a fudge sundae to celebrate the loss of the first five pounds! This sort of reward is something every dieter should occasionally permit himself. After you've had a small splurge, you'll be content to count calories again.

Trim your meals by selecting calorie bargains from among the things you like. The more bargains you can include, the more food you can have. For example, consider at breakfast time a slice of melon at 35 calories, rather than a glass of orange juice at 90. Or why not have a poached egg at 75 calories, instead of a scrambled one at 110? And save the Danish pastry for a snack later on—maybe for two snacks, with half each time.

At noon, you can have just as much food and feel as well fed with a roll and a fruit salad with cottage cheese as with, say, a hot roast-beef sandwich. You'll save 200 calories. If you build dinner around broiled chicken instead of chicken a la king, you're 100 calories ahead. And if you select baked fish rather than pork chops, you've saved a walloping 350!

And so it goes. By building meals around calorie bargains, giving yourself rewards and sticking to a schedule you like, you can complete the tailoring of the diet you really need. The most workable way is to plan menus a week at a time, keeping your activities in mind. Do you bowl every Thursday and wind up the evening with your teammates over hamburger and beer? Put it down and work the rest of Thursday around it. Trim a little off the rest of the week to pay for dinner out on Saturday. Your life determines the diet, not the diet your life. Plan it to suit you, and it will serve you well.

Following any diet—even one especially made for you—is not easy. Here are some hints. At the beginning, omit salt. With unsalted food, you don't want so much. Eat slowly, preferably with someone, so you'll have conversation—something to occupy your mind—besides the eating. If you must eat alone, read or listen to music when you can. Keep your meals small, so you can allow yourself a lot of extra nibbling. Serve meals on smaller plates: they'll look larger and keep you happier.

A great deal of overeating is done out of boredom. Don't let yourself be bored. The start of a diet is a good time to begin an activity: get the garden in shape, or paint a room. When your hands are busy—and dirty—you're not as apt to want food. And the extra activity burns up calories. Finally, weigh yourself only once a week. You'll have lost enough weight to feel successful—and nothing succeeds like success!

Success here doesn't just mean loss of weight. You will also be eating your way to better health. And since thin people live longer than fat ones, you'll be able to look forward to more time with everything you enjoy. It's a big payoff.

APPRECIATE! ENJOY!

NO WONDER!

by W. E. Sangster

HAVE YOU ever analyzed the charm of childhood? Half the secret is that children can still wonder. Do you want to remain young? Learn to keep wonder in your life. Life without wonder is hardly worth living.

All philosophy, said Socrates, began in wonder. Why was man not content to eat and drink and breed like other animals? Because he wondered, because something inside him tortured him with the desire to know.

In his early and dim awareness of God, primitive man was conscious of Someone high and eerie, and this consciousness both daunted and fascinated him. It said to him, "Come hither" and "Stand back." Both—and both together. No honest thinker went in search of God who knew beforehand whether it is more terrible to see the One before Whom the angels veil their faces or to learn that man is all alone in this mysterious universe.

So it is with scientific research. Curiosity is still its great dynamic. Said Einstein: "The most beautiful thing we can experience is the mysterious. It is the source of all true science."

There are people all over the world eating their hearts out to travel and see wonders which are far away, yet most of them are blind to wonders near at hand. In familiar events of the familiar world about me, which I dismiss as utterly trifling,

Shakespeare would find the material for a play.

How can one keep wonder in life? Is there any mental strategy for seeing all things with mystery and the morning dew upon them?

Holidays are one way. But not chiefly to go places; rather, *to come back with film-free eyes.*

G. K. Chesterton used to live in Battersea, a section of London. One day as he was packing for a holiday a friend asked where he was going.

"To Battersea," he replied.

"The wit of your remark escapes me," said the friend.

"I am going to Battersea," said Chesterton, "*via* Paris, Heidelberg, Frankfort. I am going to wander all over the world until once more I find Battersea. I cannot see any Battersea here, *because a cloud of sleep and custom has come across my eyes.* The only way to go to Battersea is to go away from it."

No one will miss the deep wisdom behind that show of nonsense. The ideal end of a vacation is to come home not with a grudge in the heart because it is over but with the eager thrill of being back. Does home look fresh again? Even a little strange?

But then, of course, one need not go on holiday to work the miracle. Robert Haven Schauffler tells of a shop assistant in Zurich whose hobby was painting and who lived in resentment because of all the ugliness he had to pass on his way to work. One day illumination came. A taste for art, he reasoned, was not given him in order to resent ugliness but to see beauty where others were blind to it. He resolved to find ten pictures he could paint every time he walked that familiar course. It became fun finding them. A lissome youth helping his mother from a red bus. A ragged boy aping a pompous policeman. A burst of sunlight making a halo around the head of a frizzy blonde. Pictures everywhere.

Most snapshotters fail not in estimating distances, apertures and exposures but in taking what is not a picture. With the seeing eye comes wonder and, with more wonder, a keener eye.

To keep wonder in my life I constantly go back in thought to the moment when I first heard a quite wonderful thing. One day long ago I called on a friend and learned that his young son had made a "wireless set." Would I like to listen? I would, never having heard a radio. But what would I make of those dots and dashes? I smiled benignly on the youngster while he awkwardly placed the earphones on my head and began to fidget with what he called the crystal.

Then it came—a burst of music! I stared at the boy in incredulity. And I have recalled that incredulity a thousand times since. When I pause now before turning the knob and think myself back to the pre-radio days, the breath-taking astonishment of broadcasting breaks over me anew.

Here is another device I use to preserve my sense of astonishment. I have five senses unimpaired. Whenever I think of being deprived of one of them, I awake freshly to the wonder of having it. Deafness? I put all my mind in my ear and wonder at the marvel of sound: the hum of the bee, the purr of a great engine, the subdued murmur of household chatter. Blindness? I shut my eyes awhile and then open them to the sun and the shadows, the rolling countryside, the smile at the corner of my wife's mouth.

Finishing a meal, a man once said to me: "I've practically no sense of taste, you know." Ever since, I've been tasting better. I deliberately savor flavors. Smell and touch I am developing, too, and storing in my memory. I can smell at will the lavender farms I visited a year ago. I can touch again the stubby doormat head of that little boy we took into our home for a holiday. Most of the things I foolishly spend my time wanting are not worth one of the treasures I already possess.

Nor do my discoveries end there. I have found that to look at things as work is always to look at them through dark glasses. I am no longer surprised at the old rancher who looked down into Bryce Canyon, Utah, and said that it was "a hell of a place to lose a cow in." He saw that great work of nature only through the spectacles of drudgery, and those spectacles shut out the light of wonder.

Years ago I visited Carisbrooke Castle on the Isle of Wight. In its small museum were several suits of armor. Looking at them, I was enthralled; my mind threaded the long avenues of the past. But my reverie was interrupted. A charwoman on holiday came in, took one glance at the armor and said to her friend: "Cor blimey, I wouldn't like to have to clean *that* every week!"

Foster your capacity for wonder. Stand and stare at the sea, for instance. It is one of the great refuges of the mysterious on this earth. It is six miles deep in places and who can doubt that it hides creatures never seen by the eye of man? The sea serpent, of course. And what else?

Foster wonder—of the world, of yourself, of humanity, of the Deity. Chesterton said: "The world will never starve for wonders—only for the want of wonder."

One of the unanswered questions of life is: "*When* is old age?" My answer would be: "When we have ceased to wonder."

Harold Nicolson says that his grandmother lived in a state of "incandescent amazement." She not only remembered the first steam packet but lived to hear of M. Blériot flying the Channel. The amazement with which this remarkable old lady exulted in the surprises of our astonishing world kept her young. If the young people around her became blasé, she would rap her ebony stick and demand that they greet the surprises of this Jules Verne world with something of the excitement which she felt herself. She lived to be 99.

Those who wonder are always exultantly asking, "What next?" They have a childlike eagerness. Nor will they be disappointed at death. To them, death itself may seem the most exciting adventure of all.

THE SPECIAL

JOYS OF SUPER-SLOW

READING

by Sydney Piddington

EVEN FOR the pressure-cooker world of advertising, it had been a frustrating, tension-building day. I took home a briefcase full of troubles. A major contract was in danger of being lost at the last minute, two executives of a company with whom we hoped to clinch a deal were being elusive, and a strike threatened the opening of a business that held my money and my future.

As I sat down on that hot and humid evening, there seemed to be no solutions to the problems thrashing around in my brain. So I picked up a book, settled into a comfortable chair and applied my own special therapy—super-slow reading.

I spent three hours on two short chapters of *Personal History* by Vincent Sheean—savoring each paragraph, lingering over a sentence, a phrase, or even a single word, building a detailed mental picture of the scene. No longer was I in Sydney, Australia, on a sticky heatwave night. Relishing every word, I joined foreign correspondent Sheean on a mission to China and another to Russia. I lost myself in the author's world, *living* his book. And when finally I put it down, my mind was totally refreshed.

Next morning, four words from the book—"take the long view"—were still in my mind. At my desk, I had a long-view look at my problems. I concluded that the strike would end sooner or later, so I made positive plans about what to do then. The two executives would see me eventually; if not, I would find other customers. That left me free to concentrate on the main thing, saving the contract. Once more, super-slow reading had given me not only pleasure but perspective, and helped me in my everyday affairs.

I discovered its worth years ago, in the infamous Changi prisoner-of-war camp in Singapore. I was 19, an artillery sergeant, when the city fell to the Japanese on February 15, 1942. Waiting with other Australian POWs to be marched off, I tried to decide what I should take in the single pack permitted. The only limit was what a weary man could carry the 17 miles to Changi. Our officer thoughtfully suggested, "Each man should find room for a book."

So I stuffed into my pack a copy of Lin Yutang's *The Importance of Living*—a title of almost macabre appropriateness—and began a reading habit that was to keep me sane for the next three and a half years. Previously, if I had been really interested in a book, I would race from page to page, eager to know what came next. Now, I decided, I had to become a miser with words and stretch every sentence like a poor man spending his last dollar.

During the first few days at Changi, I took Lin Yutang out of my pack three or four times, just gazing at the cover, the binding and the illustrated inside cover. Finally, as the sun went down one evening, I walked out into the prison yard, sat down on a pile of wood and, under the glare of prison lights, slowly opened the book to the title page and frontispiece. I spent three sessions on the preface, then two whole evenings on the contents pages—three and a half pages of chapter headings with fascinating subtitles—before I even reached page one. Night after night I sat there with my treasure. Fellow prisoners argued, played cards and walked about all around me. I was oblivious, I disappeared so completely into my book that sometimes my closest friends thought I had gone bonkers.

I had started with the practical object of making my book last. But by the end of the second week, still only on page ten, I began to realize how much I was getting from super-slow reading itself. Sometimes just a particular phrase caught my attention, sometimes a sentence. I would read it slowly, analyze it, read it again—perhaps changing down into an even lower gear—and then sit for 20 minutes thinking about it before moving on. I was like a pianist studying a piece of music, phrase by phrase, rehearsing it, trying to discover and recreate exactly what the composer was trying to convey.

It is difficult to do justice to the intensity of the relationship. When Lin Yutang wrote of preparations for a tea party, I could see the charcoal fire, hear the tinkle of tiny teacups, almost taste the delicate flavor of the tea. I read myself in so thoroughly that it became not a mass of words but a living experience.

It took me something like two months to read Lin Yutang's book. By then, his philosophy on tea-making had become my philosophy on reading: You can do it fast, but it's a whole lot better done slowly. I held to the method, even after we had persuaded the Japanese to give us several hundred books from the famous Raffles library in Singapore.

The realization dawned on me that, although my body was captive, my mind was free to roam the world. From Changi, I sailed with William Albert Robinson, through his book *Deep Water and Shoal*. In my crowded cell at night, lying on a concrete floor, I felt myself dropping off to sleep in a warm cabin, the boat pitching under me. Next day, I'd be on deck again, in a storm, and after two or three graphic paragraphs I'd be gripping the helm myself, with the roar of the wind in my ears, my hair thick with salt. I wouldn't let go of the helm until we sailed into the calmer waters of a new chapter. If I had read with my old momentum, it would have been like viewing Sydney Harbor from a speedboat, instead of experiencing it from the deck of my own yacht.

My voyage took me just short of eight weeks. Had I raced through the book at my former speed, I could never have experienced the blessed release of Robinson's reality becoming so vividly mine.

Sitting on a woodpile in the prison yard or crouched on my haunches in any unoccupied corner, I slow-read biographies, philosophy, encyclopedias, even the *Concise Oxford Dictionary*. One favorite was W. Somerset Maugham's *The Summing Up*. I was no longer on a rough prison woodpile, wasting away from hunger; I was in an elegant drawing room on the French

Riviera, a decanter of old port at hand, listening to a great writer talking just to me about his journey through life, passing on the wisdom he had gained.

An average speed reader might dispose of *The Summing Up* in 50 minutes. But he wouldn't be living that book with the writer, as I did during the nine weeks I took to read its 379 pages. (A slow reader himself, Maugham wrote scathingly of those who "read with their eyes and not with their sensibility. It is a mechanical exercise like the Tibetans' turning of a prayer wheel.") I handled *The Summing Up* so much that it fell to pieces in the tropical heat. Then I carefully rebound it with dried banana leaves and rubber gum. I still have it, the most treasured volume in my bookcase.

I developed the habit in Changi of copying passages that especially appealed to me. One of these, from Aldous Huxley's *Ends and Means*, told how training is needed before one can fully savor anything—even alcohol and tobacco:

"First whiskies seem revolting, first pipes turn even the strongest of boyish stomachs.... First Shakespeare sonnets seem meaningless; first Bach fugues a bore, first differential equations sheer torture. But in due course, contact with an obscurely beautiful poem, an elaborate piece of counterpoint, or of mathematical reasoning, causes us to feel direct intuitions of beauty and significance."

I defy anyone to pick anything really significant out of a book like that by speed reading. It would be like playing a Beethoven record at the wrong speed!

Once, something I copied proved useful in camp. Our own commander had ordered us to give any spare clothing to our officers so they could appear immaculately dressed before the Japanese. The order incensed everybody. I pinned over my bunk some words from T. E. Lawrence's *Seven Pillars of Wisdom:*

"Among the Arabs there were no distinctions, traditional or natural, except the unconscious power given a famous sheik by virtue of his accomplishment, and they taught me that no man could be their leader except that he ate the ranks' food, wore their clothes, lived level with them, and yet appeared better in himself."

That night hundreds of slips of paper bearing these words

were pinned up all over Changi. The affair was over, a possible nasty conflict averted.

Beyond giving me the will to survive in Changi, slow reading helps me today. Of course, super-slow reading is not for the man clearing out his briefcase or dealing with the Niagara of paper flowing across his desk. I can skim an inter-office memo as fast as the next person. But when faced with a real problem, to clear my mind of everyday clutter I will sit down quietly at home and slowly read myself into another world.

As Lin Yutang wrote: "There are two kinds of reading, reading out of business necessity, and reading as a luxury. The second kind partakes of the nature of a secret delight. It is like a walk in the woods, instead of a trip to the market. One brings home, not packages of canned tomatoes, but a brightened face and lungs filled with good clear air."

That is what super-slow reading is all about. Try it. As I read somewhere, a man is only poor when he doesn't know where his next book is coming from. And if he can get out of a book everything the author put into it, he is rich indeed.

TAKE MUSIC

INSTEAD OF A

MILTOWN

by George R. Marek

THAT MORNING, I was sure the end of the world had come. My boss had fired me; and, with the pessimism of youth, I was convinced that I would never find another job. I was marked for failure. (I was 19 years old.)

That evening I had a date to meet a friend at Lewisohn Stadium, to hear the New York Philharmonic. Job or no job, I decided to go.

At first, as I sat there, the music merely lapped against the stone wall of my anxiety. But with the final number of the program, the "First Symphony" of Brahms, I began to listen in earnest. As the music reached me, I reflected that I had heard the symphony often before, that I was probably to hear it often again under different conditions—and that it always had been, and would be in the future, the same satisfying music. *It* did not change; only *I* did. I was impermanent; the symphony was permanent. I drew comfort from this.

I measured the event of the day more calmly. Was it as important as all that? Couldn't I do something about it? As I walked home, the dull blanket of despondency weighed less. Somehow I would manage to find another job.

Since then, I have often marveled at the power that lies in music to raise the spirits, to comfort shaken nerves, to serve as a rope on which hope can lift itself. I am, of course, not the first to marvel. Most of us remember Congreve's "Music hath charms to soothe the savage breast." Horace spoke of music as "the healing balm of troubles." "I feel physically refreshed and strengthened by it," said Coleridge. Even Goethe, who was not particularly musical, said that music made him unfold "like the fingers of a threatening fist which straighten, amicably."

Music may be used in two different ways.

The first way is the road taken by the music lover. He need not be able to tell a fugue from a fandango. But to him, the hearing of music is an experience that grips his mind and tears at his heart. He cannot remain indifferent.

How does one become a music lover? There is but one way: listen to music! Only direct experience, not study or explanations or any sort of prop, will lead you to music.

I have two suggestions for the beginner. First, listen to the *same* composition often, until you can respond to it emotionally. Do not expect to encompass a symphony at first hearing. And do not be discouraged or feel guilty if, while listening to an unfamiliar symphony, your attention wanders. Initially, absorb from it as much as you can—and coast through the rest. There will come a time when the clouds roll away and the landscape lies clearly before you. In music, the familiar is the enjoyable. Don't dart from one composition to the next. Stay with it!

Second, choose—in the beginning, at least—romantic music. This is repertoire that begins with Beethoven and ends with Sibelius and that, in its wide orbit, includes the most popular works—those of Schubert, Brahms, Dvořák, Tchaikovsky, Verdi, Wagner, Berlioz and a dozen other composers of the 19th century. Such music, with its rich coloring, its exuberance, its sweetness, its exciting oratory, makes an immediate appeal.

But it is not safe to predict what *you* will like. We do know that people tend to respond more easily to Chopin and Puccini than to Handel or Haydn. Yet your experience may differ. I know one woman whose enthusiasm for music flared when she became acquainted with Scarlatti and Vivaldi. She happens to be very modern in her tastes, and possibly these early-18th-century products furnish a counterbalance.

Of all the arts, music is the freest. Most music does not

"mean" anything—except in its own world and on its own terms. But because it has little to do with what we call real life, because it is free of the weekday, it can effectively take us away from our lives, from our nine-to-five worries. Because music travels on winged feet, it can make us forget where the shoe pinches.

The other way of using music is as background accompaniment—like a tepid bath in which you induce a drowsy reverie. You hardly listen to what you hear, any more than you consciously listen to the surf of the sea. Almost any kind of music can be used for such a purpose, though most people prefer a smooth blend of sound. We meet such music in the most unlikely places—in the dentist's office, in the airport and the bus depot, at the meat market.

In factories, such music helps to relieve the boredom of routine labor. So, too, in the home, people mix the sound of violins with the sound of the dishwasher. But mental processes—creative or calculating—seem to be aided as well. El Greco hired musicians to play for him as he painted. Many men, thinking their problems through, like to have the radio or the phonograph going. Many background-music records—"Music for Dining," "Music for Reading" and the like—help to calm nerves and assuage fatigue.

John Oldham, England's favorite satirist of the 17th century, dropped his doubts when he wrote:

> Music's the cordial of a troubled
> breast,
> The softest remedy that grief
> can find,
> The gentle spell that charms our
> care to rest
> And calms the ruffled passions
> of the mind.

OPEN YOUR EYES

TO THE BEAUTY

AROUND YOU

by Santha Rama Rau

THERE IS a famous story in Japan about a man renowned for the magnificent chrysanthemums he cultivated. His fame reached even to the Imperial Palace and the emperor asked to see these remarkable flowers. Before the emperor arrived the man went into his garden and cut down his treasured chrysanthemums, leaving only one, the most beautiful, to delight the eyes of the monarch.

To foreigners, perhaps, this story needs explanation, but to the Japanese the point is immediately clear—the appreciation of something beautiful is so important a human activity that there is nothing surprising in the destruction of hundreds of plants so that the emperor may enjoy the one flawless flower undistracted by lesser blooms. A friend once explained the matter to me. "Almost anyone," he said, "has at least some appreciation of art, but the Japanese have made an art of appreciation."

In Western society one is apt to feel that to be creative one must be active and have something to *show* for the effort—one must write or paint, compose music, or even be a good cook. But what of the people who read the books, see the pictures, hear the music or eat the cooking? Their sensitive and developed appreciation is a "creative" offering just as hard to come by and, to the Japanese at least, just about as valuable.

To a visitor in Japan this sense of appreciation lends a surprising and new perspective to life, a richness and unsuspected depth. An American Army wife told me about one of her most unexpectedly pleasant experiences in Tokyo. She was invited by a Japanese friend to attend the meetings of an "incense-smelling society." This group of Japanese women had employed an expert to instruct them, and gathered regularly to enjoy the fragrances of scented wood smoke—cedar, lime, verbena, plum and many more—learning their special characteristics, appreciating the subtle changes of quality in a piece of wood a hundred years old as contrasted with a fragment cut the day before. From these meetings my American friend came to understand a whole new approach to the pleasure and appreciation of daily living, to the smells, sounds, textures or sights that previously had not seemed worth her notice.

The Japanese have developed a deeply individual enjoyment of universally available pleasures. In Japan you might be invited to a moonviewing party, for instance. You watch the moon rise and no conversation is expected of you. It is assumed that your mind is fully occupied by watching the changing light the moon throws on gardens, countryside or rooftops. People recognize that your entire attention is needed to absorb the shifting shadows, the play of clouds across the moon, the growing luminosity of the night sky. Some houses, in fact, have a special "moon-viewing window," a treasured architectural feature silently expressing the value of the experience of profound appreciation of beauty.

The first snow has elicited countless poems and paintings in Japan and remains a celebrated occasion calling for the exercise of talents that, in the West, are too often considered passive rather than active. A woman in Kyoto made me realize the importance of this annual experience in her life. She had a small pavilion in her garden built to offer her the best view of the snow. She would sit there in silence with her friends, sipping a tiny cup of the special *sake* that the Japanese brew exclusively for snow-viewing. Beaten up with a raw egg, it is supposed to enhance your appreciation of the changed look of the land under snow. "After this," she said, "it is possible to continue with the memory in your head for the rest of the year."

These refinements of appreciation extend far beyond the accidental beauties of nature into the smallest details of one's daily life in Japan. If, for instance, you are invited to dinner you will see at the bottom of your bowl of consommé a slice of vegetable cut into some beautiful or fantastic shape. A hostess is as much complimented by the guests who say, "How beautiful!" and don't taste the soup as by those who say, "How delicious!" and eat it all.

If you make the most plodding purchase in a shop, you will see the salesman wrap and tie the package with a skill that makes it almost a work of art. When you write a formal letter your calligraphy will be as much appreciated as the actual message. All trifles, but nevertheless to the Japanese all potentially moments of beauty.

At certain seasons of the year your neighbors will probably invite you for an "airing of household treasures"— when whatever the family considers particularly beautiful will be displayed for a while to friends. You will drink tea and admire—with or without conversation, according to your wish—perhaps some ancient masks or unusually lovely kimonos, possibly some picture scrolls or pieces of brocade. Afterward it will all be packed away again, for the interior of a Japanese house is so carefully measured in its elegance that there is no place for a permanent display. A fine table, a picture, a vase of flowers, a couple of bright silk cushions—this is the extent of decoration in a Japanese room. The point is still the same: you can't appreciate something unless you allow your eye or your mind or your ear an undistracted concentration.

All this is not simply the expression of an over-fussy formalism. It is the recognition of the value of constant awareness, a sensitivity to even insignificant aspects of an ordinary activity or occurrence.

This approach is so well accepted in Japan that even in the most highly developed arts a degree of participation is expected from the spectator. In a Japanese poem or dance, for example, the poet or performer will give you only a few fleeting indications of the mood or meaning he wishes to express. The rest is up to you—your own faculties for appreciation, sharing, enlarging are assumed to be up to the challenge of completing the experience in your mind, of embellishing it with special meaning. The place of the observer is thus considerably enlarged. By translating the poem or dance into your own singular experience, you are no longer merely a passive spectator but an active participant.

Apply the same principle in your life, the Japanese believe, and it becomes not a passive progression from day to day but an active, stimulating and creative way of living.

LIFE STAGES

WHY KIDS

ARE 20° COOLER

by Joan Mills

H-E-E-R-R-E'S SUMMER!

Before this morning's sun was half up, the dogs were dragging their tongues in the dust. And now I'm melted into a shape only a hammock can support, watching three kids. Hardly a stitch on any one of 'em. They're skedaddling through the sprinkler, wet as frogs and jumping twice as high. Air conditioning is for adults. Summer is for kids.

I wish *I* were a wet skedaddler again, scampering through the sprinkles in my underwear. It wouldn't be proper, of course, at my age. But what's to commend propriety when it's 93° in the shade? Seems to me that in summer adults are more proper than smart. Kids know that nothing makes more sense in summer than forgetting to be sensible. That's why they're 20° cooler than anybody.

Just how *do* children beat the heat?

Well, first they shed those encumbering conventions that are more stifling than the sun. Then they're free to go about in airy innocence and whatever else feels good. They refresh themselves with nonsense. They—ah, they do all the lovely, carefree, delicious things we grownups would do if we could.

And they do it by instinct. No eight-year-old ever has to consult a Field Manual for Surviving Summer to think of

253

something cool to do. He already knows.

Remember how it was? Like: walk barefoot to the store for a frozen ice on a stick. It's important that you be barefoot. The sidewalk must sizzle your soles so you can be even gladder that your mouth is icy-cold. Halfway home, when the last sherbety blob slides from the stick, catch it in your hand and rub it into your shirt. What a wonderful feeling!

Or drag the old washtub out of the cellar. Set it under a tree, tip the hose in, and add yourself—clothes and all. While you're sitting cool, watch a worm wiggle by. That passes the time and is mildly interesting, besides.

Find a large dog. Soak him down and stand next to him as he shakes himself dry. Kids have never found a dog that wasn't tickled silly to perform this small favor for a human.

I sense again through children how simple and wonderful such summer pleasures are. How do they get that marvelous let-out-of-school feeling? Why, they acquire a hoard of comic books to leaf through in the hayloft. The pictures help interpret the text, the hay is fine to lie on, and the horse doesn't interrupt with foolish questions.

Or, with a couple of friends, they spend the afternoon under your porch, feeding flies to the spiders and playing tick-tack-toe in the dirt.

They drop a stone into a deep well and listen for the faraway, moss-muffled *thunk*.

If mother has to drive to the bank, the laundry, the grocery, the dump, hang your bare feet out one window while the dog hangs his head out the other. Whenever your car is stalled in traffic, kneel on the back seat so you can wave at the driver of the car behind you—it will take his mind off his heat rash.

Take a zigzag stroll around town, sticking your head in every birdbath you see. Thumb the spouts of public drinking fountains to drench yourself and others. Find mud puddles to stomp in. Track the mud through your house to the bathroom and get in the tub with a ballpoint pen. You can while away an absorbing hour drawing pictures on the porcelain.

Summer is happiest when shared with friends. Children cultivate the pals to whom they can say at any old five o'clock, "Hey, you wanna eat over my house?" or who will say to them,

"Hey, you wanna sleep over our back field?"

When it's a child's turn to have friends "eat over," the scheme is: first, fill up on charred hot dogs. After supper, you lie in the grass and watch the fire die. Then you gather at the end of the driveway to play tag until the ice-cream man comes.

For "sleeping over," each sleeper supplies his own smelly blanket. Whoever is host provides mosquito repellent and something for breakfast, like a box of raisins. What's customary is to spread blankets in the chosen yard or field at nine, chase fireflies until eleven, and then settle down to talk until three.

Any child knows that the saddest thing about summer is that it doesn't last forever. After Labor Day, he is expected to put on new shoes, get a haircut, go on to fourth grade.

Such a fate is easier to face if you collect some souvenirs—bottle caps, birds' eggs, a one-armed starfish, ticket stubs from the Saturday movies—so you'll never, ever forget What I Did on My Summer Vacation. And have something to talk about: "Hey, wow, you wanna see my garter-snake skin? Or my best kite, only it's busted? And look, here's where I got dog-bit running through Doc Wilson's sprinkler."

There's one thing, though, that I myself forgot to save. I wish that on some long-ago, high-summer day, a day that was hot and smothery-damp, smelling of cut grass and sun-warm hollyhocks, I had scooped at least a pint of air into a mason jar. Then I could open that jar today and inhale deeply the scent of summer past.

Oh, surely then I'd feel like a kid again. Surely then my heart would once more give a thump of innocent delight, and I could toss away my most confining middle-aged proprieties, and seize upon a zillion breezy notions. Surely then I'd have the wisdom to be cool.

GREEN

WINTER

by Elise Maclay

OLD PEOPLE have much to tell those of us who are not yet old. In these word portraits, a sensitive writer offers us glimpses of ourselves later on. The portraits, she explains, "are reflections of the spirit of men and women I have known—some for many years, some for only an instant of intimacy. I recorded these particular moments because they are precious, and worthy of being shared. But they are far from unique. For if we have the heart to see beyond the cataract-clouded eye, the shaking hand, the slipped-mooring memory, we will find wisdom, courage and insight shimmering all around us."

The title is from a poem by Robert Southey:
>"That in my age as cheerful
> I might be
>As the green winter of
> the Holly Tree..."

My Children Are Coming Today

My Children are coming today.
They mean well. But they worry.
They think I should have a railing in the hall. A telephone in the kitchen.

They want someone to come in when I take a bath.
They really don't like my living alone.
Help me to be grateful for their concern. And help them to
understand that I have to do what I can as long as I can.
They're right when they say there are risks. I might fall. I might
leave the stove on. But there is no challenge, no possibility of
triumph, no real aliveness without risk.
When they were young and climbed trees and rode bicycles and
went away to camp, I was terrified. But I let them go.
Because to hold them would have hurt them.
Now our roles are reversed. Help them see.
Keep me from being grim or stubborn about it. But don't let me
let them smother me.

God Love You, Gram

I read a letter in the newspaper from a lady who signed herself
"Gram" and said she was 73. She has learned, she said, one
helpful hint about how to live with a fractured arm, with a cast to
the elbow. Slide a stocking, wide top first, over the cast to keep it
clean and to make it easier to get your coat on. Snip out the toe
so you can move your fingers. One more bit of advice: don't
climb on kitchen chairs!
Oh, Gram. You plucky, lucky lady. To take a broken arm at 73
as a matter of course.
No self-pity. Only ingenuity. And the impulse to help others in
the same pickle. And humor. What were you doing on the
chair? Taking down curtains? Putting up pictures?
God love you, Gram.
Which, of course, He does.

Some Other Day

Preserve me from the occupational therapist, God.
She means well, but I'm too busy to make baskets.
I want to relive a day in July when Sam and I went berrying.
I was eighteen, my hair was long and thick and I braided it and
wound it round my head so it wouldn't get caught on the
briars.

But when we sat in the shade to rest I unpinned it and it came
    tumbling down.
And Sam proposed.
I suppose it wasn't fair to use my hair to make him fall in love
    with me, but it turned out to be a good marriage...
Oh, here she comes, the therapist, with scissors and paste.
Would I like to try découpage?
"No," I say, "I haven't got time."
"Nonsense," she says, "you're going to live a long, long time."
That's not what I mean, I mean that all my life I've been doing
    things for people, with people. I have to catch up on my
    thinking and feeling.
About Sam's death, for one thing.
Close to the end, I asked if there was anything I could do...
He said, "Yes, unpin your hair."
I said, "Oh, Sam, it's so thin now and gray."
"Please," he said, "unpin it anyway."
I did and h_ reached out his hand—the skin transparent, I could
    see the blue veins—and stroked my hair.
If I close my eyes, I can feel it. Sam.

"Please open your eyes," the therapist says;
"You don't want to sleep the day away."
She wants to know what I used to do,
Knit? Crochet?
Yes, I did those things, and cooked and cleaned and raised five
    children, and had things happen to me.
Beautiful things, terrible things.
I need to think about them, arrange them on the shelves of my
    mind.
The therapist is showing me glittery beads.
She's a dear child and means well,
So I tell her I might.
Some other day.

Our Secret

Hey, Lord, we have a secret.
There are some things about being old that are fun.

Yes, fun.
The world gets off your back. They neglect you.
You don't have to keep up appearances.
So you can go back to the fun of being a child.
Watching a spider spin a web.
Making shadow pictures against the light.
Exploring the back yard as if it were a new country.
Eating applesauce and cream instead of dinner.
Dawdling.
Staying up all night. Counting stars.
Staying home from a dull party to play chess with an old friend.
Wearing a funny hat.
Why didn't You tell me that besides all the things I hate about
    being old, there'd be some fun in it, too?
I know, I know.
I wouldn't have believed You.

Walking Home

I was going to take the bus and then I didn't, because I didn't
    have the money.
I mean, I had the money but I didn't think I ought to spend it.
The fare's fifty cents now, half of a dollar, and for someone of
    my means (or lack of means) that's a lot.
So I said to myself, "All right, I'll hike."
I wasn't looking forward to it though,
I was a little tired, and I figured I'd be bored.
Putting one foot in front of the other isn't the most interesting
    thing in the world when you've gone the route a hundred
    times or more before.
And then You put on that light show, God.
It was beautiful, the sky all apricot and gold, the trees
    silhouetted.
In the space of an hour, light wheeled, danced and was done and
    one star shone.
It would be an understatement to say I'm glad I decided to walk
    home today.
And if I tried to say anything about Your goodness and glory, I'd

*have to shout and sing, which I'm not about to do. Ecstasy is
not a thing folks understand in a fellow who happens to be
seventy-six, which I happen to be.*

*But, God, sometimes, between me and You, I'm singing-
shouting glad to be alive.*

A Sense of Love

The grandchildren haven't turned out the way we thought they
would. Their parents, my children, are hurt and angry, ashamed
and worried about it. I'm not. I like these kids. The way they are.
Open and honest. Disorganized and gentle. Scruffy and kind.
They don't seem to mind spending time with me. We talk about
real things. Dreams. Peace. The sky. They tell me living is more
important than accomplishing things. I agree.

Their parents are outraged by this, so I don't go into it. I
say, "The kids came." The parents say, "Good; at least they have
a sense of duty."

I think they have a sense of love.

MS READ-a-thon— a simple way to start youngsters reading

Boys and girls between 6 and 14 can join the MS READ-a-thon and help find a cure for Multiple Sclerosis by reading books. And they get two rewards — the enjoyment of reading, and the great feeling that comes from helping others.

Parents and educators: For complete information call your local MS chapter. Or mail the coupon below.

Kids can help, too!